Precipice

A Murder Mystery
Book Eight in the 'Reporting is Murder'© Series

By
Eugénie D. West

THE SAMOTHRACE PRESS

This is a work of fiction. Names, places, events, motives, characters and descriptions in this book are products of the author's imagination and/or are used fictitiously. Any resemblance to actual events, places, entities or people, living or dead, is purely coincidental and beyond the intent of the author.

For SNJ, MHJ, CJK
& RMJ
with love

About the Author

The author of 'Precipice,' Eugénie D. West, was a news reporter for a weekly newspaper for more than 15 years. All of the books in her 'Reporting is Murder!'© series, of which 'Precipice' is the eighth, are inspired by actual cases the author encountered during her time on the news beat, or events which deeply affected her.

The treatments given these cases in West's books are fictional, with motives, details and outcomes that are not the same as the real ones. West writes her novels under a *nom de plume* borrowed from a paternal great-great-great grandmother.

'Precipice' features West's protagonist, sleuthing journalist Gracie Barufaldi, along with her on again off again boyfriend Jack and West's trademark ensemble cast of intriguing characters. These all interact with each other and carry forward their own personal stories against the backdrop of a surprising death—only afterwards discovered to have been murder—and its eventual solution.

Like most of the books West writes, the featured murder isn't the only crime in the story, nor is the thread of Gracie and Jack's relationship the only sub plot. As in life, other misdemeanors, dramas and passions intervene, making for a richly woven tale that is satisfyingly blended and concluded.

West is inspired by people she has known and places she has been, but the characters in her books are fictional: amalgams of qualities, characteristics and traits from scores of acquaintances, strangers and other personalities. They are created to fit with and further the story. To read any more into them, or to attempt to identify real people in West's characters, is foolhardy.

West holds a Ph.D. in English and enjoys history, languages, music, science and travel. Like Gracie, she lives in a rural part of the northeastern United States, is a bit of a techno-geek, and is an accomplished cook.

Visit West on her Amazon Author Page, and find her on Twitter, Facebook, Pinterest, Goodreads and on her blog, ThebooksofEugnieDWest.blogspot.com.

Also in the
'Reporting is Murder!'© Series
by Eugénie D. West:

Baby's Breath
Coercion
Black Card
Where There's Smoke, There's Murder
Spin
Tide's Reach
Natural Causes

§

And as
Deborah L. Courville
(historical fact-based fiction):

A River In Time
Treachery in Time

PRECIPICE

Chapter One

The sun shone brilliantly and a lively, late May breeze ruffled the edges of the tent, bringing with it the scent of lilies and roses. At least half the mourners who had been at Springfield's Assembly of God Church for Michael Garnier's funeral that morning had joined the procession to nearby Netherfields Cemetery for the interment, and as many as could fit now crowded together at the grave-site under the white tent, and listened to Pastor Plumb. The rest circled the tent in a gently undulating ring of somber black: they were respectful, and silent except for the occasional sob or whisper.

Even though Mike hadn't died in the line of duty, a Massachusetts State Police Officer was still one of a brotherhood, and on this Friday, a week since his death, both the church and the cemetery were graced by the State Police Honor Guard; there were as many law enforcement officers in their dress uniforms with black bands crossing their badges and surrounding their biceps as there were civilians, all come to pay Mike tribute.

Mike's death was especially tough on the State Troopers, as just the year before, an MSP Corporal and a Trooper had been shot at as they were leaving the Cheshire Barracks B-4 at the end of their shift. Both men had survived, but with life threatening wounds that would take months of rehab and several surgeries to correct.

The shooter, thought to have been a lone gunman, had not been apprehended, although an extensive search had been mounted. It was presumed he had fled the state, and probably the country, and although the 'BOLO' or 'be on the lookout' for the suspect was still active, police had virtually nothing to go on, and the trail had gone cold.

Now, Gracie stood next to Jack, in the row behind Mike's immediate family and that of his wife, Sandy. They had had similar positions in the church, along with other college friends from Dartmouth, many of whom knew both Mike and Jack. And, as he had during the short church service, Jack held tightly to Gracie's hand as they listened to the Pastor and watched as the honor guard stepped forward, removed the U.S. Flag from Mike's coffin, and folded it neatly, precisely, reverently into its fateful triangle.

Jack was somber but stoic, and he'd got through his part of the brief eulogy at the church with only the smallest catch in his voice. He was quiet during the rifle salute and while the bagpiper played 'Amazing Grace.' When State Police Sergeant William Wright handed the folded Flag to Mike's widowed mother Della, though, Gracie teared up, and Jack clenched his teeth, a muscle tightening in his jaw.

Then they lowered the coffin, and a member of the State Police Band began to play 'Taps.'

Jack lost it: Gracie heard an odd sort of hiccuping noise, and quickly looked at him. His chin was high and his throat was working furiously as though trying to swallow the grief. His eyes swam and Jack clenched his teeth. Gracie gripped his hand more firmly.

By the time everyone who wanted to had dropped a flower, a card or a clod of earth on the mahogany coffin it was almost completely obscured. The mourners left the grave-site to begin their healing, and left Mike's earthly remains to the ministering of the cemetery grounds-men.

"What a day," Jack sighed as he climbed into Gracie's Jeep a couple of hours later, after the luncheon reception given by the families at Springfield's Hampton House.

"It sure seemed very long," Gracie agreed, giving him a small smile. "And so sad."

The day had been the culmination of a week of heart-wrenching activity. Jack had been called to the scene of a fatal hiking accident the previous Friday. He had just wrapped up his investigations on two murder cases and he and Gracie had been finishing dinner at her house when Gracie's scanner had gone off as well as Jack's phone.

Knowing from the codes used by the dispatchers that he could expect to find a body out on Greylock Mountain, Jack hadn't known the deceased was his good friend Mike Garnier until he had arrived on the scene. Then, the relatively smooth machinery of an accident investigation had taken over, allowing Jack to stand back and process his thoughts, and begin to process his grief.

Gracie had been assigned to cover the accident for the weekly newspaper she wrote for, the *Intelligencer*. She had been able to get a copy of the initial police report from the Adams PD as well as the coroner's report; this latter had ruled Mike's death 'accidental by misadventure' though it had given the cause of death as 'multiple trauma.'

It was that note that made Gracie, and Jack, suspicious. As Gracie had said when Jack had first told her of Mike's death, Mike was an expert hiker, outdoorsman and rock climber. The thought of him falling to his death while hiking the north face of Mount Greylock—something he did several times a year—while not beyond the realm of possibility, was so unlikely that it raised a considerable red flag for both Jack and Gracie. Additional information that only Jack, Gracie and Mike's wife Sandy were privy to also made the death suspicious, at least to them.

They knew Mike had been investigating rumors of alleged corruption within the Juvenile Court System in neighboring Hampshire County. He'd been doing so unofficially, not as a member of the State Police, and on information provided to him by Sandy, who was a Caseworker for the Hampshire County Juvenile Probation Department.

Of course, Sandy hadn't shared sensitive information like the juveniles' names or personal information, but other things like questionable adjudications of certain cases, had at first worried her, and then troubled her so deeply she felt duty bound to share her concerns with Mike. She hadn't wanted to go to the head of her department, in case he was involved in the peculiarities she suspected.

Sandy had also hoped that, as a logical, level headed State Police Trooper, her husband Mike could just look at the facts, without emotion, and tell her if her suspicions had any merit.

Mike had listened, and thought Sandy's suspicions were well-founded. He'd begun poking around—unobtrusively, he had thought—doing his own off the record, unofficial investigation into a possibly corrupt scheme.

The fact that Mike may have ruffled some guilty feathers in spite of his caution, plus his years of experience as a climber and hiker had made Sandy, then Jack, and then Gracie, suspicious of the autopsy ruling. They did not think Mike's death had necessarily been a 'misadventure.'

Mike's mother had quailed at the thought of an intrusive autopsy, and Sandy had gone along with her mother-in-law to keep whatever peace they could wrangle at this heart wrenching time. Dr. Tom Spears, Berkshire County's Medical Examiner, had noted in his autopsy report that because of the 'overwhelming external physical evidence' that Mike's death had been caused by 'multiple trauma resulting from an accidental fall' and because of the family's wishes, no more than a cursory external autopsy would be performed.

So Jack had no hard evidence that foul play had figured in his friend's death. All he had were logical deductions and an instinctive feeling. And he could hardly open a murder investigation based on that.

"Hey, listen: I was thinking about going up there tomorrow," Jack said now, as Gracie turned into his long driveway and approached the trailer he called home. It sat on a lovely piece of property which Jack had bought with the clear intention of building a house in the near future. Meanwhile, a top of the line double wide served him, and his half dog-half wolf, Woof, well enough. "Probably not the way you'd planned your Memorial Day Weekend, but..."

"Up to Mt. Greylock, you mean?" Gracie queried, although she knew exactly what Jack meant.

The Adams PD CSU had included Jack on site while they'd been examining the area above and around where Mike's body had been found, even though once the death had been ruled accidental, his presence as County Detective hadn't been strictly necessary. Now that hikers could return to that part of the North Face Trail, Gracie thought she understood why Jack would want to go back and see the spot in its natural state.

"Yeah," Jack replied now. "Maybe you'd like to come with?" he asked. "If you're not busy, I mean,"

"I don't have any plans," Gracie said, adding that she had tossed any holiday weekend plans out the window once she had learned of Mike's death the weekend before. "I thought about stopping into Greylock Manor," she went on. "This weekend is their Spring Thyme Herb Festival," she reminded Jack. A couple of years previous, she and Jack along with his parents, had attended the Festival, and since she was on the Greylock Board, Gracie liked to show support, and help out if she could, whenever the historic home held an event. "But...I don't know if I can handle the mountain," Gracie admitted a second later as she put the Jeep in 'park' and switched off the engine. She was in good shape and certainly did her share of hiking, but the North Face Trail was rated 'experienced hikers only' and she wouldn't exactly call herself that.

"I've hiked it," Jack returned. "Several times: with Mike, with those Eagle Scouts he worked with, and alone. I'll be there to help you," he coaxed. His smile was a sad one, and small.

"I've only rappelled a few times," Gracie cautioned him. Rappelling was required on a couple of sections of the trail.

"But you like it," Jack reminded her. "Seriously, I think you'll be fine: you're a better hiker than you think you are," he added, and gave her another, somewhat happier, smile. His dark blue eyes held her chocolate brown ones for a moment, and she smiled back.

"You have such confidence in me," she said, sounding as though perhaps he shouldn't.

"With good reason, Gracie," Jack replied, still looking at her.

God it was good to have her here, he thought. She had spent most of April in England visiting her cousin Verena, and he'd really missed her. Once she'd returned, May had been filled with two murder investigations that had meant neither of them had had much free time.

Now, it was the long Memorial Day weekend and the start of the summer. They hadn't been romantically involved for several months, ever since Jack had found out that Gracie's friendship with Boston lawyer Ben Holmes had turned into something more. Jack and Gracie had at that time been dating for over a year, and although they'd never discussed the matter, he had just assumed theirs had been an exclusive relationship. So when he'd discovered she had started dating Holmes, too, he had broken it off with her.

But they had remained friends. Good friends, for Jack felt Gracie knew him like no other, and he liked to think he knew her, as well. And upon her return from England, the fact that she had broken up with Holmes earlier that spring had come up in conversation. Jack hadn't asked why, hadn't said anything, but he'd felt his heart, and his hope, grow lighter with the knowledge.

Their relationship had never been an easy one. Since Gracie was 'G.B. Barufaldi,' the news reporter for the weekly newspaper the *Intelligencer* and covered Berkshire County, and he was the Berkshire County Detective, they were work associates. As such, they had constantly had to battle things like confidential information, conflict of interest, and the appearance of impropriety. But Jack had loved Gracie from the first second he'd seen her a few years before, and doubted he would ever stop. And now, even though they had broken up, maybe he would have another chance. And this time, he vowed, he would do it right.

"Okay," Gracie agreed about the hike, sighing. She paused. "Are you sure you're okay? I don't think you should be alone tonight," she added gently.

Jack gave her a wry smile. "I'd be rotten company," he answered. "And I'm not alone: I've got Woof," he added, getting out of her Jeep and walking to his front door. He unlocked it, and was greeted by his wolf-dog, who put his front paws briefly on Jack's shoulders and then ran to say hello to Gracie. Then he ran off into the grass surrounding the trailer for a brief constitutional.

"I'll bring all my hiking gear and harnesses, so you don't have to worry about any specialized equipment," Jack told Gracie from his front step. He was waiting for Woof to finish and return, so he could go inside. "Just wear your hiking boots." He paused. "And if you want, we can stop into the Festival on our way back," he offered.

"Okay," Gracie said again, looking a bit more cheerful. Clearly, she was not thrilled at the prospect of climbing up the north face of Mount Greylock, but she knew Jack would take care of her and see she came to no harm.

From inside the trailer, Jack's phone began to ring. He whistled for Woof and then waved to Gracie. "I'll pick you up at 9 a.m. tomorrow, okay?" he asked her, and she nodded. "Thanks, Gracie," he said, and Gracie smiled in return and climbed into her Jeep for the short ride back to her home.

Chapter Two

The phone call had been Sandy, wanting to meet with Jack to give him some of Mike's personal things she wanted him to have, now that she'd packed up the contents of their small apartment. Jack had mentioned his planned hike to Mt. Greylock the next morning, and invited her to come with him and Gracie. He had added that they could make the transfer of the personal belongings afterwards.

'You're sure you want me to have those things?' Jack had asked, his voice full, when Sandy told him her plan.

'You were his best friend, Jack,' Sandy had reassured him. 'I know Mike would want you to have them.'

Sandy had agreed to join Jack and Gracie on their hike, noting that she would probably be an emotional mess, but that she also realized seeing the place where her husband had met his death would give her closure.

Given the fact that she was leaving the area quite soon, the Saturday morning hike would likely be her only chance.

Sandy was headed back to Moose River, ME, where her parents still lived. They ran a kayak rental and outdoor adventure trip business they had built up from scratch, and Sandy felt a change of pace was due her and so planned to join them and help out.

Sandy was an accomplished white water rafter, hiker and climber, and it had been a shared sense of adventure which had initially attracted Sandy and Mike to each other. She'd finished her four years at Western Maine College with a degree in Social Work, then married Mike and moved south to Massachusetts with him. She'd counted herself fortunate to have found a good post with the Hampshire County Juvenile Probation Department, and she and Mike had rented a small apartment that was mid way between her work in Northampton and Mike's SP Barracks in Pittsfield. Eventually, they had planned to buy property and build, but that dream would now never come true.

In the days surrounding Mike's death, if asked about the impending return to her home state, Sandy had just told everyone that she'd decided she needed a complete change. However, the truth was that Sandy was frightened: Mike had been a spectacular hiker. Sure, accidents happened, but somehow the timing of it, right after he'd begun his unofficial inquiry into the odd things Sandy had become suspicious of at the JP Department, had made her wonder if his death had somehow been connected to his investigation. Had someone—she couldn't imagine who—wanted to keep Mike from finding something out? And how could she be sure that whoever might have wanted that, wouldn't now come after her? Surely they had to realize that Sandy had been the suspicious one who urged Mike to investigate.

On Saturday morning, however, conversation and speculation were limited as Sandy, Jack and Gracie trekked up the north face of Mount Greylock. When they reached the summit, they followed the path along the top of the trail to a lookout point, the spot where Mike had fallen from. Although she had been dry eyed, though quiet, on the trek up, it took Sandy several minutes to compose herself once they arrived at the spot. Jack and Gracie gave her all the space and time she needed; they were themselves quite emotional, and Jack in particular felt that Mike's spirit was still near.

Gracie stayed close to both Sandy and Jack, but couldn't help surreptitiously examining the lookout spot. Certainly, there was loose rock all along the flattish point that jutted out over the canyon below. Although it was the end of May, the lookout was over 3000 feet high and in the shade: there was still a little ice here and there, which could make footing treacherous. There were waist high rails meant to afford hikers a secure spot from which to view the truly amazing vista spread out before and below them. The rails would seem to preclude any type of fall, but the CSU team on scene had theorized that Mike had possibly stepped beyond the rails, perhaps to get a photo of something, and had slipped, and fallen. Mike's camera had been found with his body, in the knapsack he had slung over his shoulders.

Saturday, Jack, Gracie and Sandy all stayed behind the railing. The Friday evening before when he'd reported to the scene, Jack had clambered out and over to the edge of the lookout, and had rappelled down to the narrow shelf which had caught Mike's body and been its final resting place. Jack now had no desire to repeat that experience. The three of them would return to the main trail and rappel down the designated path. They would be able to see the place from which another hiker had spotted Mike's body, and the shelf where the body had lain until recovered, so there would be no need to go there directly.

"It sure is beautiful up here," Gracie breathed, thinking of how quickly life could change, and enjoying the silence, vastness and beauty that she felt was unique to the North American wilderness.

She took a couple of photos, managing to catch a golden eagle riding the thermal currents coming up from the canyon, and thinking fancifully to herself that the majestic creature was possibly Mike's spirit. She whispered that the eagle made her think of Mike: Sandy shot her a tearful smile, and Jack just nodded, but his eyes followed the eagle's progress until it passed a bend in the canyon and winged out of sight.

They returned to the main trail and rappelled down to the canyon floor, then trekked the two miles to the lower Mount Greylock Ranger Station where they'd begun their hike. By now it was one o'clock and by mutual previous agreement the three stripped themselves of their bulky hiking gear and crowded into Jack's truck, headed back to Gracie's for lunch. Since that had been their meeting point that morning, it only made good sense, and Gracie was happy to provide fresh pea soup, a chicken asparagus white grape salad she'd assembled the evening before, and cheddar cheese croissants she'd baked that morning. For dessert, she offered iced lemon cake and coffee.

"We'll miss you, Sandy," Jack said as they finished their coffee and dessert and moved onto Gracie's screened porch. It was a clear day and Woof and Gracie's large orange tabby cat Pumpkin--who oddly enough were good pals--had claimed a large patch of sunshine. They were sprawled companionably on the hardwood floor, paws intertwined.

"Yes, I was hoping you could join the Pittsfield Junior League this year," Gracie chimed in. "I had your sponsorship letter all written!"

Sandy smiled, and settled herself in one of the comfortable Adirondack chairs. She clutched a bright orange butterfly shaped pillow as she spoke.

"I'm afraid," she admitted, looking furtively at Jack and Gracie.

Both her friends nodded. They had suspected that fear might be behind Sandy's quite abrupt decision to leave Hampshire County, her job, and the apartment she'd shared with Mike. Fear, and memories. "I figure if I go back home, to Maine, and kind of disappear, maybe they'll leave me alone and forget about me," Sandy finished in a whisper.

"Who's 'they?' " Gracie asked just as Jack said:

"But no one knows you were the one who tipped off Mike."

Sandy smiled as Jack and Gracie's comments 'stepped' on each other.

"I know they don't, but I was a Case Worker in the Juvenile Probation Department, and Mike's wife. I'm sure they suspect that I was the suspicious one, that I was the one who got Mike to investigate," she explained.

Then she turned to Gracie. "And as for who 'they' are, I'm not sure." She bit her lip. "Sometimes I wish I hadn't said anything. Then Mike might--"

"Don't think like that, Sandy," Jack broke in. It wasn't her fault that Mike, hearing her suspicions that juvenile offenders were being sent to the Detention Center without real cause and against the recommendations of Case Workers, had decided to investigate. And it surely wasn't Sandy's fault that Mike had died.

She nodded, grateful for Jack's support. "Mark has to know," she continued softly, meaning her boss, Mark Broadstreet, who was the head of Juvenile Probation. "That's why I didn't go to him with my concerns. He's the one who makes the recommendation to the Judge as to what sentence the kids receive."

"I thought the Case Workers did that," Gracie put in.

Sandy shook her head. "Well, we suggest," she offered, exaggerating the last word, and rolling her expressive blue eyes. "But Mark makes the final decision."

"Mike told me he didn't want to approach Rita Licora," Jack said thoughtfully. And he knew why: Mike had suspected that Rita, the Hampshire County Detective, was having an affair with Broadstreet, and so had figured that if Broadstreet were up to anything shady, Licora very likely would know about it.

"Right," Sandy affirmed, and echoed her dead husband's suspicions.

"Well, what about the Hampshire County Commissioners? Or the DA?" Gracie asked.

Sandy took a deep breath. "I think Mike was considering saying something to Jenkins," she answered, referring to Don Jenkins, the Hampshire County DA. "But then--" she broke off, and bowed her head.

After a few beats of grieving silence, Sandy looked up and forced a smile. "Well, anyway, Jack--" she reached into the knapsack that she'd brought with her, "here's what I wanted to give you."

She handed Jack the Walther PPK that Mike had prized, his Nikon digital camera, a sueded leather outback 'cowboy' hat he'd brought back from a vacation to Australia, and the Baume & Mercier Chronograph Watch Sandy had bought for him when he'd been promoted to Corporal with the State Police.

"You don't want this?" Jack asked, indicating the watch. It was worth quite a lot, and was a beautiful piece of jewelry as well as a wonderful time piece.

Sandy shook her head, her short brown hair feathering against her cheeks. "I can't wear it," she said simply. Mike had been as tall as Jack, and stocky. Sandy, by contrast, was just over five feet three inches and wiry-thin. Even if she had links removed from the band, the time piece would look ridiculously big on her tiny wrist. And perhaps, for her, the memories were just too close.

"Thanks, Sandy," Jack said, his voice hoarse. "I don't know what to--"

"I want you to have these things," Sandy cut him off, firmly, dashing away tears from a freckled cheek, and smiling again. "And Mike would want you to have them."

Chapter Three

"What am I interrupting?" Jack asked quickly into his phone. It was the following Tuesday evening, and he could hear noises in the background that indicated that Gracie was with other people.

"Club meeting," Gracie replied guardedly into her iPhone. "Is it important?"

"Mmmm...yeah. I just thought you'd like to know there's been another death down in Stockbridge."

"Another one?" Gracie echoed, frowning. She remembered Jack telling her in one of his emails the last week she'd been in England about a young woman who had died under somewhat suspicious circumstances. There had been no apparent cause of death: she hadn't been mugged, or shot or knifed: she'd just collapsed in her home in Stockbridge, a small town to the south in Berkshire County.

Friends had said the twenty-four year old had been complaining of feeling weak and a bit dizzy for a couple of days. They had become concerned when she hadn't shown up at a party she'd been invited to, and hadn't called to explain why.

The autopsy had revealed nothing remarkable initially, although the tox screen had shown elevated levels of ethylene glycol in her blood. Dr. Spears had examined her organs and found calcium oxalate crystals in her kidneys and brain. He had ruled cause of death as 'multiple organ failure' caused by the ingestion of the ethylene glycol.

Spears had not determined the manner of death yet: one couldn't rule out accidental ingestion, but one could also not responsibly rule out intentional poisoning, he had explained. The case was still open, and Jack had been working to see if he could figure out if anyone might have had a motive for killing the young woman.

Her death had been one of the open case files that had nagged at him from his 'in' box for the month of May, and although his investigation hadn't stopped, it would be fair to say it had stalled in the past month with the two murders that occupied his department.

Now, if Gracie understood him right, Jack was telling her that another young woman had died, possibly under similar circumstances, just barely more than a month later. The stalled investigation was now very much alive, and on the top of Jack's to-do list.

"Right," Jack confirmed, but he wouldn't say much else over a mobile phone. "You might want to make some calls tomorrow morning," he suggested obliquely. "It went out over the scanner, so I'm sure your buddy at the *Gazetteer* will be asking questions, too," he added wryly.

He was referencing Gil Butcher, the editor at the *Intelligencer's* rival paper. The *Gazetteer* covered mainly Pittsfield, although lurid or sensational news--like this second mysterious death--also earned coverage.

Butcher, who envied Gracie's hard earned contacts in Berkshire County, sought to discredit her whenever he could in order to deflect attention away from his own ineptitude. He also had an annoying sense of entitlement, feeling that because he was an Editor, and Gracie merely a Reporter, sources should tell him things they wouldn't tell her, or at least tell him as much as they told her.

The fact was, most people in the Pittsfield Courthouse, the Police and other contacts used by the media had learned to trust Gracie over the several years she had been reporting. They didn't trust Butcher, largely because their experience with him didn't merit it: he got many things wrong, was a poor writer, and was sanctimoniously obnoxious on top of it all. It wasn't hard to understand why Butcher had been moved to the small weekly *Gazetteer* from a larger weekly and before that a daily newspaper, all owned by the same New England communications company.

Butcher and Gracie were unfriendly rivals, and Gracie took an extra measure of joy in scooping the *Gazetteer,* or writing a more detailed or in depth story, whenever she could. Writing a more correct and complete story was never difficult.

"Erm, okay, Jack, I'll do that, thanks, " Gracie said, uneasily. She felt like she was talking in code. "It won't be a really late night," she added. "When I get home shall I call you?" The Club meeting was unofficial, since it was summer time, and was being held at another member's home.

"You can, and I'll fill you in so you'll be prepped for tomorrow," Jack agreed. "I've already put in a call to Poppinfresh," he added, using their special nickname for the Berkshire County DA. His real surname was Popovitch, but his resemblance to the chubby, white dough-ball mascot of a national baked goods company was sufficient to have made Gracie dub him 'Poppinfresh' a few years back, and the nickname had stuck. At least with Jack and Gracie.

"Oh?" If Jack was getting the DA involved, that meant he suspected something. "You think they're connected: this one, and the one in April?" she asked.

"We'll talk later," Jack said with cryptic promise, and disconnected.

"Hey, Peter, can I walk you to your office?" Gracie asked, smiling her most winning smile and aiming herself at the DA the following morning. Popovitch, whose full name was Peter Paul Popovitch and who disliked being called anything besides 'Mr. Popovitch' by anyone he held in such low esteem as he did Gracie, grunted in reply.

Since Gracie wasn't sure exactly what the grunt meant, she decided it meant 'yes' and followed Popovitch out of the Commissioners' office. The DA as well as the Sheriff, the Public Defender, the Warden, Judge Norcross and others had been attending a meeting of the Berkshire County Prison Board, and the meeting had just adjourned. Gracie had snagged Popovitch on his way out of the second floor conference room, *en route* to his third floor office suite.

Popovitch waddled towards the elevator, wheezing as he did so.

"I generally take the stairs," Gracie murmured as she followed him onto the small car and surreptitiously checked the weight limit: 900 pounds. They should be okay. Popovitch had to weigh close to 400 pounds, though, Gracie thought as they rode up the single flight in silence.

Rudely, or perhaps because he couldn't have squeezed over and made enough room to let her by, Popovitch exited the elevator before Gracie, but she walked purposefully right behind him as he entered his office suite.

Millie, his long suffering secretary, gazed up at him with a well schooled look of dispassion, and handed him several pink message slips. When she caught sight of Gracie, though, she broke into a wide smile.

"Good morning, Millie," Gracie said cheerily.

"Jack's on the phone, but I can tell him you're here," Millie offered, still smiling. She liked Jack, a lot. And she liked Gracie, too. She had thought it was wonderful when they had started dating, and had been sad when they'd broken up, but she was glad they could still be friends, and was always happy to see the clever young reporter.

"I'm here for the Boss today," Gracie said, indicating Popovitch's massive--and hastily disappearing--back. She rolled her eyes at Millie, who almost giggled, and nodded her comprehension. Then Gracie caught up to the DA as he entered his private office.

"Make it fast, Barufaldi: I've got a lot on my plate," Popovitch growled, thrusting the files he'd carried to and from the Prison Board meeting (but had not opened) onto the already crowded surface of his desk.

He apparently saw no irony whatsoever in his statement.

'A lot on your plate?' thought Gracie. He must mean lunch, she reasoned to herself: Jack did most of the work in this office, she knew. As County Detective, he was the DA's right hand but in this case he was more like the DA's entire arm. Maybe both arms. And possibly his legs as well.

"Erm, right," she said cooperatively. "I just wanted to know if you think the death of that young woman last night in Stockbridge is connected to the death of the other girl a few weeks back?" she asked. "Also in Stockbridge. About the same age: 24 years old, I think. Her name was Sally Sullivan?"

"Connected?" Popovitch echoed dimly.

It wasn't a foreign word: why did Popovitch have that perplexed look on his face? Gracie waited.

"Why would I think they're connected?" Popovitch asked a moment later.

Ah, he was fishing to see what she knew, Gracie thought.

"Erm, let's see now," she pretended to think very hard, screwing up her face into a frown. Then: "logic?" she asked brightly. "Look, Peter," she continued, making a lightning fast switch from overplayed satire to professionalism, "we've got two young women, both in their early 20's, who die within a few weeks of each other, in the same town with no immediately apparent manner or cause of death. " She paused. "D'you think that's a coincidence?" she queried rhetorically.

"It could be," Popovitch shot back in irritation. "We haven't determined any connection between the two," he added, truculent. "We have to wait for cause of death in the latest case."

"Well, the symptoms described over the scanner by 911 are consistent with ethylene glycol poisoning, and that was the COD for Sullivan's death," Gracie offered. That much was true: a little research on the internet had given Gracie the information on ethylene glycol, the main component in antifreeze. Jack had played her a recording of the 911 call in the second case. The deceased had been at the local gym, which she attended three times a week, when she had left her aerobics class because she'd felt unwell.

She had apparently returned to the locker room where she had passed out on the floor; she was found about a half hour later, and the gym manager had made the 911 call when the woman had remained unresponsive despite efforts to revive her.

But Popovitch didn't need to know of Jack's involvement: Gracie could have just as easily heard the 911 dispatcher's broadcast herself. And if she hadn't been at the Club meeting, she probably would have, on her scanner at home.

"Are you looking for any connections?" Gracie asked again, prodding.

Popovitch stared at her for a split second, clearly dumbfounded. He had no idea, Gracie realized, that the symptoms described in the new case were similar to those in the case from April. As Gracie's pal Joey would say, 'man oh Manischewitz: what a jerk.'

"I can't comment on an ongoing investigation," Popovitch said a second later, the rote response falling easily off his tongue. He stopped speaking and looked slightly surprised at his cleverness, and then smug.

Probably thinks he's shut me up, Gracie thought to herself. More fool him.

"So, you aren't considering the two deaths related," Gracie said in mock seriousness, and pretended to make a note on her steno pad.

"I didn't say that."

"Well, then, you *are* considering that the two deaths might be related?" Gracie asked, feigning confusion.

"I didn't say that either."

"So, then, you have no idea whether the two deaths are related or why they might be or what your office is pursuing by way of investigation of these deaths, does that about sum it up, Peter?" Gracie asked, her tone sweet but her eyes blazing.

The DA didn't answer, but he curled his lip and favored Gracie with a glower.

"I'm not asking you to reveal your entire strategy or name sources, Peter: I'm just asking if you think there's a connection!" Gracie exclaimed, exasperated. "If you don't answer me, I'm going to print that you refused to comment because you have no idea what the substance of the investigation is," she challenged.

"You wouldn't dare!" Popovitch snarled back at her.

"I would, and you know it!" she shot back. "So tell me something," she finished, her voice back to reasonable and soothing, but not wheedling: Gracie never wheedled. Or whined.

"Superficially it seems there may be a connection but we haven't in any way--in *any* way--confirmed that," Popovitch said, finally. When he wanted to, he could actually make sense, Gracie thought, scribbling down the quote. "We will wait for COD in the second death and then, if it is antifreeze poisoning, we will go from there."

Gracie smiled slightly at the DA, who was still glaring at her. "Was that so hard?" she asked sweetly but sarcastically. "I'll contact Dr. Spears to see when he'll have an autopsy report and a COD," she added. "Thank you for your time."

Later that afternoon, Gracie had acquired the autopsy reports on both women to compare. Spears, as usual, had been extremely accommodating about giving Gracie both reports. She'd assembled a quick dinner of whole grain rigatoni with grilled chicken, red pepper and artichoke hearts and was now savoring a salted caramel brownie from Bistro Adam for dessert: she usually bought a half dozen and froze them whenever she stopped at the eatery for lunch.

She looked at the two documents side by side on her laptop's wide screen. Pumpkin, who obviously thought she could aid somehow in the analysis, jumped up and curled in the 'boat' position on the sofa beside Gracie.

It now appeared that the first death, that of Sally Sullivan, had not been an isolated occurrence.

The second body had been that of Pattie Ford, 22 years old; the cause of death had been ethylene glycol poisoning and subsequent organ failure. Again, Spears had not determined the manner of death, but now that there were two cases, he had re-classified both as 'suspicious.'

According to Spears' report, the concentration of ethylene glycol in Ford's blood had been 875 mg/L when he'd run her blood serum through the gas chromatograph. As he had with Sullivan, Spears had done an examination of Ford's internal organs, specifically the kidneys, liver and brain. He'd discovered calcium oxalate crystals in the kidneys and brain, as well as some tubular necrosis in the kidneys. The morphology was almost identical to Sullivan's.

From her research online, Gracie understood now that someone could ingest relatively small quantities of antifreeze over several days, or even weeks, and just feel sick. Symptoms, like those Sally's friends described and those in Pattie's gym had observed, ranged from feeling dizzy and weak to being extremely thirsty, peeing more than usual, having diarrhea, mouth sores and even seizures.

However, ethylene glycol was metabolized by the body, and it was the metabolization which eventually caused the substance to become toxic, and which eventually would kill the one who had ingested it. Those metabolites, or metabolized substances, affected many organs as well as the central nervous system and cardiopulmonary function. Ethylene glycol became glycoaldehyde and finally glyoxcylic acid, formic acid and oxalate. It was the last three which were deadly.

What were the chances, Gracie considered as she munched the gooey brownie and absently stroked Pumpkin's head, that two people from the same town would both accidentally ingest a lethal dose of antifreeze? Slim, she figured. She knew from talking to Jack earlier that evening that he had already contacted the public health nurse in the county to rule out something like water supply contamination. If that were the case, both Jack and the public health nurse had thought that more people would have become ill, but they'd had the water system tested anyway, and it had come up clean.

Gracie was bothered by the fact that both victims, so far at least, were very similar in age although not in outward appearance. Both had been in their early 20's. Both had been petite and had had very good figures, although one had been a blonde and the other a brunette.

Gracie thought that fact was important: she didn't know quite why just yet, but determined to do more investigating to see if she could uncover any more similarities or connections between the two dead women.

Chapter Four

Jack, like Gracie, felt sure there was a connection between Sally Sullivan's death in her apartment and Pattie Ford's death at the gym. As Gracie had said, how likely was it that two people in the same small town would die of antifreeze poisoning within a few weeks of each other?

Occasionally, one heard about dogs or cats or even wild animals who, attracted to the antifreeze because of its sweet taste and smell, died from ingesting even the small amount that had leaked from a car radiator. Jack thought that most people were fairly careful nowadays about leaking coolant, and many had switched to the newer, non toxic type of antifreeze.

And it was hardly likely, he thought to himself Thursday morning on his way into work, that Sullivan and Ford had been licking antifreeze up off driveways. They had to have ingested it in an otherwise benign food or drink. The water supply to Stockbridge had tested ok. Neither Sullivan nor Ford had lived in a home with a private well which could have been contaminated: both had been on the municipal water system.

Spears had told Jack that he couldn't give him any kind of time frame for when the poison had been encountered by either Sullivan or Ford because both could have been exposed to small amounts over a period of weeks before finally succumbing. Sullivan's friends had said back in April that she'd been feeling ill and 'not herself' for about a week before her death. None of Ford's friends or coworkers had been interviewed yet: that was on Jack's 'to do' list.

Unfortunately, although Spears had ruled the deaths 'suspicious,' with such a small staff in the DA's office Jack couldn't really afford to focus on the matter until he had more to go on. He was involved with a months-long investigation alongside the State Police Narcotics Task Force, and together they were just days away from a huge county wide drug bust, so most of his energy needed to be devoted to that. They were looking to nab several dealers, some users and possibly one or two of the area's larger suppliers, if their luck held. He knew it was the proverbial Hydra: cut off one head and another grows in its place, but at least he could feel good about eradicating some of the drug network.

So far, no word about the upcoming bust had leaked out. Jack hadn't even told Gracie, although he thought that he probably should tell her pretty soon. Like him, she was stretched thin, being the only news reporter covering the county for the *Intelligencer,* and she appreciated a 'head's up' if something important was happening.

Jack arrived at his office. It was early: just 8 a.m. Millie was already there, and with a smile, Jack saw that she'd started the coffee. The rich brown aromatic brew was foaming into the carafe and he could smell the welcome fragrance the moment he set foot in the office suite.

He exchanged pleasantries with Millie, who kept her age a dark secret but had been the secretary in the DA's office for more than four decades Jack figured she had to be nearing 70. Then he got his messages and sat at his desk to review his appointments for the day. Millie brought him a large mug of black coffee. He smiled.

"You don't have to do that, Millie," he said quietly. "But thank you."

"You're welcome, Jack," Millie replied. "I rather enjoy bringing coffee to you, Jack, precisely because you never expect me to," she added fondly, and retreated to the outer office and her desk.

Jack's schedule for the day looked like what he called a 'paper day.' In other words, he didn't have any meetings or field work planned, so theoretically would be in the office all day doing paperwork. And with 30 some warrants related to the drug bust being readied to go before Judge Norcross for his signature, Jack would need to be at his desk.

He sighed, and opened the first file. Maybe, if he got them all reviewed this morning, the Judge could sign them all this afternoon and the bust would go down tonight. If that were the case, he thought, scanning and noting the completeness of the first file, he should really call Gracie, and just tell her to be prepared for a lot of arrests and a big story.

By rights, he supposed he should call the *Gazetteer,* too. Maybe he'd ask Millie to make that call: Jack liked Gil Butcher about as much as Gracie did, which was not at all.

He sighed, and got busy.

By late Thursday afternoon, all the warrants and their attendant paperwork had been checked, submitted and signed; Constables and State Troopers were starting the process of serving the warrants. Jack, who had ordered lunch in and had hardly moved from his desk all day, decided to bring home the files on Sullivan and Ford and review them in comfort. He could also make a list of people he would want to interview in the Ford case, and with a little luck he could get started on that the next day, if the drug bust went down successfully.

He stood, and stretched. It was 4 o'clock, and the sun had gone behind a bank of clouds which likely presaged rain overnight. Jack took a deep breath and looked out the window of his courthouse office. The leaves on the tree just outside were a beautiful, fresh color, and even though the early summer afternoon was overcast, it was greenly fragrant and lightly warm.

He would dearly love to get to the gym for a racquetball game. He felt a sudden pang, almost a physical sensation, of loss. Mike had been his reliable, and favorite, racquetball partner, almost always up for a game or two if he and Jack were both off duty at the same time. At least once a week they'd also shared a pizza and a couple of beers at The Docket or some other handy watering hole, discussing work, and Sandy, and Gracie, and a host of things in between including current events, outdoor sports, and books.

Jack sighed again, and looked down. God, how he missed Mike.

He could probably find a new racquetball partner at the gym: there was often another person on his or her own looking for a partner to play. But it wouldn't be the same.

He headed out the door with his files under one arm, and decided that he'd go home to Woof, change, and then go for a run over at the High School's track. Then it would be dinner, and the review of those files.

Settled in his mind, Jack got into his unmarked cruiser and headed home.

About 9 pm Gracie's iPhone rang. She and Pumpkin had just finished watching an installment of 'The Adventure of English' on the History International Channel, and she switched off the satellite TV as she leaned over to grab her mobile device.

It was Jack, who was ready now to tell her about the big drug bust currently in play. On purpose, the activities surrounding it were being kept off the scanners and radios, with only coded comments which could relate to anything, or nothing, being made.

"I wondered if something was up," Gracie said by way of reply when Jack had finished telling her about the warrants, and advising that she check with the local magistrate in the morning to see who had been picked up. "There was a lot of chatter on the scanner, and on the police band tonight, but it all sounded kind of meaningless, lots of 'what's your 20's' and 'finished with that detail' which they don't normally broadcast."

Biting back a grin, Jack realized she was right. But he trusted that only someone as observant--and as wickedly sharp--as Gracie would have noticed that.

Then they turned their conversation to the Sullivan and Ford cases.

"I haven't made much progress yet," Jack complained, frustrated. "I've gone over Sullivan's friends' statements, though, really carefully and caught something that I missed before," he admitted.

"Well, you have been kinda busy," Gracie put in supportively. It was true: just a week or so after the Sullivan death had come across Jack's radar, Senator Jesperson's suspicious death had occurred, and then the mis-identified body in the local arboretum had been discovered.

"Here it is:" he rustled a page. "Sullivan's girlfriend Tanya Oakes said when Officer Moss was asking about Sullivan's hobbies that she was really into physical fitness."

"I believe that," Gracie commented. "Both of the girls were in very good shape, from what I could gather from the autopsy reports."

"Right. But Oakes told Moss that Sullivan had belonged to the Sure-Fit Gym."

"That's the gym where Ford was found," Gracie replied quickly. "She was a member, too."

"Right."

"Ah-hah!" Gracie crowed.

"You think it's significant," Jack said, sounding as though he certainly thought it was.

"Absolutely. It's a great connection!" Gracie enthused. "When are you interviewing Ford's friends, and the staff at the gym?" she queried.

Jack sighed. "I'm going to start with Ford's family and friends tomorrow if I can. The funeral's Saturday so for their sake I'd like to have my part in all of this over by then. But I won't have time to get to the gym until maybe next week."

Gracie didn't hesitate. "I'll do it," she offered happily.

Chapter Five

This was the tricky part: Gracie wasn't a detective for the county, she was a reporter. As such, she was empowered to ask questions, of course, and investigate her own theories and leads, but the impetus to do that could not be information Jack had shared with her.

Of course, anything she obtained on her own she could freely choose to share with Jack, but he had to be careful about getting 'tips' as it were from 'the press.' That wasn't normally a practice that law enforcement encouraged.

A couple of times he had referred to Gracie as a 'confidential informant' and had even gone so far as to start a file on her as he would with any CI, just to be on the safe side.

Both Gracie and Jack had always been well aware of the limitations that ethics put on their relationship. They regarded it as a challenge rather than a hindrance, however, which meant that they usually came up with a solution.

Thursday night's conversation was no different.

"I'll do it," Gracie said happily, meaning she would go to the Sure Fit Gym and talk to staff and members about the deceased, Pattie Ford and Sally Sullivan. "I have time tomorrow."

Since all her stories for that week were filed, and the *Intelligencer* was hitting the newsstands the next morning, Friday was generally a 'free' day for her.

"Yeah, okay, I can see you would want to ask them about Ford," Jack came back. "Everyone knows she was found in the locker room at Sure Fit. But why would you ask about Sullivan? Only Officer Moss and I are supposed to know she was also a member at that gym."

Gracie thought for a moment. She understood his point, and she knew the interviews with Sullivan's friends wouldn't be made public while the case was still under investigation, so there would be no way she could have learned about them except through Jack.

"Well, I can go and just start asking about Ford and then maybe get to see a membership roster or something and then have a reason to ask about Sullivan. Or maybe someone there will offer the information that Sullivan was also a member," Gracie added with hope. "I mean, someone there has to have realized that both dead women belonged to Sure Fit."

Jack hemmed and hawed for a minute, then agreed. "But don't mention Sullivan until someone else does, and don't go breaking into any files to get membership lists," he admonished.

"Me? Break into files? Why, whatever could you mean, Jack?" Gracie asked, affecting innocence with a grin on her face. She knew that Jack was only too aware of some of her less than by-the-book methods for getting information.

She promised that she'd be on her best behavior, and only protested mildly that her breaking in to get records in the course of her sleuthing on a previous case had provided the clue that had broken the whole thing wide open.

Jack sighed in reluctant agreement.

"Okay, so I'll swing by the gym first, and then do my errands, and I can tell you what I've found out tomorrow night," Gracie concluded.

"Sounds good. Should I--" Jack was about to ask if he should call her, or if she wanted to call him, but Gracie interrupted.

"I've got a couple of new recipes to try out," she said. "Do you want to bring Woof for a visit and come for dinner? We can discuss everything then."

Jack smiled into his phone. With Gracie, experimental recipes almost always turned out delicious, since she was an accomplished home cook, unafraid and adventurous in the kitchen. Although being a guinea pig normally wasn't a role he enjoyed, when it came to Gracie's cooking, Jack tended to agree willingly to it.

He obligingly said that dinner would be fine, and they arranged for him to come out to her house about 5:30 pm.

"That way, you'll have time to give Woof a nice long walk through the meadow before it gets dark," Gracie added.

The staff at Sure Fit Gym was more than happy to talk to Gracie, once she told them what paper she wrote for. The *Intelligencer's* sports and leisure reporter had done a big article on their opening two years before and Sure Fit ran advertisements in the paper as well. Kim Foley and Jarrod Pinkus, the co-owners, were both in their early 30's; Pinkus told Gracie that the *Intelligencer* was the only paper his father and mother subscribed to. Ecology-minded Foley said she subscribed on line to save paper, and was an ardent admirer of the publication. She also compiled a weekly listing of her church's activities which the *Intelligencer* published, along with those from other houses of worship in the area.

"It's such a thoroughly good newspaper," Foley explained much to Gracie's delight. "I mean, the news is accurate, and you never print sensational things: it's always tastefully and discreetly done. And I love all the hometown news sections."

"It was part of my childhood, that paper," Jarrod reminisced fondly, relating that he'd been in boxing as a student, and won several competitions that the *Intelligencer* had covered.

"I have a friend who boxes," Gracie said, thinking of David MacLachlan, the young Detective Constable she'd made friends with in England. She owed him an email.

"Oh? What gym does he use?" Jarrod asked, interested.

Gracie smiled. "Erm, doesn't live around here, I'm afraid."

Having the entrée of Jarrod and Kim being loyal fans of the *Intelligencer,* Gracie proceeded to ask about Pattie Ford. Kim told her that Pattie had been a faithful attendee of Sure Fit's advanced aerobics classes, had taken a yoga class twice a week, and had also used their 'wellness spa,' which offered whirlpools, saunas and massage services. Kim affirmed that Pattie had been 'somewhat obsessed' about her body, as Gracie had surmised.

"She wasn't satisfied to be in good shape: she had to be perfect," Kim remarked, and Gracie wondered if there weren't a bit of cattiness in the gym owner's tone. "You should have heard her if she, like, got a zit: you'd think the planets had fallen out of the sky!"

Kim was an attractive, healthy looking blonde with bright blue eyes and naturally rosy cheeks and lips. She was tall and slender, but boyishly so, with few curves in her figure.

Pattie, on the other hand, had been quite beautiful from what Gracie had seen in the obituary photo, and quite curvaceous from what she was now hearing from Jarrod and Kim.

Gracie, who had thought about her approach overnight and on the drive to Stockbridge that morning, had decided she could hardly ask the Sure Fit staff if Pattie had had any enemies. That sounded too much like the police, which she was not. Instead, she asked if Pattie had had any special friends at the gym.

"Oh, lots of the guys liked her," Jarrod said with a cheeky smile.

"You?" Gracie asked quickly, wanting to catch him off guard.

"Me?" She'd caught him: Jarrod's big hazel eyes widened even more in surprise. "Oh, no, no--" he shook his head. "I make it a practice never to date any of our clients," he said virtuously. "And besides, I'm already in a relationship," he added. Gracie wondered if that were with a man or a woman, but since she had no reason to ask, she didn't.

"You and Kim?" she asked instead, pandering to the folk wisdom that a man and a woman couldn't just be friends or business partners, they had to be romantically involved as well.

Jarrod shook his head again. "Nope. Just friends. Since high school. Kim is--" he looked into the middle distance, searching for the right word. The object of his commentary had left the gym's small business office where Jarrod and Gracie were still seated, to handle a customer at the front desk. "Well, she's a great business partner, and a good friend, but she's very religious," he offered, then he chuckled. "I'm afraid she'd never be in a relationship with a heathen like me."

Again, Gracie could hardly ask him what he meant, but it didn't seem to have anything to do with Pattie, so she dropped it.

"I don't suppose you could show me a membership roster?" Gracie asked quietly. "I mean, there might be people on there I know, so it would be easier to ask them about Pattie, you know, what she was like, etc. etc. For the article," she added, solemn. "You and Kim have been incredibly forthcoming, but not all people are, and if I already know the person it might be easier to talk to them, than just going up to a stranger and asking..."

Jarrod regarded her for a moment. "We keep our membership confidential," he replied, sounding disappointed at not being able to cooperate. "But I will tell you one strange thing."

"Oh?" 'Strange' could be good.

"Pattie was friends with Sally Sullivan," Jarrod said. "You know, the woman who was found in her apartment a few weeks ago?"

Gracie nodded. Just as she'd hoped: someone had brought up Sullivan's name.

"Did they take the same classes?"

"Sally and Pattie were both in yoga," Jarrod offered. "And they both used the spa a lot, but then, it's really popular."

"Was Sally, like Kim said Pattie was, 'obsessed' with her looks?" Gracie asked. "In a good way, I mean," she hastened to add, not wanting to run into the 'don't speak ill of the dead' shibboleth.

Jarrod waggled his head from side to side, deciding. "She was, but Pattie tended to be rounder if you know what I mean, so she really had to watch that her figure didn't get too curvy."

Gracie nodded to show she understood.

"Sally's metabolism was faster or something, I think: she could eat anything and never really put on weight. She didn't do aerobics, just the yoga, and I think she walked a lot, and her figure stayed the same."

Like Pattie's, Sally's figure had been nicely proportioned and from what Gracie had seen in the obit photos, she had been a remarkably lovely girl as well.

"Well, thanks, Jarrod," Gracie said, and stood.

Kim re-entered the office, smiling. "Got another new member!" she announced cheerily.

"Great!" Jarrod replied. "See what I mean, Gracie: she's an amazing saleswoman and a dynamite business partner," he said of Kim, whose smile broadened.

"You're not leaving already?" Kim asked Gracie, looking disappointed. "I'm sorry, I--" and she gestured towards the front desk, where she'd been occupied.

"Oh, no, no, business first!" Gracie exclaimed. "And you and Jarrod have been so wonderful, talking with me, I really appreciate it," she said again, striking just the right spot between sincere and gushing.

"Well, at least let me give you a tour of the place," Kim continued. "We've been open just for two years, but we're doing really well and we're proud of what we've accomplished, and of course, of the services we offer."

Gracie, who actually had lots of time that day, allowed herself to be shepherded by Kim through the front lobby and into a long hall which had airy high ceilinged rooms on either side of it. Some, Kim pointed out, were used for aerobics classes, or yoga. They passed another room which had a boxing ring and several related types of equipment in it.

"That's Jarrod's favorite room," Kim joked as they passed it.

The next room had circuit weight training machines, on which several people were huffing and puffing their way towards fitness.

Kim led Gracie into the center of the complex, and gestured to the men's locker room, then took her into the women's.

"Is this where--" Gracie began to ask and Kim nodded. "Yes."

They were quiet as they walked through, but of course the area where Pattie's body had been discovered was no longer marked. Long makeup tables with dressing room style lights, a bank of sinks and a row of private shower stalls and toilets completed the locker room, and then Kim and Gracie were back out on the other side of the gym's spacious single floor facility.

"Here we have a little juice bar," Kim said, indicating a small area with bottled water and various types of juices and power drinks in a glass fronted refrigerator. There were two blenders on the counter as well, and a selection of glasses, and a large bowl of fruit.

"What're the blenders for?" Gracie asked.

"Some of our members like to mix the juice with yoghurt," she said, pointing to a row of small white containers of plain Greek style non fat yoghurt on the bottom of the refrigerator. "Makes a smoothie."

"Of course! That's brilliant."

Kim beamed.

The women's spa section came next, and was the last stop on the tour. The men's facility, explained Kim, was identical. There was a steam room redolent with eucalyptus, a jacuzzi, a small wood-paneled sauna, and three 'treatment rooms' where members could book a massage.

"You've really done a great job on the place," Gracie praised.

"Thanks!" Kim smiled, flicking back her long blonde hair as she escorted Gracie back through to the front office. "You know, for Jarrod it's mostly about getting fit and being strong, and I encourage that, too, but for me, it's kinda like a mission," she confessed, glancing at Gracie to see if she understood.

Gracie nodded. "Well, doesn't the Bible talk about our bodies being God's temple?" she said to Kim, recalling what Jarrod had said about his partner's religious leanings.

Kim brightened and nodded. "Yes, exactly! I feel it's important to have a healthy mind, a healthy soul and a healthy body," she added. "And here at Sure Fit, we help people do that."

Chapter Six

"So what are we eating?" Jack asked Friday evening, seating himself, at Gracie's direction, at her large barn board kitchen table. They had just finished a two mile 'walk' with Woof across the meadow that abutted the gardens around Gracie's house, and up to the craggy promontory that overlooked the Hoosic River.

Upon returning to Gracie's home, Jack had wiped off Woof's muddy paws and released him to gobble down his dinner and then flop in front of the small fireplace in a corner of the kitchen while Gracie started cooking. For his part, Jack had uncorked a bottle of Barolo and sat sipping, watching and talking to Gracie.

Pumpkin had appeared as Gracie was pouring kibble into Woof's bowl. The cat crunched her way through the specially formulated organic cat food in her dish--which had a line drawing of a cat on it and the logo 'Purrfect'-- and then joined her canine buddy in front of the small kitchen fireplace. It wasn't on, as the day had been warm, but it was one of the duo's habitual spots.

"Well, this I made before you got here," Gracie answered, removing a small covered bowl from her stainless steel commercial grade refrigerator. She put the bowl in the middle of a large plate and then surrounded it with baked pita bread triangles she pulled from a zip lock bag. She had toasted them earlier as well. "It's baba ghanouj," she answered.

"Same to you, but I need a little more info," Jack quipped. The creamy dip looked good, but he appreciated knowing the ingredients before he ate, as a general rule.

"Just try it first," Gracie urged.

Shrugging, he did. It was lemony and garlicky with a roasted sort of flavor, and very good.

"Okay, it's good, I like it. Now what is it?" he asked again, laughing, and taking a sip of wine.

"It's roasted eggplant all mushed up with spices and sesame seeds and stuff," Gracie replied. "We've got a couple of new members in Club who are Syrian, and the other night at the Banquet they were talking about some of their favorite dishes, so I kind of got interested," she added in a self-deprecating tone.

"Oh! Well, I like this, so what's for the main course?" Jack asked, agreeable.

Gracie took a sip of the Barolo and then got up to continue cooking. "I have to do the cake first, so it can bake while we eat," she said by way of answer. Within minutes, she had combined the usual ingredients for a cake batter along with orange zest, orange juice and some mysterious spices from her cupboards, beaten it all together, and poured it in two round cake pans. Into her convection oven they went.

"Now I can start on dinner, which is chicken sofrito and tabbouleh," she replied gaily.

Jack recognized 'chicken' but the rest was gibberish. Still, if it was like the baba-whatever he was eating, it would be all right with him.

"So, what did you learn at Sure Fit?" he asked, finally. They had both somehow instinctively not immediately started discussing any 'business' until they'd had a chance to go for that long walk and decompress from the stress of the week.

"Nothing earth shattering, or I would have told you right away," Gracie admitted. She opened a plastic container and removed chicken breasts she had pounded thin and marinaded earlier that afternoon as she spoke. The marinade had been a mixture of olive oil, lemon, turmeric, cardamom, salt and white pepper, and the chicken breasts smelled amazing, even uncooked. They were destined for the indoor grill in Gracie's recently renovated kitchen.

Next she poured a cup of bulgur wheat into a pot of boiling broth on her range top. She told Jack about her conversation with Jarrod and Kim.

"So Sullivan and Ford knew each other," Jack murmured. "Interesting."

"Maybe there are other connections between them that we can discover, too," Gracie commented. "Did you find anything out from the family?" She knew Jack had talked to Ford's family and close friends that afternoon, which she imagined hadn't been a cheerful task.

He shook his head. "Not really. Ford was a secretary at a local car repair place," he told Gracie. "She wasn't dating anyone in particular; her brother said she had a lot of 'casual dates' but no one special. Friends said her big hobbies were working out at the gym and going on cruises once a year for vacation."

Gracie lifted her sable eyebrows and gave Jack an inscrutable look. "Sounds pretty boring."

He nodded. "I can't see why anyone would have any reason to kill her," he admitted. "And the same for Sullivan," he added, referring to the woman who'd died several weeks before. "She was the assistant produce manager at the Food Mart in Stockbridge. No boyfriend although her family and friends said she did go out to area clubs, at least once a week, usually with a couple of other people."

He had pulled financials on both Ford and Sullivan once Ford's body had been found, and the theory that the two deaths could be connected had been fleshed out. Nothing in either woman's credit report or band statements had indicated any reason at all for murder.

"Hmmm..." Gracie had sliced hothouse tomatoes and fresh cucumbers while Jack had been speaking. Now she whizzed up a mixture of oil, lemon juice, parsley, mint and scallions, then took the bulgur off the range top, drained it, and tossed it into the bowl with the parsley and everything else. She stirred it and Jack could smell the lemon and the scallions: fantastic.

"Maybe next week I'll start asking about Sullivan at some of the clubs her friends said she liked," Jack went on, thinking out loud.

"Good idea," Gracie said. "And maybe talk to some of the people at Food Mart?" she suggested as she put the warm bulgur mixture in a large casserole type dish, then layered the cucumbers and tomatoes on top. She set the dish aside, covered loosely with cling film. "And I guess the people at the auto place where Ford worked," she added.

"Yeah, you never know: maybe we'll find out someone's been embezzling money and Ford or Sullivan found out and got killed," he commented, recalling a case they'd solved together the previous summer.

Gracie grinned. "Nah: lightning doesn't strike twice, and besides, it's unrealistic to think that both Sullivan and Ford uncovered embezzlement schemes!" she declared.

It was time now to grill the chicken, so Gracie took care of that part of the meal prep while Jack set the table. He used, as Gracie had requested, the yellow and green striped linen napkins and matching place mats, and cleared away the few remains of the appetizer. Then he filled their wine glasses again as Gracie plated the grilled chicken with the now room temperature tabbouleh. She drizzled an olive oil-lemon mixture over the salad, and sprinkled chopped parsley lightly over the entire dish.

"This looks great," Jack said as they started to eat, and he was pleased but not surprised to find that the taste lived up to the appearance. "Wow, this is really good, Gracie. What other Syrian recipes are you going to make?" he asked jokingly.

Gracie just smiled. "I'm not sure. Farida has offered to have the annual cookout next month at their place in Sherwood Forest, so I'm sure there'll be more Syrian food there, even though everyone brings stuff," she added, speaking of one of the new Club members she'd been talking to. Farida was married to Koshy Salama who, along with his brother Chacko owned a big construction company. Their house in one of the most expensive suburbs of Pittsfield was supposed to be like something out of 'Beautiful Homes' magazine. "You could come with me, if you like," Gracie added. Her tone was carefully casual.

She wondered what Jack would make of her invitation. It was true: they weren't dating any longer, and it hadn't been a pleasant breakup, but they'd salvaged their friendship and she thought if anything they were closer than ever. She couldn't think of anyone she'd rather have come with her to the Club Cookout this year than Jack.

Except maybe David MacLachlan. But he was back in England, Gracie thought to herself. She really did have to email him, tonight, before she went to bed.

"Sherwood Forest?" Jack echoed, not directly responding to Gracie's suggestion at first. He whistled. "Pricey real estate," he commented, and Gracie filled him in on the Salamas' business. "Ah, yes, I've heard of that company," Jack commented. "They're pretty much the only game in town out here," he added. There were only a few other major construction firms in the western part of the state, and Salama Construction seemed to do most of the large--and well paying--jobs.

"So, you want to come?" Gracie asked again as she got up and took the cake out of the oven. They'd finished the meal and the wine bottle was empty, so Jack brought their plates and glasses over to the sink. "Coffee?" Gracie asked, switching subjects like she often did, with no preamble.

"Please," Jack answered. Then he leaned back against the blue quartz countertop and watched as Gracie rummaged in a cupboard for her Bialletti coffee maker. "Oh, we're even having Syrian coffee?" he asked, spying the unfamiliar package of ground coffee she had in her hand.

"Well, as close as I can come. I don't have a samovar," she said, sounding wistful. "But I think this Italian jobbie will work okay," she added. "I got the coffee special at this little grocery store on the West side that Farida told me about, so at least that's authentic."

She wasn't going to ask again. If he wanted to come with her, fine. If not, she'd go solo: she had before and it was no big deal. Not every Club member was married or in a relationship. But she would enjoy Jack's company, which is why she had asked him.

Jack was silent.

Gracie determined that the cake had cooled enough for her to pop both rounds from their pans onto a rack. She did this, and then measured the coffee and water into her Italian coffee-maker and set it on the range top to brew. As she got out a small bowl and started mixing shredded coconut, honey and almonds with orange juice, Jack cleared his throat.

"I'd like to go to the cookout, yeah, Gracie. But as what?" he asked.

Jack knew Gracie had broken up with Ben a few months before. Was she even thinking about another relationship, and if so, did she want to resume the relationship she'd had with him?

"Oh, it's not a costume party," Gracie answered, smiling, and deliberately misunderstanding him. "You just come as you."

"Ha ha, very amusing," Jack replied sourly. "You know what I mean, Gracie," he said, his voice huskier than he would have liked. She still got to him: she always had and she always would.

Gracie turned from her ministrations at the mixing bowl and faced him. The track lighting she'd had installed a couple of years back when she'd had her new kitchen put in illuminated his face clearly, and she could see his remarkably deep, denim blue eyes.

"As friends, Jack," she replied softly. "Really, really good friends, the best of friends," she added, still gentle. "That's enough for now, for me." She paused. "Is it enough for you?"

She knew Jack was still in love with her: he had told her so himself. The fact that he was in love with her was the reason he'd broken up with her when he'd found out she'd started seeing Ben Holmes. And while Gracie loved Jack--deeply--she wasn't sure if she was ready to make a commitment to him, or to anyone. That had been an underlying difference, even at the start of their relationship. But until she had started seeing Ben, it hadn't seemed to matter.

Breaking up with Ben had shown Gracie that she wasn't ready: yet. She hadn't been ready to commit to Jack, and when the moment came she hadn't been willing to commit to Ben. Or he to her, for that matter, unless it was on his terms. Gracie knew she was stubborn, but she'd learned that she had to find a man who wanted her as she was, not as he thought she could be under his tutelage.

Now, Jack nodded. "It's enough, for now," he replied honestly. He wasn't going to tell her that he wanted her in his life in whatever way she was willing to be in it: that sounded too needy. He'd accept the terms of 'the best of friends' for now, and his 'for now' was meant to warn her that eventually, irrevocably, he would want more.

Gracie smiled. "Good. I'm glad, Jack." She looked at him for another second, and then the coffee pot made a hissing noise as the boiling liquid poured into the chamber. Gracie turned, and took the pot off the range. "Okay, that's done."

Over dessert--Gracie had drizzled the coconut-nut-honey-orange juice mixture over the still warm cake slices, which had made a good cake practically ambrosia--she asked Jack if he'd ever had the pictures developed that Mike's fiancée Sandy had given him, along with the Nikon D-90.

"You know, I didn't get around to it, and I actually was going to ask you, if there aren't too many photos on the camera card, if you'd do it for me," Jack replied, finishing off his cake. "Your equipment is as good as what they have at the photo shop, and I thought if any of the pictures were really good, you could print out a few and we could send them to Sandy." He paused. "Who knows? There might even be some of the two of them on there, or of her."

Gracie nodded. "I can do that. Just give me the camera card." She understood, she thought, that the underlying reason Jack wanted her to do the photo processing was that the pictures Mike had taken--some on the day he died--were too precious, too close, to hand over to a stranger.

Jack grinned. "It's in my wallet," he replied, pulling the leather case from a back pocket of his jeans. "I stuck it there so if I drove by the camera shop I could drop it off, but I never did. And then I decided to ask you if you'd do them up for me."

Gracie nodded again. "I'm happy to." She stood, and collected the dishes and cups. "Let me get these washed, and we can look at them now, see what we've got, okay?"

"Oh, that would be great!" Jack said. "But let me wash: you dry and put away," he suggested, and Gracie agreed, and grabbed a clean tea towel.

Chapter Seven

By the time Gracie and Jack had viewed the photos on Mike's camera card, and Gracie had had a chance to enhance a few that Jack selected and print them out for Sandy, all thoughts of emailing David back in England had flown from Gracie's head. So Saturday morning, after she'd sipped a bit of her coffee and got her brain started, Gracie placed a call to David's flat over in Shoeburyness, a small town near where her cousin Verena lived, northeast of London. It was just after two o'clock in England.

"Hallo," David's voice answered on the second ring.

"Hi, David: I owe you an email, but I decided to give you a ring instead," Gracie greeted him. He sounded exactly the same as he had a month ago when they'd said goodbye on Verena's doorstep.

"Och, Gracie!" He sounded extremely pleased. "I'm glad you called, how are you?" he went on, his Scottish accent quite apparent. It was one of the things about him Gracie had found so charming.

Still did.

"I'm fine. How are you?" she countered.

"Ach, I'm all right. Missing you, though. You haven't got locked in any car boots ('kaahr buits') lately then?" he asked jokingly.

"No, I've been able to avoid that," Gracie returned with a laugh. That incident, while placing her in considerable danger at the time it had occurred, was quite funny in retrospect, she discovered.

"And how's your friend, the detective, Jack?" David asked innocently. He knew Gracie and Jack were friends, but Gracie had never intimated that there was or ever had been anything more between them, and David, gentleman that he was, hadn't asked. But David had sensed somehow that Jack was important to Gracie.

"He's okay. Mike's death was hard on him," Gracie answered. She had emailed David about the State Trooper's death on Mount Greylock. "The funeral was last week," she added, and went on to tell David about their trip up to Mt. Greylock's north summit, and the golden eagle, and her fancy that it could have been Mike's spirit.

"I believe that, Gracie, so I don't think you're daft for having that idea," David reassured her. "Remember, I'm Scottish: we have wee beasties and ghoulies in the nicht ye ken," he said, lapsing into an even broader dialect.

"Oh, now, you're not Robbie Burns," Gracie laughed.

David laughed with her. "Mount Greylock sounds beautiful. I'd love to see your country someday."

"It's a big country: maybe you could start with my state," Gracie replied, and held her breath. They'd briefly discussed him coming to visit her, just before she'd left Verena's to come home, but she hadn't known whether the topic had been part of an emotional leave-taking or a genuine desire on David's part. As for herself, she felt both apprehensive and delighted at the prospect of seeing him again.

"I'd like that, Gracie," David replied, but said nothing more. He was too well brought up to invite himself, so he would wait for Gracie to extend an offer to visit. If she did.

"So, what cases are you working on? Any more murders?" Gracie asked, deflecting the discussion away from the subject of a visit.

She and David spoke at some length about the cases he was working on and the two big stories Gracie had going: the drug bust and the mysterious deaths of Sullivan and Ford. David thought the two deaths could be connected, just like she and Jack did. He said that if it were his case, he'd definitely look for other links between the two young women.

"What about your friend's hiking fall, then, was it truly a terrible tragic accident?" David asked, returning to the subject of Mike's death. He remembered what Gracie had told him about Jack's suspicions.

Gracie sighed. "It was ruled death by misadventure, with the cause of death multiple trauma, but I told you that in an email."

"Aye."

"When we were up there, on Mt. Greylock I mean, it seemed that Mike could have slipped and fallen, since there was loose shale and a little ice, even at the end of May. But I find it hard to believe that Mike would have gone that far out onto the edge without a reason, and I can't imagine a reason."

"You said the CSU team thought he'd been taking a photo of something?"

Gracie nodded, but of course David couldn't see her. "They thought that maybe that was why he'd stepped as far to the edge as he must have, and then lost his balance. But Jack just brought over the camera card from Mike's Nikon last night and we looked at the pictures. I didn't see any that would have required him to go out to the edge like that," she mused.

"Aye," David agreed. "And when you think of it, Gracie, if he'd been taking a photo right before he fell, his camera would have been out, and it likely would have been smashed to smithereens, wouldn't it?" he offered.

"You're right," Gracie agreed. "That thought crossed my mind, too. According to the accident report, his camera was found in his backpack, which he had on."

"So, then, it's unlikely he was taking a photo," David returned. "Unless, of course, he slipped when he was putting the camera in his backpack, or putting the backpack on," he continued.

"Yeah, that could be, too." Gracie sighed again. "So, what are you doing today? It's a Saturday afternoon, why are you home?" she demanded, chuckling. "You should be out doing something exciting."

"I went to the gym this morning, yeah? And then I came home and had something to eat," David replied, but it wasn't much of an answer.

There were several single guys at the gym where David belonged, and boxed several times a week. Occasionally he'd go clubbing with them, but their objective--to meet girls--wasn't something David found himself as interested in now as he had been before he'd met Gracie.

He kept telling himself that Gracie was 3000 miles away, and he should meet someone who at least lived on the same continent. But when he did go out, even though he had an okay time and met some pretty women, no one interested him beyond that.

"What are you doing?" David asked Gracie, meaning her plans for the rest of the weekend.

"Well, I've got a lot of gardening to do," Gracie replied, and explained that in addition to mowing the grass, there were a number of seedlings she needed to tend to. "And there are always weeds to pull," she laughed. "And I've been thinking of having some work done on the house, as well," she added, realizing that this summer would be the perfect time to have the conservatory and hot tub put in on the East side of her house. As she said the words, she decided that when she had hung up with David she'd call her contractor, Larry, and see what he thought.

"Ah, then maybe not a good time to visit just now?" David said, returning to the subject of him coming to America to see her.

Gracie blinked. He was serious.

"I don't know when my contractor will be able to do the work," she explained, and outlined the project as she envisioned it, briefly. "But once I speak with him and get a time frame, maybe we can talk again about you visiting," she replied. "I'd prefer you to come once it's finished: then you can help me christen it," she said playfully, meaning the hot tub.

"I do have vacation time coming," David said, keeping his voice as even as he could with the image of himself and Gracie in a hot tub in his mind's eye. "I'd just need to give DI Jonas a month's notice of it."

Larry thought the idea of a conservatory with a hot tub was a great one: he always had, ever since Gracie had first expressed her wish to make such an addition, a couple of years before. When Gracie finally reached him late Saturday afternoon, they'd talked over the project for about a half hour.

Larry had helped Gracie with all the renovations to her 300+ year old house, ever since she had bought it and moved in some years before. Her neighbors Bob and Anna had recommended him to Gracie after friends of theirs (who also became friends of Gracie's) had raved over the work he'd done for them, and for their neighbors.

The first 'big job' Larry had tackled, after the health and safety things like the wiring, the heating system, the plumbing, and a new roof had been finished, was the Oak Room. This had required knocking two smaller rooms into one very large room which was then finished in blonde oak and featured a massive river stone fireplace on one wall. Larry had also installed a fabulous parquet floor which he had, under Gracie's direction, continued up over the half step of the Oak Room's threshold, and out into the main foyer.

Then Larry, along with his trusty crew, had gone on to the refurbishment of the rest of the interior of the house, which had been sadly neglected over many decades. Gallons of paint, acres of carpet and tons of new fixtures later, Gracie's historic home was a showplace, yet it retained its cozy welcome feeling and remained true to its New England pioneer roots.

And Larry had to admit, not only did Gracie entrust him with the work, she looked to him for design guidance, a creative aspect to the construction work he didn't often encounter. He was very appreciative of this, and also of the fact that Gracie was always willing to learn and help out. And, unlikely though it may have been, over the years Larry and his wife Betty Jo had become friends of Gracie's.

Some of his 'crew' had worked on Gracie's gardens as well, landscaping them to her specifications and making a series of specialty areas where herbs, perennials and annuals bloomed and thrived on what had once been overgrown weeds.

Their biggest accomplishment in landscaping had been the salvaging of an old stone wall which once upon a time had marked the drive in front of Gracie's house. Larry's crew had taken it apart stone by stone and re-assembled it off the southeast corner of the house, where it now created a 'secret garden' effect. This sheltered area, offset with an old cast iron gate they'd reclaimed from a salvage dump, was where Gracie had her herbs and her roses and other tender things which needed protection from the wind. They had installed an ornamental fountain in the center of the walled garden; in another part of the property which was more open, there was a larger ornamental pond with a small waterfall.

The next big project had been Gracie's new kitchen: completed a couple of years ago, it featured top of the line appliances, blue quartz counter tops, pillowed subway tiles as a back splash, and an indoor grill.

Now, Larry and Gracie discussed the proposed conservatory or 'sunroom' as Americans called it, with a small hot tub in it. As Gracie envisioned it, French double glass doors would open off the formal living room and open into the conservatory, which would be sited where forsythia bushes currently grew, along the eastern exterior wall of the house. Besides the construction of the conservatory itself, wiring would have to be run to the new addition as well as heating ducts. And of course, the exterior wall of the farmhouse would have to be knocked out to install the French doors. But since this section was an early twentieth century addition to the home and not part of the original 1679 structure, Gracie didn't feel bad about that idea.

After they had roughed out the plan, Larry consulted his calendar.

"Well, it's already June," he thought out loud. He mentioned another project he had going at the moment, and several more scheduled for the upcoming weeks. "But if we order the conservatory, it'll take about a month to ship over, so I'd say we could start in early July."

"And how long do you think the project would take?" Gracie asked.

Larry hemmed and hawed a bit. "I doubt it'd be done by the Fourth," he cautioned. He knew Gracie usually held a big open house/cookout for the Fourth of July, as he and Betty Jo were always invited. And he remembered her disappointment the year her kitchen was in a shambles because of the renovations and she couldn't hold her 'house party.'

"I didn't have Memorial Day weekend," Gracie confided, "because of Mike Garnier's death. I had hoped for the Fourth of July, but I'm willing to wait for Labor Day," she added, trying to sound cooperative.

"Well, why don't you find the conservatory you like and email it to me. I'll see if I think it's workable: remember, this is New England, Gracie, not Old England. The weather's not the same," he admonished. He explained that he would have to make sure the glass and insulation, not to mention the materials themselves, were up to code and could withstand the temperature variations and weather conditions common in western Massachusetts. "Then I'll email you back, and you go ahead and order it. And as soon as it comes in, I'll switch around what jobs I can, and get it done as fast as possible. OK?"

Smiling, Gracie agreed, and hung up. Then she fired up her laptop, and started searching for exactly the conservatory she wanted.

Chapter Eight

"You missed the boat on this one, Butcher!" Gil Butcher's publisher--and boss--yelled through the telephone at his lackluster Editor. It was Monday morning and Butcher, who was nursing a hangover and looked like he'd spent the entire weekend in the wrinkled, slightly rank clothes he was still wearing, had taken his publisher's call only reluctantly.

"I wanted to wait until all the warrants were served and do one big story instead of two or three." Butcher made his excuse feebly.

"Which would be fine if you worked for *Reader's Digest*," snarled his publisher in reply. "Last I checked, the *Gazetteer* was still a newspaper, and that means we print the news, as it happens or as close to it as we can!"

Butcher said nothing, but he ran his stubby, nicotine-stained fingers through his unkempt, greying hair. He needed a haircut, he realized. He felt his chin: and a shave.

"You could have done what the *Intelligencer* did, say that more information would be coming once all the arraignments had been held," the publisher went on. "Why didn't you do that?" he asked reasonably, but his anger still simmered quite near the surface.

Why hadn't he done that, indeed, Butcher thought to himself. Probably because the warrants went out on Thursday night and the *Gazetteer* had already come out for the week. So he hadn't seen the big rush, even though he could have put a 'breaking news' article on the internet version of the paper. And because he was lazy, and hadn't felt like allowing actual work to interrupt the bender he'd had planned for the weekend.

"We'd already published for the week," Butcher started to reply feebly.

"We could have put it on the website," spat out the publisher.

Butcher said nothing.

"I'm tired of having G.B. Barufaldi scoop us every other week, Butcher," the publisher went on. "You'd better get yourself up to speed or you'll find yourself out of a job," he finished firmly. "Don't say I haven't warned you. I can't be more fair than that."

"Yes, Mr. Behr," Butcher answered miserably. The publisher hung up. Butcher replaced the phone in its cradle and sat back in his desk chair. If he lost this job, he would lose his last chance, at least in the newspaper world: he'd been fired, or 'downsized' from the other writing and editorial jobs he'd held, all for newspapers in the same publishing group. He knew that other communications conglomerates were aware of his track record, and he knew that it was highly unlikely anyone else would hire him.

He hated being stuck out here in what he derisively referred to as 'the sticks.' He missed Hartford, CT: *The Hartford View* had been a weekly, too, but at least Hartford was a city, not a one horse town whose big claim to fame was that it was near the Turnpike. Being put in charge of the *Gazetteer* had been a demotion, and Butcher resented it mightily: all the more so, because deep in his heart he knew he deserved it.

The *Gazetteer* could have been a good little paper, too, as Mr. Behr, his publisher, was always trying to tell him. Behr wanted the *Gazetteer* to focus on Pittsfield but Butcher felt there wasn't enough real news in the small western Massachusetts town and so sporadically covered other news in Berkshire County and even Hampshire County to the East. This, Behr had told him, diluted the paper. He should focus on the *Gazetteer's* strengths and make it a real hometown newspaper with in depth local interest stories you wouldn't get, or get as much of, in the *Intelligencer*, which covered all of Berkshire County and contiguous Hampshire County.

But Butcher didn't agree with that, more out of pride than out of any newspaper marketing savvy, and so he tried to cover as much territory as the *Intelligencer* did. The results were disastrous. The paper was bland, full of factual errors and often played 'catch up' to other news sources. Readership was down, and so was advertising revenue.

Butcher's reporters kept leaving him, too, mostly because his people skills were worse than his personal hygiene, but also because Butcher himself wasn't much of a reporter or writer. He was a sloppy and unsure editor, and was surely no teacher. His one fairly decent reporter, Joe Pilecki, had stayed for three years, but had just left to write for a daily up in Brattleboro, Vermont. So Butcher was once again understaffed, and had to do everything from covering courthouse notes to writing up big stories to doing the 'Mrs. MacGillicuddy's Cow Turns 30' type stories.

Although he tried to tell himself that this was the reason his work was generally below average, the truth was, Butcher just didn't have any talent for the newspaper business. He'd gone into it because a family friend had got him his first job following a dismal and barely deserved graduation from Southern Connecticut Community College with an Associate's degree in English. Butcher hadn't gone to college to get an education: he'd seen it more as a vehicle to party and find girls. Which he had. But when graduation rolled around, his GPA had been 2.5, the minimum to wear the cap and gown. And he'd garnered an appendage he certainly hadn't planned on: his first wife, who was glowingly pregnant with his conceived-under-the-bleachers baby.

It had pretty much been downhill from there, since Butcher had never developed crucial values like personal responsibility, integrity or any kind of work ethic.

And now, as he gazed around the sparsely populated newsroom of the *Gazetteer* on what should have been a busy Monday morning two days before going to press for this week, he became even more depressed and angry.

It was all Gracie Barufaldi's fault, he told himself perversely. He put an antacid in his mouth, then another, and tried to chew his hostility away. It didn't work.

If Barufaldi weren't such a good reporter, he wouldn't look so bad. And it wasn't that she was that good, he told himself, desperately trying to believe his own version of the truth: she had unfair advantages, help from sources he should have, too, he thought petulantly.

The fact that Gracie had built up the relationships with her sources over time and had earned the high esteem in which she was held and the trust she was afforded, Butcher conveniently ignored. And as for unfair advantages, Gracie and Jack had always gone out of their way to make certain that neither his nor Gracie's ethics had ever been compromised by their relationship, even when they'd been dating. Just like she and Paula, the County Prothonotary: they were good friends through Club and also had a professional relationship, and were always careful to define and keep the boundaries.

But much of that type of thought was, literally, beyond Butcher's capability. He saw the world very much as a young child does: black and white, punishment and reward. And, like a child, he always looked to others to take responsibility when things went wrong.

By Monday afternoon all but one of the warrants out for the thirty-some drug dealers had been served, and Gracie spent quite some time doing the second part of her story on the big roundup. Then she finished up her profile on Pattie Ford, and filed everything electronically. Her paper came out Friday morning, and technically, her deadline was Wednesday evening though she could push it to Thursday noon if she had to. She was certain more stories would pop up before press time, but for now, she had made her rounds at the Pittsfield courthouse and the police station and magistrates' offices, so she could relax.

After doing a little weeding in the flower bed directly off her screened porch, and eating dinner, Gracie decided to look through Mike Garnier's pictures again. She had a thought that although she had made copies for Sandy of some photos Mike had taken, Jack might also like some of Mike's pictures for himself, to remember his friend by. She had already run her own shot of the golden eagle through her photo enhancement and editing program and printed it out, and was vaguely contemplating putting together a little album of sorts for Jack, with the photo of the eagle on the front cover.

She settled in the Oak Room on one end of the comfy leather sofa and opened the photo file on her laptop. Slowly, she scanned the pictures. Mike had taken several from the pinnacle of the north face of Mount Greylock: she recognized the spot, particularly since she had just been up there a few days before. He'd also taken a couple of close-ups, apparently on his way up the mountain, of ferns and rocks and one kind of far away shot of a blue heron.

Gracie was able to enlarge and enhance this, and she cropped and fiddled with the color and contrast on the other photos as well until they were the way she wanted them.

Two of the shots Mike had made from the top of the trail were very similar, and Gracie had to really study them both before she selected one over the other.

One showed the opposite ridge, a part of the canyon, and just the tip of the far curve of the ridge on which Mike had stood, and from which he'd fallen. The other, apparently taken with the wide angle feature on Mike's fancy camera, centered on the same view, but included the tips of some hemlock trees which stood to the right of the lookout point, and almost the entire curve of the ridge top to the left with evergreens, and deciduous trees coming into leaf.

Gracie squinted at the latter. Were those trees? Leaves? Shadows? She closed her eyes and then opened them again: if you concentrated on the pattern of light and dark within the stand of trees on the ridge top to the left, it almost looked like two human shapes, camouflaged within the forest.

"Nah..." Gracie admonished herself aloud, but the image bothered her. She sighed, and pulled the photo out of the 'lineup' of her regular photo editing program, and accessed a specialized digital imagery program she'd bought, mostly just to play around with. It had the capability of breaking down a digital photo into discrete pixels and then doing any number of things with them, including sharpening edges, reversing light and dark, sensing a variety of standard patterns, and changing colors.

The brain does a lot of 'correction' of the images the optic nerve feeds to it. For example, humans actually see everything upside down, but motion and gravity sensors in our bodies 'tell' us which way, literally, is up. So our brain 'flips' the image and we then see the world right side up. Or, when we are reading something with a missing or misspelled word, the brain will often automatically supply or correct the word.

The fancy digital enhancement program was meant to break down a digital image so completely that it would go beyond the automatic corrections made by our brains and enable a photograph to be examined in a more objective manner.

Black and white, as it were.

Gracie put Mike's photo into this program, and then cropped and enlarged it so the photo consisted only of the area she was concerned with, the part where it looked like two figures were crouched among the trees. She took it down to pixel level, sharpened it to the max, and then went back to normal view to see if it had made any difference: the outlines were a little clearer, at least to her eye.

What made it hard to discern the images was the pattern of light and dark from the leaves, and the shadows they cast. Frowning, Gracie went back down to the pixel level and removed the color from the photo. Then she reversed positive and negative. This made the light parts of the photo dark and the dark parts of the photo light. It could end up being just as confusing as the original, she thought as she zoomed back out to normal view. Or it could throw whatever outline or shape was there into a more recognizable image.

It took a minute to process what she was seeing with everything reversed. It was like looking at a film negative. But Gracie quickly saw that her initial impression of two figures among the trees had been correct: with the light/dark reversal, the figures stood out more.

One more filter. If it worked, it would hardly be conclusive, but it would be another piece of evidence, perhaps. She selected the pattern recognition feature and then selected 'human figure.' Her computer whirred briefly as the software completed its analysis. Then the picture, still in reversed exposure mode, reappeared and dotted red lines outlined the two areas Gracie was concentrating on.

She gasped. Apparently, two people, one crouched low and the other half-standing, had been hiding in the trees on the other end of the ridge when Mike Garnier had been, atop the north face of Mount Greylock. What had they been doing there? Were they hikers, too? And more importantly, if Mike had slipped and fallen, as the police had theorized, why had those two people in the trees failed to render aid or go for help? The time stamp on Mike's photo put them in the vicinity at time of death.

Surely they would have seen his fall. And surely, if Mike had fallen, he would have made some kind of noise: a cry for help, or at least the sound of loose rocks falling as he slipped. Even if the people in the trees had been looking in another direction at that moment, they surely would have heard something.

But the hiker who had called 911 when he'd seen Mike's body had made that call more than 24 hours after Mike had fallen to his death, according to the police report and the time of death established by the coroner. And if Gracie recalled correctly, the 911 caller had been hiking alone; Mike's photo showed two people in the forest on the ridge top.

Stunned, Gracie sat back against the sofa cushions and stared at the image on her computer screen. There was no way any better view of the people's faces could be obtained, even with her fancy software: the shot had been taken from too far away and the faces were camouflaged by the shadows. But there was no doubt in her mind that there had been two people up on Mount Greylock along with Mike that fateful afternoon.

And there was no doubt in Gracie's mind that even though their faces remained a mystery, she was looking at a photo of Mike's killers.

Chapter Nine

Jack had driven straight over to Gracie's when she'd called him about 9 pm Monday night and told him what she'd found in the photo Mike had taken. Once he had arrived, Gracie repeated with him the steps she'd taken to enhance the photo, and showed him the finished product.

Like her, Jack had been stunned.

"I knew he hadn't just slipped and fallen," Jack murmured, low. "He was murdered. And it probably has to do with that whole Juvenile Detention Center thing he was investigating."

"And you really think you can't tell Rita Licora?" Gracie asked, meaning the Detective who was Jack's counterpart in Hampshire County.

Jack shook his head. "I don't know about her." He paused. "Mike was pretty sure she was seeing Mark Broadstreet--Sandy's old boss? The head of Juvenile Detention. If something is going on that's--"

"Hinky," Gracie replied.

"OK, 'hinky,'" Jack echoed. It was as good a word as any. "Then Broadstreet has to be involved, and Licora has to at least know about it, even if she's not directly part of it."

Gracie nodded. "And the DA in Hampshire County?" she asked. She'd mentioned him before, but Jack hadn't sounded enthusiastic about contacting him.

Jack got a funny smile on his face. "Don Jenkins?" He sighed. "He's okay I guess. I don't know if he's involved, but I suppose I could see if I could find out." He shrugged.

"You don't like him?" Gracie asked, curious. She hadn't ever actually had occasion to talk to or interact with Jenkins, now that she thought about it, since Hampshire County wasn't in the area she covered for the *Intelligencer*.

Jack gave a wry chuckle. "It's just that he reminds me of that guy on 'Dragnet' you know? 'Just the facts.' " He shook his head. "Really old school, too."

Gracie nodded.

Jack looked again at the enhanced photograph. "You know what this makes me think of?"

"No, what?"

"Remember President Kennedy?"

Gracie nodded. She knew about Kennedy and his assassination, even if she was too young to have lived through it.

"Remember some conspiracy theorists insisted that there had been a second gunman on the grassy knoll who had also fired on the motorcade?" Jack asked. Kennedy and his assassination had long been a subject that fascinated him.

Gracie looked unsure. "Vaguely."

Jack looked at the picture Mike had taken again. "They've done all sorts of things to the photos and films taken that day to see if they could pull up an image of a person standing on that grassy knoll as the President's car went by," Jack explained. "But of course, they can only do so much, even with the best, most modern technology, because the original photos and films aren't digital." He pointed to the photo Gracie had worked on. "This is digital, which is why you were able to manipulate it so well."

Gracie nodded. "Okay, so what do we do with it?" she asked, meaning the shot of the two people in the trees. "We already know there was no 911 call or report of a hiker in distress until the one late Friday afternoon from the guy who found Mike," Gracie recalled.

"And Mike left Thursday morning," Jack put in.

"Yes, the photos are date stamped for Thursday. The last one--" she quickly opened another window on her laptop's screen and scrolled down a list. "The last one was taken on Thursday at about 3 pm."

Jack was quiet for a moment. "I think we have to have an autopsy done, to see if there is any evidence of murder," he said, low.

"Would there be? I mean, if someone had just pushed him off?" Gracie asked.

Jack shook his head. "No, not if they just pushed him. But if I wanted to murder someone and make it look like an accident, I'd want to be sure the person was really dead before I staged the 'accident,' " Jack replied.

Gracie nodded. "So you're thinking someone hit Mike on his head first or something, and then threw him into the ravine?"

"Or strangled him. Any external bruises would have been masked by the bruises sustained as he fell against the rocks. And after he'd been out there overnight..."

There had been quite a bit of scavenger damage to Mike's body, Gracie knew.

"But Mike's buried. We'd have to get the body exhumed to do an autopsy," Gracie said almost in a whisper. Once before she'd been involved in a case where a dead body had been re-examined. In that situation, a second autopsy had been done with the result that a different cause of death had been found, and a young woman falsely accused of the crime had been cleared.

"Mmmm...Mike's mother can request it," Jack replied, thinking out loud. "Can I borrow this?" he asked, pointing to the enhanced photo. "I'd like to show it to her, and tell her what we think and see if she'll agree to have Dr. Spears do a full autopsy."

"Of course," Gracie answered. "And if she does agree and Dr. Spears does find evidence of murder, then what?"

Jack sighed. "Well, then, we know it wasn't an accident, and we start looking for someone who would have wanted to kill Mike," he answered solemnly.

"Now, I'll be in my meeting, Ruth, but you've got the computer and if you need anything, you just pick up the phone and buzz Debby and she'll help you with whatever you need," Itty Azar said in a soothing tone. His wife, Ruth, had rolled her wheelchair up close to a small desk in one corner of Itty's office and was busily logging on to the internet. She spent hours each day on Facebook, MySpace, and on her own blog, 'The Wheels Go 'Round' which chronicled her disabilities and her daily struggle with Multiple Sclerosis.

"Yes, Itty," Ruth said with an absent smile. "I know." She was, after all, familiar with the routine: Itty had been bringing her to work with him most days for the past several months, ever since her MS had got so bad that being on her own for more than a few minutes at a time wasn't a good idea. The computer she used was an 'extra' one, her husband had told her, from the office of someone who'd been the victim of downsizing the year before. And the internet connection was already there, so what did it matter if she logged on?

Ruth occasionally felt a twinge of guilt at the arrangement: after all, she wasn't a Hampshire County employee and yet she was in the county courthouse, using a county computer and the county internet provider nearly every day. Itty always brought her lunch, but a few times a day she'd ask one of the secretarial staff to bring her a glass of water, or a snack from the vending machine in the break room. And even though she paid for the snacks, of course, and often for something for the secretary, too, Ruth still felt it was somehow wrong: she was taking that person away from her job to tend to her.

On the few occasions she'd tried to discuss this with her husband, particularly at the beginning of what would become her daily trips to work with him, Itty had dismissed her concerns, saying that because he worked so hard for the county and was so valuable, no one would question it if he bent the rules a little.

'I'm a county commissisoner,' he had told Ruth. 'I give hours and hours of my own time to this county. The least I can ask in return is a corner of my own office for my own wife. You're not bothering anyone, anyway,' he had concluded.

And Ruth truly did try not to be a bother. But despite what Itty thought, sitting in his office all day, even with the internet, got boring after a while.

She had suggested that she go to an adult day care facility: there were a couple of very nice ones in Northampton, so it wouldn't be any trouble for Itty to drop her off on his way to work. And she knew those places had activities, even speakers, and most importantly they had other people for her to talk to. In Itty's office, even though all the secretaries and the rest of the staff were friendly, Ruth hesitated about talking with them too much, and taking them away from their work.

But Itty had nixed the day care idea, although he hadn't given her much of a reason. Ruth didn't think it could be because of the cost of such places: Itty always seemed to have plenty of money, and their insurance might even pay for part of it. And on the days he couldn't bring her to the office where she was either with him or within earshot of staff, Itty paid for a private home health aide to come to their house. That surely had to cost more than the day care would.

Now, Itty had left to go to the weekly Commissioners' meeting. Ruth turned to the computer she thought of as 'hers.' She logged on, and then sighed. A cup of tea would be nice: should she see if Debby had time to make one for her?

Before his death, Mike had asked Jack if he could pull financial records on Mark Broadstreet, the Hampshire County Juvenile Probation Chief. Jack had, but nothing had looked out of line.

Monday night when Jack and Gracie were discussing the case and he reminded her about this, Gracie decided to do a little investigating on her own. Jack was still busy with the Ford and Sullivan deaths. She knew he was slated to check out Ford's apartment Tuesday. Sullivan's family had already cleaned out her flat, but Jack was hopeful that they still had her things in storage and would let him go through them, looking for any clue which might help in the investigation of her death. Jack felt sure that Sullivan's and Ford's deaths were connected, he just didn't know how. Yet. And he felt sure they had both been murdered, but he couldn't prove it. Yet.

Tuesday Gracie got busy on her laptop. If, as Mike had theorized, something strange was going on with the Hampshire County Juvenile Detention Center, she ought to be able to find indications of that, even if she couldn't find actual proof.

She researched the Center itself first. It had been built three years before by Salama Construction with money granted to the county through the Massachusetts Commission on Crime and Delinquency. The building had cost just over $14.5 million and had 70 beds. It accepted inmates from the entire western Massachusetts area and in some cases from other New England states; the main portion, however, came from Hampshire County and the Springfield area.

The MCCD grant had required a 25 percent county match: this translated to $3.6 million which the county had obtained via a low interest loan. Hampshire County planned to pay back the loan through boarding costs of the inmates at the Center. A fee to accomplish this was built into the rates.

So far, from what Gracie could find, Hampshire County had been on time and paying appropriate amounts. The loan wouldn't be satisfied for several more years, but nothing appeared out of line or in arrears.

Next, she logged on to the Salama Construction website. She knew already that Farida Salama, one of the newest members in Club, was married to the owner, Koshy Salama. But on the website, she discovered that his brother Chacko was a co-owner. Still, that didn't mean anything. Neither Koshy nor Chacko had any sort of criminal record. Both had been born in the U.S. Chacko had gone through a divorce a couple of years before, but that was the only peculiarity, if one could call it that, Gracie could find.

Finally, she did a Boolean search on 'Hampshire County Juvenile Detention Center' and came up with a myriad of websites which mentioned the Center. Some listed its staff and services. Others were articles which had been written before and during the time the Center had been built, dealing with the need for such a facility. Still others were focused on Epiphany, the for profit group that ran the Center and was headed by the Center's Director, Sasha Yedid.

A visit to the Epiphany website revealed next to nothing. There was a photograph of a large group of people gathered for the ribbon cutting at the Center. Identified in the photo were the county commissioners for Hampshire County: Itty Azar, Stu Bernhardt and Lilly Sonnheim. Also identified, standing next to the commissioners in the front row, was the Director of Epiphany, Sasha Yedid, Mark Broadstreet the Juvenile Probation Chief, and Chacko and Koshy Salama of Salama Construction.

Sighing, Gracie gave up for the moment and decided to make herself some lunch. Then, since the unpredictable New England weather had turned sunny again, she thought she would go out to her garden and make another stab at doing some weeding.

Chapter Ten

Wednesday Gracie did some grocery shopping at the large organic supermarket in Pittsfield. Her smaller needs were met by the shelves of Cheshire's 'Market Basket' grocery, but for more exotic items, she generally sought out one of the national organic grocery chains.

As she was contemplating the avocados and thinking up ways to use them in various dishes, she heard her name. She turned.

"Gracie? It *is* you!"

"Farida! Hello, how are you?" Gracie said with a smile, greeting the woman who had just joined Club. "You shop here too, huh?"

"Yes. Between here and the little store I recommended to you, I can get anything I need," Farida agreed.

"Oh, and I should have called you or emailed you," Gracie put in, contrite. "That place was just great! I had fun looking at all the different things, and the coffee was delicious. The meal came out well, too," she added, and told her friend about the chicken sofrito she'd made for Jack.

Farida seemed pleased.

"So, anything new? What are your plans for the summer?" Gracie asked. "Besides the big cookout, I mean," she added with a laugh. The Club Cookout, which Farida was hosting this year, was a month away.

"Well, two weekends ago my cousin got married out on Cape Cod," Farida told Gracie chattily as they wheeled their carts through the produce section. "They have a house there and have invited us to go for a visit, so we may do that if Koshy can take a little time off."

"He's awfully busy, isn't he?" Gracie asked companionably.

"He does work very hard, Gracie, but I think he takes great pride in his work."

Gracie nodded. "Salama Construction built the Juvenile Detention Center in Hampshire County, didn't they?" she asked rhetorically.

Farida smiled. "Yes, one of the biggest projects the company has ever done," she answered proudly. "There's talk of a new wing of Springfield General going up next year and Koshy says he'll bid on it: that would be very exciting."

Again, Gracie nodded. She plucked a couple of broccoli crowns from the display and put them in her cart.

"And you enjoyed the Club end of year Banquet?" Gracie asked.

Farida answered emphatically: "oh yes, very much. I am so happy to be a member!" She went on to explain to Gracie that since marrying Koshy about ten years before, around the same time he'd started up Salama Construction with his brother, she had felt quite isolated. "I had the children, of course, but I longed for adult companionship. And there was Koshy, but he was always so wrapped up in business," Farida said. "I missed my sister and the rest of my family in Weymouth," she told Gracie, naming her small hometown south of Boston.

"I should imagine you did," Gracie said sympathetically.

"Yes. I saw everyone again when we went to the wedding two weeks ago, and it was wonderful. And now I'm in Club, I hope to make many new friends," Farida finished, still smiling. Then a thought struck her. "I have pictures! I just picked them up," she added, rummaging in her handbag and then drawing out a brightly colored packet which appeared to hold a number of photographs. "I can show you my sister," she told Gracie, who bit back the goodbye which she'd been just about to give. A few more minutes wouldn't hurt, and Farida seemed so happy and excited.

Gracie duly admired the usual slightly lopsided and out of focus photos of bride and groom, attendants, parents, uncles, aunts, and so on. In all honesty, she had to admit that Farida, who was herself quite attractive, had a knock 'em dead gorgeous sister. Talia was younger than Farida, and had been one of the eight bridesmaids at the gala wedding.

"She's absolutely stunning," she told Farida sincerely.

"She got all the looks in the family," Farida sighed.

"Oh, come on, I wouldn't say that!" Gracie protested as Farida showed her more pictures, these from the reception. Gracie smiled and nodded and then put out a staying hand. "Who's that?" she asked, pointing to a man seated next to a woman in a wheelchair at one of the tables. He looked very familiar to Gracie, but she couldn't immediately place him.

"That's Koshy's second cousin, Itty Azar and his wife Ruth," Farida answered simply.

"Itty Azar, the Hampshire County Commissioner?" Gracie asked, wanting to be sure. He looked so different in evening wear!

Farida nodded.

"They're second cousins, Gracie, that's not a crime," Jack said reasonably later that day. Gracie had finished her shopping and returned home, then driven the short distance to the *Intelligencer's* offices in Lenox and asked her editor, Dave Tiller, if she could spend some time in the newspaper's morgue.

The morgue was the place, often just a store room or a big closet, where a publication kept all of its back issues. At the *Intelligencer,* the newspapers had been bound in large annual leather volumes. Recently, all the old editions--and the *Intelligencer* had been started by Dave's great-great-grandfather in 1838--had been converted to microfilm. For the last decade, everything was on computer disk and there was both a microfilm reader and a computer available to researchers.

It hadn't taken Gracie too long to find the article she had wanted: four years before, their Hampshire County reporter Abe Todd had done a story on the commissioners and the bid opening for the new Juvenile Detention Center. Todd had listed the bids, which had been received from five construction firms. Salama's bid had been the lowest, by nearly a quarter million dollars. By law, the county was compelled to accept the lowest bid on this type of project, presuming the bid met all the requirements.

As far as that went, Gracie thought, that checked out.

She looked even further back, but there was only a mention, a couple of months before, of the 'RFP' or Request for Proposal going out on the project; as far as she knew, that would have been the public's first notification that such a project was in the wind.

She made a note of the date. But she wondered if Commissioner Azar, who had signed off on the grant application as prepared by Broadstreet, had told his cousin about the proposed Juvenile Detention Center in advance, maybe even giving him inside information, so that Salama Construction could be sure to submit a winning bid.

That was unethical, and possibly criminal, but she didn't think there was anything that anyone could do now: all of that had happened years ago and any evidence was long gone. At any rate, Gracie didn't like to think of her friend Farida's husband being involved in anything underhanded.

But she'd still called and told Jack what she'd learned. And now, his response was disappointing.

"Don't you think Azar might have told his cousin about the Detention Center project?" Gracie protested, and outlined her theory that inside information from his cousin had given Salama Construction an edge in the bidding process.

Jack sighed. "I suppose it could be so, Gracie, but as you said, finding the proof would be next to impossible now." He paused. "I saw Mrs. Garnier today," he said then, sounding grim.

"Oh, Jack," Gracie interjected, sympathetic. She didn't imagine it would have been a very jolly interview.

"She was really shocked when she saw the picture," Jack went on. "And then she got angry, because she thought there were two people on Mt. Greylock who could have helped Mike. And then she was horrified, when I explained that the photo was probably of Mike's killers."

"So she accepts that it might have been murder?" Gracie asked gently.

Jack sighed. "Yep. Turns out she always wondered, because Mike was such a good climber. But of course didn't say anything because the forensic team and the coroner seemed so certain it had been an accident."

"Well, it does make sense. Unless you know--knew--Mike," Gracie agreed. "Not only was he an accomplished hiker and rock climber, he was super safety conscious."

"That was the most important thing he stressed whenever he took a group of Scouts out on a hike or a wilderness experience, or taught climbing, or anything: safety first. Safety no matter what," Jack echoed.

"So, will Mrs. Garnier ask Dr. Spears to do a full autopsy, and request an exhumation?" Gracie queried.

"Tomorrow: she said she'd call him tomorrow." Jack paused again. "I tell you, Gracie, burying him once was bad enough. This will be a nightmare."

"I know, Jack: but at least if Dr. Spears does a complete autopsy and finds evidence of foul play, you'll be able to open a real investigation and find out who killed Mike. And that would make him happy, and proud. And it will help you, too, to get him justice. So try to feel good about that," she counseled.

Jack grudgingly said he supposed Gracie was right, and told her he'd keep her apprised of developments.

"If Dr. Spears gets the paperwork done quickly, Judge Norcross might sign the exhumation order by Friday, and we could schedule it for Monday morning," Jack added.

Contrary to Gracie's supposition at the beginning of the week, no other events presented themselves prior to press time, so she was free to carry on with her investigation into the Hampshire JDC. After she'd exhausted every file she could uncover on Salama Construction, the Center itself and Epiphany, the company that ran the Center, she decided to see what she could dig up on all the individual people involved with the JDC in any way.

Jack had pulled financials on Mark Broadstreet, and Gracie knew he hadn't noted anything unusual or strange. But that didn't mean Broadstreet wasn't hiding money in an account outside the US, or under a different name, or for that matter in a shoe box under his bed. Gracie thought she'd check out the rest of the people involved first, before she tried to get a line on offshore accounts and other more underhanded ways of secreting ill gotten gains.

She started with the Hampshire County Commissioners: Itty Azar, Stu Bernhardt and Lilly Sonnheim. Both Bernhardt and Sonnheim came up clean. Azar's financials looked okay at first glance, but a little digging pulled up an account on which he was a signatory, even though it was an account in his wife Ruth's birth name: Ruth Romano. In order to make that link, Gracie had had to find Itty and Ruth's marriage certificate on which her original surname was listed, and then run a financial check on that name. Finally, once she'd located the account in question, she'd checked to see who else had access to the account, and found Itty Azar's name.

None of this was especially legal, or illegal, although the privacy laws were quickly catching up with electronic data. But the way Gracie looked at it--and this was something she and Jack and even she and Ben had argued about--if she could get the software to find weaknesses in financial institutions' firewalls and then exploit those weaknesses to uncover information, that was fair game. The information she gained access to was no different from what a potential employer might be able to find by running a credit check on an employee. She just gained her access through somewhat unorthodox methods, because she was not a credit reporting firm.

And second, of course, she always rationalized her marginal activity (as she liked to call it) by asserting that the ends justified the means. If her unorthodox methods helped her help Jack or the police find criminals and bring them to justice, well, all well and good.

So Ruth Romano's account was quite healthy: it showed a $40,000 opening deposit on a date four years before: and the date looked a bit familiar. Gracie grabbed the notes she'd made at the *Intelligencer*'s morgue. Bingo: the RFP on the Hampshire County JDC had been published on May 11. All bids were due in by June 30. They were awarded on July 6, by the commissioners, during a public meeting.

The $40,000 deposit had been made on May 12.

A second $40,000 deposit had been made July 10.

It looked like Itty had been 'rewarded' for throwing the bid to Salama Construction, first when the RFP went out and then when the bid was awarded. Of course, this was only circumstantial and Gracie would have to see if she could trace the source of these deposits before she could be really sure--and before she could tell Jack.

Chapter Eleven

Gracie noted that it was getting quite late: her clocks were all chiming midnight, starting at about five before the hour and finishing with her beloved crystal regulator at about three minutes past. But she was too involved in her research on the people involved in the building and maintaining of the JDC to stop now.

Carrying her laptop with its screen still showing the transactions for the account in Ruth Romano's name, Gracie moved into her kitchen and switched on her electric kettle for a cup of tea.

There had been a pause in deposits to the account for over a year after the bid had been awarded, she saw as she scanned the document on her screen. If Gracie's theory were correct, this would have been during the construction phase of the JDC when no money was coming in. So it made sense that no 'kickbacks,' if that was what they were, would have been issued.

A significant withdrawal of $12,000 had been made in December of that year and Gracie wondered what that had been used for.

Starting in the following year, regular monthly deposits, on or about the 10th of each month, of another $40,000 were entered into the account. These deposits began two months after the opening of the JDC, according to Gracie's notes from the morgue.

Withdrawals after that were sporadic, and most were for just a few thousand although one for $135,000 and another for $87,500 caught Gracie's eye. She wondered what those had been for, too.

When the water boiled, Gracie poured it over a PG Tips tea bag and waited for the tea to steep. She gazed out her greenhouse window onto her quiet, early summer garden. The irises were the most prominent feature of the garden right now, most with buds showing, and some in bloom. A full moon was up and washed everything with warm silver.

Hearing activity besides the tapping of Gracie's fingers on her computer keys, Pumpkin had arrived in the kitchen, ostensibly to offer companionship. But she really wanted to see if Gracie had put any treats in her food bowl and was rewarded when Gracie popped two of the crunchy morsels which advertised themselves as 'dental delights' into the ceramic dish.

Her tea steeped, Gracie added a splash of half and half and sat at her barn board table where her laptop awaited. Back to the Romano account.

She noted the dates of the largest withdrawals, thinking that she would see if she could find records of any large purchases around these same times: cars, jewelry, furs, and similar luxury items.

Then she turned to the Salama Construction principals, owners Koshy and Chacko. She felt a little guilty prying into Koshy, and therefore Farida's financial information, but breathed a sigh of relief when nothing untoward presented itself. Even when she checked Farida's birth name, she didn't get a hit. So it looked like they were on the level. At least so far.

Chacko's financials were pretty clean, too, but Gracie made a note to herself to check for offshore accounts for him as well as for his brother, and for Broadstreet.

The last person Gracie ran a check on was Sasha Yedid, the Director of the JDC and head of Epiphany. She appeared to have virtually no debt: she owned her home and car, paid off her credit cards in full every month, and paid for the private school she sent her child Ishtar to a year in advance.

Gracie scanned Yedid's file: for someone whose salary from Epiphany and the JDC was only $98,000 a year, she seemed to live very well. But perhaps there was something Gracie wasn't seeing, like a divorce settlement?

She switched out of that program and went into the one that allowed her to check for criminal and civil actions on a person. Sure enough, Yedid was divorced: four years before, from Chacko Salama.

"Whoa, now, that's interesting," Gracie murmured, sipping at her tea.

Pumpkin, who had curled up on the small rug in front of the kitchen fireplace, even though the fireplace wasn't on, miaowed, startled at Gracie's exclamation.

"Not you, baby," Gracie said to the cat. "But Mummy's found something odd," she added, turning back to the laptop.

There had been no settlement award listed. Of course, Chacko could always have given Sasha a lump sum and not made it part of the official court record. But checking Yedid's financials for the period in question Gracie could find no large deposit that might indicate this.

She sighed. Sasha Yedid was obviously into conspicuous consumption: she drove a Lexus, lived in a home last valued at $1.2 million, went to Canyon Ranch every three months, and had credit card charges from stores like Neiman's, Horchow, and Saks. If Chacko had given her the house and maybe the car, for example, in the divorce, Gracie still didn't think Sasha's salary from Epiphany would cover the credit card purchases, the spa trips and the private school for Ishtar. Maybe Chacko paid for that, too? Still, it seemed like Yedid was spending way more than she made, and on a regular basis.

Despite the tea, Gracie still felt weary, and her eyes burned. She yawned. She ran one more check on Ishtar Yedid, and found nothing. Then she tried Ishtar Salama and found a savings account on which her mother, Sasha Yedid, was signatory.

At the last statement date it contained $1,650,000.

Mike's body was exhumed on Monday and Dr. Spears, sensitive to the nature of the case, did the autopsy that afternoon. Although it pained him a great deal to do it, Jack had asked to attend the autopsy and of course Dr. Spears was more than happy to allow this.

X-Rays of the entire body were taken first. While these developed, Dr. Spears started with the usual observations of the abrasions and contusions on the body, which were still discernible, and noted any scavenger damage as he had in the initial cursory examination of the body.

He was about to start the Y incision when his Diener came back with the X-rays. "You might want to take a look at this first, Doc," she told Dr. Spears and with a nod to Jack, she put the films up on the light board.

Dr. Spears scrutinized the first film of Mike's head and shoulders and then began nodding. He turned to Jack.

"You see this?" he asked, pointing with the tip of one gloved finger to a portion of Mike's neck, just under the skull.

Jack nodded.

"See that?" he pointed to what looked, even to Jack's untrained eye, like a break in a bone.

Jack nodded again and instantly knew what he was looking at: a broken hyoid bone.

"Hyoid's broken," he said to Dr. Spears, who smiled at him the way a teacher would smile at a favored student.

"Correct. This man was strangled."

"Are you sure?"

"Well, yes. But we'll open him up and do a visual check of the bone. I should be able to rule out post mortem occurrence, even after the time that's elapsed, from internal muscle bruising and from the bone itself."

"Why would someone strangle him if he was already dead?" Jack asked in a voice which itself sounded strangled.

Dr. Spears smiled. "They wouldn't, Jack. But if someone wanted to take issue with the X-ray and my ruling of strangulation being the cause of death, they could try to say that the injury to the hyoid bone was encountered during Mike's fall down into the ravine."

"And was it?"

Dr. Spears shook his head. "I don't think so. In fact, I doubt it very much. But a physical exam will rule out that possibility, which is why I'm going to do it."

Jack nodded, and they returned to the exam table and Mike's body. Jack stood a little bit away and kept his face mask firmly attached. Gracie always told him to put a little mentholatum under his nose to mask the smell of rotting flesh during an autopsy but he'd forgotten the ointment. And in any case, the fact that the corpse before him was that of his good friend Mike was something he just couldn't get over.

His stomach somersaulted neatly, and Jack tried to both take a deep breath and not breathe.

"I'm just getting a little air," he said to Dr. Spears. "Be right back," and he dashed for the door.

The autopsy suite had a small side door which led directly to the car park of Pittsfield General. Jack, without even a glance for the Diener who was doing paperwork at another desk, opened this little door and stepped out gratefully into the early summer morning. He exhaled and then inhaled deeply.

Better.

"Peter, got a sec?" Jack asked. It was very late Monday afternoon, and he'd just returned from the autopsy. Re-interment was to be done privately the following morning.

The DA, who was unhappy to still be at his desk at the unconscionable hour of 4:15 pm, lifted one overgrown eyebrow and tried to give Jack what he thought of as his 'bulldog' look. It merely made the DA look dyspeptic.

"We've got some new evidence in the Garnier death," Jack told his boss, unaffected by the 'look' and stepping a few paces into the DA's office. He held the file containing Dr. Spears' revised autopsy report as well as the findings from the original case file, but he knew Popovitch wouldn't care to see it.

"Unh?" Popovitch grunted. He appeared to have been deeply engrossed in something on his computer screen, but as this was turned away from him, Jack couldn't see what the fascination might have been.

Popovitch pressed a button, and the screen went to the 'wallpaper' mode, which had little logos of the statue of Justice all over it and a chiron running across the middle that said, 'Berkshire County District Attorney Peter Paul Popovitch'.

"You know Mrs. Garnier asked for a full autopsy, right?" Jack began again. Popovitch just looked at him. "Well, Dr. Spears did that this afternoon: Judge Norcross signed the exhumation order last week and the exhumation was this morning."

Popovitch nodded. Jack noted that when he did this, the fat under his chin rolled over his shirt collar like rising dough over the perimeter of a bowl.

"He found evidence that Mike had been strangled--and that was the cause of death. He's revised his means of death in the case to 'homicide.'"

"So we have to re-open the case?" Popovitch asked, not sounding pleased.

"Well, of course, Peter," Jack blurted out before he could edit his words or tone. "I mean, it's a murder investigation now."

But as Berkshire County DA, it was Popovitch's say so that was needed to re-open an investigation, no matter how much Jack, as County Detective, might want it.

"Mmmmm..." Popovitch sighed. "You were buddy-buddy with that Garnier, weren't you?" he asked in a seeming non-sequitur. But Jack knew how Popovitch's mind worked. He would bet that Popovitch wanted Jack to recuse himself from investigating Mike's murder on the grounds of their friendship. Then he would decide to investigate the case himself, which would be tantamount to doing no investigation at all.

"Well, we were at Dartmouth together," Jack admitted, never missing an opportunity to flourish his Ivy League college degree in Popovitch's face. Popovitch had gone to U. Mass and then Northern Ohio Law School. "But since then we'd lost touch and only saw each other occasionally," he finished. He wasn't exactly lying: he and Mike had lost touch right after college. But then when Mike found himself assigned to the Pittsfield Barracks of the State Police and Jack was in Pittsfield as Police Chief--and later County Detective--they had renewed their friendship. And 'occasionally' could mean once a week, couldn't it?

Popovitch looked disappointed. He frowned down at the dirty blotter on his desk. "Oh. So there's no need for you to step away from the investigation?" he asked, sounding prim.

Jack made a dismissive face and shook his head. "No, not at all, Peter." He'd be damned if he let anyone else handle it!

Popovitch sighed and rose from his chair with two grunts, a push off from his desk, and what Jack was almost sure was a small fart. "Well, all right: you have the paper work for me to sign?" he asked grudgingly, as though re-opening the case were a huge favor he was granting rather than his sworn duty to serve justice.

Silently, Jack handed him the sheet of paper which had been on top of the file he held.

Popovitch glanced at it, then signed it with a flourish and handed it back to Jack. "I wish you good luck," he said, sounding as though he meant the exact opposite of his words. "I can't imagine who would have wanted to kill him."

Jack nodded, not needing or wanting to explain to his boss what had persuaded Mrs. Garnier to request the exhumation and that full autopsy. Right now, except for Gracie, he trusted no one, and would keep to himself the information about the two figures in the forest just a few hundred yards away from the spot where Mike 'fell' to his death on Mt. Greylock.

Chapter Twelve

Completing her usual 'rounds' to get the weekly updates for the areas she covered for the *Intelligencer* took a little longer on Tuesday because Gracie travelled into nearby Hampshire County to check a few things out on her own.

She had looked up the address for Salama Construction's main office in Northampton. Conveniently, this was near the Hampshire County Courthouse and the Juvenile Detention Center. Chacko Salama lived in Southampton, not more than a five minute drive away. Sasha and Ishtar Yedid, Chacko's ex-wife and daughter, lived in Knightville, a little to the west. Itty Azar lived in Goss Heights, just south of Knightville.

Gracie's plan was to check out the homes and, if she could locate them, the cars of each of these 'parties of interest' as she thought of them, and make a note of it. Soon, she knew, she'd have to share what she'd uncovered about Itty Azar's and Sasha Yedid's —the former Mrs. Chacko Salama's—bank statements. But she wanted to have a little more to go on as well.

When she'd checked out Salama Construction's website, she hadn't found anything peculiar. However, a list of their recent projects read like a list of the top construction jobs in western Massachusetts. Several had been in Hampshire County, while others had been in Franklin, Hampden and Berkshire Counties. Gracie wanted to drive by their offices, mostly just to see what it looked like, and also to see what kind of cars the people who worked there, drove.

Often, she'd found, people spent extra income on a high end vehicle and she wondered if she'd discover any luxury cars at the construction company: that could be a clue to hidden income for certain employees.

When she arrived at Salama Construction, she found a large building and an even larger lot with two warehouses and several trucks and heavy equipment vehicles. Its location just north of the county seat was extremely convenient, she had to admit, but the employees' parking lot was a disappointment: it looked fairly middling to Gracie.

She spotted a number of Toyotas and Hondas, several Hyundais, a few Fords and Chevys, a Lincoln Navigator that Farida had told her belonged to Koshy, and a Porsche Cayenne. Gracie let out a long breath and checked the license plate: it matched the information she'd gleaned from Chacko's financials and credit report. This $160,000 luxury SUV belonged to him.

Next, she drove the few miles into Northampton proper. It was a pretty little town, much influenced by nearby Smith College and the seasonal skiers who frequented Mount Tom. In the courthouse parking lot she found, again, the usual mix of vehicles including a couple of new Jeeps and several Impalas and Avengers which she knew had to be law enforcement vehicles. Several of them had the telltale extra wing mirror, or a grille separating the front and back seats, and their roofs were generally bristling with antennae.

When she'd checked Itty Azar's bank statements and found the one registered to Ruth Romano, his wife's birth name, she had noted that Itty drove a Cadillac Escalade. She found it in the car park, and noted the name of the dealership on the rear license plate holder. That withdrawal of $12,000 from the Romano account still gnawed at her, and as she regarded the top of the line silver grey SUV, Gracie wondered if she could match the withdrawal to the purchase date of the Escalade.

Not that that's what the vehicle had cost: it was in the $90,000 range, she thought. But the $12,000 would have been a good downpayment, or most of one, allowing Azar to have reasonable car payments.

He was smart, Gracie thought, preparing to exit the lot: he had known not to march in to a car dealership waving $90,000 in cash to buy a luxury vehicle. That would have raised a red flag for sure, because no county commissioner should have that kind of cash on hand unless he were independently wealthy. And Gracie knew that unless you counted the Romano account, Itty Azar was not—apparently—independently wealthy.

There was a midnight blue Mercedes SUV in the parking lot, too, Gracie noted as she swung by. She scribbled down the license plate number, planning to check it later. Not that such a ride was out of the realm of possibility for a county employee, but it did seem a bit much. A Jaguar nosed into an end space caught her eye as well: probably whoever owned it had another vehicle for the winter, Gracie mused, since Jags were notoriously bad in cold and snow. But this one, a classic XKE, was a beauty: golden tan with a cream interior. It looked like it had been lovingly restored and was being equally lovingly maintained. Again, she wrote down the license plate: a bit excessive, if it belonged to a county employee.

Gracie spotted a squat, dumpy man with thinning wiry grey hair and bulbous blue eyes exiting the side door of the courthouse as she drove around towards the main road. He was wheeling a slight, white-blonde woman in a wheelchair and Gracie suddenly realized it was Itty Azar. And his wife, Ruth, née Romano. Gracie wondered briefly what the commissioner's wife had been doing at the courthouse, but then realized that she could have been meeting him for lunch or something. Still, it was only 11 a.m., and they had both been coming out of the courthouse. Maybe she had had county business?

Well, that wasn't her concern, Gracie thought, pushing the incident out of her mind. She drove quickly down Route 10 to Southampton, and found Chacko's home in a luxury community of townhouses. She quickly located the main office, and parked, walking briskly up to the door and entering since the sign read, 'open.'

"Good morning," Gracie said, smiling and affecting an accent not unlike her English cousin Verena's, although several social ranks above it. "Might I have a brochure on your complex? My aunt is considering relocating to this area and may consider buying here," she extemporized to the attractive middle aged woman seated at the reception desk.

"Of course!" the receptionist said. "But I'm afraid we have no vacancies at the moment. When is your aunt planning to move?"

"Well, the cruise she's on goes through June," Gracie answered, inspired. "And she generally summers at her villa in Italy, so not until the autumn, I expect," she replied, taking the glossy four color folder the woman handed her.

The receptionist brightened. "Well, we may have something by then," she said. She looked around although the office appeared deserted except for the two of them. "Between you and me, one of our owners just recently had to move to an Alzheimer's Care Facility. She sold her place to an investment firm and they're planning amazing things for it: it's going to be quite the showplace when it's finished. Perhaps that would suit your aunt?"

Gracie nodded. "Yes, perhaps." She held up the brochure. "Well, thank you for this. I'll pass it on to Auntie, and we'll be in touch if we're interested," she said, smiling again, and walking quickly back to her Jeep. She couldn't wait to see what kind of set up Chacko had going, or to run a check on recent sales at 'Mapledurham Estates' to see what kind of money Chacko had had to fork over to buy into the place.

Next was a visit to Goss Heights, where Itty and Ruth Azar lived. Unfortunately, there was no way to get from Southampton to Goss Heights easily or directly: one of the less attractive features, really, of New England driving. Gracie did, however, find a road which headed south, to Westfield and then a turn off to a dirt road which cut over to Montgomery. Here, another paved road led northwest to Goss Heights.

Thanking her lucky stars for having a Jeep, Gracie arrived in Goss Heights in about 20 minutes and located the Azar home quickly. It was in a typical upscale residential area with homes varying between quite new and about 75 years old, in all different styles. Most of them had fairly large lots, many wooded, which Gracie knew would push up the real estate value.

The Azar house was a large brick affair which appeared to have been modified to accommodate Ruth's wheelchair. A two car garage, accessed by a steeply sloping driveway, was under one portion of the house, and extensive shrub plantings surrounded it. There was a large grassy area which verged into woodland.

Gracie drove by slowly, but it appeared no one was home. She clocked an in-ground outdoor pool and what looked like a recent addition at the rear of the house with peculiar fenestration: all the windows were high up in the wall, and made of frosted glass. She made a note to herself to pull construction permit information for Hampshire County and Goss Heights and see what Itty'd built recently on to his home. She recalled the $135,000 withdrawal, and another for $87,500 and thought that perhaps some home improvements could be tied to these.

Route 112 between Goss Heights and Knightville was a 'scenic route' and it lived up to its name. Gracie located Sasha Yedid's home in Knightville just after noon.

This was a brand new construction with every bell and whistle one could wish for, from what Gracie could see from the outside. Done in whitewashed brick face with a fancy copper and metal roof, the two story home was styled like a French château and extensively landscaped with costly weeping Atlas Cedars, rhododendrons coming into spectacular red bloom, and junipers.

Gracie spied a large covered patio to one side, an in ground pool with a pool house or cabana, and a hot tub adjacent to it, and a meticulously manicured cedar shaving path which led off at an angle through impossibly green grass to a small brick barn. Behind the barn was a corralled area and in that area was a beautiful bay horse, happily cropping the new spring grass.

OK, so Sasha Yedid lived far beyond her means. Gracie knew that keeping a horse meant thousands of dollars a year in upkeep, food, vet bills and so on. She would bet that little Ishtar was learning to ride, and made a note to check out area riding schools and see if she could find her registered. And she had to remember to check out Briarwood, Ishtar's private school.

All this on eighty something thousand dollars a year? Gracie didn't think so. That little savings account of Ishtar's was funding the Yedid lifestyle. And either Chacko had given Sasha a whopping divorce settlement off the record, or Sasha was getting kickbacks from the JDC.

That place was to be Gracie's last stop. Located as it was on the western edge of Northampton, it would complete her circle of investigation and put her back on Route 9 west, which would take her to Route 8 north, and home.

She found the JDC and again saw a mix of vehicles in the employee lot. The Lexus SUV she knew belonged to Sasha Yedid was gone: probably the Director of the JDC was out to lunch, Gracie thought. She made a U-turn and headed out of the lot, trying to decide if she should stop for lunch now or wait until she got home. The appearance of a restaurant called The Green Street Café, and even more importantly, Yedid's SUV parked in the contiguous lot, decided the question.

Gracie pulled in, parked, and headed for the front door.

She was shown immediately to a small table in the airy, beautifully appointed restaurant. Scanning the menu, Gracie realized that the place specialized not only in locally sourced food but also in French cuisine. How fortunate that Sasha Yedid liked nice restaurants.

Gracie looked around the restaurant, which was filling up slowly. Judging from the prices on the menu, it wouldn't be everyone's first choice: lunch would run Gracie, not including tip, well over twenty-five dollars.

She tried to see if she could spot Yedid; she recalled, more or less, what the woman looked like from the photo of the JDC opening she'd seen. But it wasn't Yedid, it was Mark Broadstreet whom Gracie identified first, sitting in a booth against the wall and just a short way down the side of the room her table was in. He was with Yedid.

How interesting, Gracie thought. Jack and Mike had presumed Broadstreet had been having an affair with the Hampshire County Detective, Rita Licora. That still could be true, she supposed, but he seemed to be very chummy with Yedid, as well. Maybe they were good friends? Maybe he was two timing Licora with Yedid? Maybe he and Licora had broken up?

Hmmm...Gracie thought as she decided on the house smoked bluefish plate and sparkling water with lime. That might be worth looking into. Jack had always said that he didn't want to contact Licora about Mike's suspicions regarding the JDC because he didn't know if he could trust Licora, since she was in a relationship with Broadstreet.

But if she was no longer in a relationship with Broadstreet, well then: she might be the perfect one to talk to.

Gracie gave her order to the faultlessly groomed waiter and pulled out her iPhone. She loved having access to the internet, and as she waited for her lunch selection to arrive, she checked her emails. Nothing too exciting, nothing that couldn't wait, but she sent off a quick text message to Jack before she put the device away. 'LOTS TO TELL, DINNER WED?' she sent, and then tucked the iPhone in her bag as her lunch was served.

Chapter Thirteen

Gracie lingered over her lunch. Not only was it delicious, but she was trying to overhear what was being said at the booth a few feet away from her, where Mark Broadstreet and Sasha Yedid were seated.

She could see that Broadstreet had ordered the house cured salmon with wilted spinach and a poached egg. He pushed the spinach to one side, which Gracie thought was typical male behavior, and the waste of a lovely vegetable. But he tucked into the salmon and egg with gusto and the dish did look very good indeed.

Yedid had a salad with blue cheese: far less interesting.

Gracie's own smoked bluefish plate was actually a plank: the sectioned pieces of fish were served on a cutting board surrounded by condiments which included a mustard sauce, a hot sauce and an herb sauce which contained dill, shallots and scallions: that was Gracie's favorite. The fish was accompanied by a small mound of field greens and sprouts in a light vinaigrette, and toasted slices of a wholemeal baguette. Gracie had to resist the impulse to plop a piece of fish along with some sauce in between two slices and make a sandwich. Maybe in a less classy place. But here, she contented herself with forking up the fish and following it with a bite of bread.

Everything was delicious.

Broadstreet and Yedid appeared to be talking about very personal topics, because their voices were quite low. Gracie could only catch a word or two here and there, but it appeared that they were discussing possible locales for an upcoming vacation: she heard them say, 'flight times' as well as 'beach,' 'massage' and 'limousine.' Of course, that didn't mean they were going on vacation together, but it sure seemed likely.

They had been seated before she had, and so ordered dessert and coffee before she did: Broadstreet had a profiterole and Yedid had fresh strawberries served plain in a crystal dish. Both had French Press coffees.

Gracie thought the profiterole would be tasty garnished by the strawberries, but she resisted ordering any dessert, opting for a 'Café Presse.'

Frankly, she was a bit surprised that Broadstreet and Yedid were meeting so openly. Then again, both were single, so there was no barrier to them dating. And the Café was pricey enough that it seemed unlikely any of the other courthouse or JDC staff would happen in for lunch and spot them.

Still, Gracie wondered if Broadstreet were still dating Licora, or in fact ever had been, or if they had broken up. As she sipped her coffee, she considered ways she could find out, without appearing to want to know.

Broadstreet and Yedid got up, and as Yedid headed for the ladies' room, Broadstreet paid the bill and left the restaurant.

When Yedid returned, the waiter had already picked up the bill and tip; he gave a smile to Yedid, who smiled cooly back, and then she, too, left the restaurant. As she passed, Gracie got a whiff of 'Joy' by Jean Patou: expensive perfume! And the pink spring suit Yedid had on had sure looked like Chanel.

A Juvenile Detention Center Director who wears Chanel? To work? Then again, from what Gracie had seen of the administrative structure of the JDC, Yedid's job was exclusively administrative: she never went into the blocks or had any encounters with the inmates. That job was left to the Warden, a guy named Ronald Sholes. He met with Yedid, of course, but her remove from the day to day business of the JDC could explain her choice of clothing. And after all, few people would realize the tailored suit was a Chanel; in fact, to the untrained eye, it would appear a somewhat plain piece of clothing.

When Gracie's bill came, she left cash to cover it plus a generous tip and returned to her Jeep. Maybe she would stop back to the imposing granite and sandstone Hampshire County Courthouse and see if Rita Licora were around. She still wasn't sure exactly what she'd say, but she had an idea.

Jack had been surprised but pleased when he'd received Gracie's text message, and had immediately texted her back, saying, 'GREAT, WHEN, WHERE?' Later on Tuesday afternoon, her reply came in: '6 pm MY PLACE BRING WOOF' and he'd replied, 'OK.'

So Wednesday after work Jack stopped at his trailer to 'freshen up' as his mother would say. For Jack, that meant a fast shower, shave, and a change of clothes from the shirt, tie and dress trousers he'd worn all day to a comfortable pair of jeans and an equally comfortable woven cotton sweater. It was getting warmer now that summer was here, but evenings could still be cool. And Gracie always kept her house cool.

He whistled for Woof and before long he and the wolf dog were traveling up Gracie's driveway.

As she often did, Gracie greeted him at the front door, her slight deshabille evidence of her efforts on behalf of dinner. After the usual greeting by Woof, Gracie led Jack and the wolf dog back through the house to the kitchen. Woof immediately made for the back screened porch, where Pumpkin was.

"There he goes," Gracie laughed. "It's a lovely evening: Pumpkin's on chipmunk patrol."

"Oh, Woof will love that," Jack agreed. He smiled at her. "I was glad to get your invitation: so what do you have to tell me?" he asked.

"Ay yay, yay," Gracie said in a passable imitation of Ricky Ricardo. "Where to begin? First, I want to thank you for sending me the updated autopsy report on Mike, and the news release that the case has been re-classified as a homicide, and re-opened," she told Jack. "I was able to get a story done and filed for this week's paper."

"Great, that's what I'd hoped," Jack answered. "I had to let the *Gazetteer* know, too, of course."

"Of course," Gracie agreed mildly. "And they come out tomorrow, and they'll probably 'scoop' me, but that's okay. I've trounced them enough in the past: they can enjoy one small victory."

"That's mighty understanding of you," Jack quipped.

"Sit down: you want some wine? Or a beer?" Gracie asked, gracious if a bit belated.

Jack opted for a glass of wine: he noticed Gracie had already started on one as she cooked. She poured him a generous glass, and then as was her habit, returned to cooking and talking at the same time.

"Well, I've been doing a lot of thinking," she began as she turned the heat off under a pot on her range and emptied out what looked like rice into a large metal mixing bowl. The rice steamed and Gracie stirred it around to cool it off as she went on. "And I did a little sleuthing," she admitted, stirring.

"Uh oh," Jack murmured into his wine glass, and Gracie shot him a look.

She recapped for him her thoughts, identical to his, that the person who had murdered Mike had wanted to silence him because of his investigation into the JDC.

Jack nodded.

"So then I started looking at the JDC, and at who was involved in its construction and its operation," she said. From a cupboard Gracie took a can of hand caught wild tuna, opened and drained it, then added it to the rice in the large bowl. She sprinkled in some spiced rice wine vinegar with Oriental writing on the bottle's label.

"It was built by Salama Construction," Jack offered.

Gracie nodded, and reminded him of her theory that Commissioner Itty Azar had somehow arranged for his second cousins, the Salama brothers, to win the bid to build the JDC. Jack still looked skeptical but he did agree that such a thing was certainly possible, even if they hadn't found any evidence of it yet.

"I'd have to go back to the records of the commissioners' meetings and the bid awards," Gracie said. "I did find the newspaper coverage of it, but nothing looked out of place."

"Well, if Azar did throw the bid, it's unlikely there would be evidence of that, even in the minutes," Jack reasoned and Gracie agreed with him.

She then told him about the two $40,000 deposits to Azar's account--or actually, Ruth Romano's account--which coincided with the publishing of the RFP and the awarding of the bid. And, she told Jack about the subsequent monthly deposits of the same amount to the same account.

"Geez, that must be over a million by now," Jack exclaimed, so appalled by the news that Gracie's methods of acquiring the information seemed hardly worth questioning.

"A million four and counting," Gracie answered. She chopped up a small bunch of glistening green scallions into very fine pieces and tossed them into the rice mixture. Another small bunch of scallions she put to one side. From a plastic deli container she removed several fresh scallops. These she quickly rinsed off and patted dry, then cut into quarters. They went into the rice mixture. Then she added minced ginger, garlic and five spice powder and a dash of Thai hot sauce and blended it all carefully with a large paddle.

Without asking, she poured each of them another glass of wine, then turned her attention to another large bowl into which she put several handfuls of maîche and sliced fresh hothouse tomatoes and cucumbers.

As she blended a vinaigrette with more ginger, mustard and sesame seeds, Gracie told him about Sasha Yedid being Chacko Salama's ex wife, and about Yedid and her daughter Ishtar's expensive lifestyle. "According to the Real Estate transaction ledger, Sasha bought the house for $850,000," Gracie explained. "But she's added a lot, including landscaping that looks like it belongs in a Flower Show, and a horse barn and paddock. Those have skyrocketed the value."

"Maybe she got a big settlement," Jack suggested, but he knew that if that had been the case, Gracie would have already said.

"Not on record anywhere. And Chacko's financials look clean, so I don't know where he would have got that kind of money." She reminded herself silently to check and see if she could find an offshore account tied to Chacko Salama. Some things it was best not to divulge in their entirety to Jack. He was, after all, an officer of the court.

"So, you think something else is going on," Jack supplied.

Gracie was feeling a number of avocados to see which ones were the ripest. Avocados were not something Jack generally enjoyed, and he watched her with what he hoped was well disguised trepidation.

"Mmmmm..." she chose two and expertly opened and de-pitted them. Then she removed the skins and cut them into thin oval shaped slices. "I was wondering if maybe there weren't two schemes running," she theorized.

"Two?" Jack echoed.

"Well, the first one was where Azar gave the bid to his cousins. Or cousin: Chacko is the lead guy on all the operations, from what I can tell, and Koshy is more the salesman for the company. He's not involved in the buying of materials or the pricing of a bid, or the running of the actual job, that's all Chacko."

Jack nodded.

"Okay, so that was one scam: Salama Construction got the contract and Azar got a nice payoff, two $40,000 deposits." Gracie paused. "But those $40,000 a month deposits started coming again like clockwork once the center was open for business," she went on. "And more than that, in Ishtar Salama's account there are regular monthly deposits of around $60,000."

"So they're both profiting from the running of the JDC."

"Right. I checked the JDC's and Epiphany's books: they look okay. Nothing untoward," Gracie assessed. "Although I want to take a closer look at how it can cost $400 a day to keep a juvenile delinquent: it seems a lot of money to me."

Gracie had put round metal dough cutters on two oversized serving plates; she lined the dough cutters with the avocado slices and packed the center with the rice mixture. She put the remaining rice mixture in a container and popped it into the fridge, then turned her attention to a paper wrapped parcel she'd just removed from her stainless steel fridge.

"Well, if Yedid and Azar are still profiting from the JDC, other people are, too," Jack put in, getting into the spirit of Gracie's theory. "I mean, Yedid would profit because she runs the place, so that's simple."

"Azar?" Gracie asked. The parcel had turned out to be ahi tuna, sushi quality, like the scallops. She plopped them on a dish and then spritzed them with olive oil and lemon before carrying them over to her indoor grill and firing it up.

"He makes sure the county continues to contract with the JDC to send its juvenile delinquents there," Jack said.

"Who else would be involved with it?"

"Well, like Sandy suspected, Broadstreet: he's the one who makes the recommendations to the Judge as to whether or not the kids need incarceration."

"Okay," Gracie agreed, tossing the ahi steaks down on her grill and hearing a satisfying sizzle. "Who else?"

Jack shrugged. "I hate to say it, but, maybe Judge Elderson? He's the one who hands out the sentences. Although he'd be inclined to accept Broadstreet's recommendations, still, he could be involved."

"Mmmm..." Gracie flipped the tuna steaks. "I haven't checked into Broadstreet or Elderson at all. Although I did see some vehicles I wanted to trace the ownership of," she added, telling Jack about her recent trip to Hampshire County and her drive-bys of Yedid's house, Chako's townhouse, and the Azar property.

Then she turned to the second bundle of scallions, quickly sliced them into thin strips and plunged them into her deep fryer, which Jack hadn't even realized was ready to go on the countertop. A couple of minutes later she removed the crispy fried bundle and deposited it on some paper towels to drain.

Jack reluctantly admitted that, based solely on circumstantial evidence, it did appear as though a few select people within the county juvenile detention and probation system were living far above their reported means. Whether this indicated anything underhanded, of course, could not be said for sure at this time, he cautioned Gracie.

She nodded. "But while I was in Northampton--it's a cute little town, Jack, with some great restaurants. Why don't we ever go there?" she questioned in an aside that took Jack completely by surprise and had him foundering. What did she mean 'why don't we ever go there?' They weren't dating. Were they? No, he didn't think so: they were friends, meeting to discuss a case both were involved with.

What would he do if she wanted to get back together? He'd missed her, oh, he'd missed her so much! But he couldn't just get romantically involved with her again without a serious discussion of exactly what each expected of the relationship, this time.

Jack was jolted out of his reverie by a great deal of movement all of a sudden. Woof and Pumpkin, knowing uncannily that food was about to be served, appeared in the kitchen, having slithered through their respective cat and doggie flaps from the screen porch. Gracie, meanwhile, had removed the metal rings from the rice mixture to reveal avocado wrapped piles of rice, tuna and scallops.

She lifted the tuna steaks from the grill and turned it off. Then she topped each of the rice cakes with a tuna steak and surrounded it with the maîche salad. On top of the tuna she put the crunchy bundles of scallions, and drizzled everything with a tamari vinegar sesame oil sauce, and brought the dishes to the table.

"Wow, where did you find this recipe?" Jack asked. Gracie's sourcing of recipes was vast, eclectic and always interesting.

Gracie smiled. "Actually, I kind of made it up. If it sucks, we can call for a pizza," she added with a self deprecating smile.

"I doubt it will 'suck' Gracie," Jack answered honestly.

"Well, anyway, back to Northampton," Gracie returned. And she told him about following Yedid to The Green Street Café and finding her lunching with Mark Broadstreet.

Jack cut into his tuna steak, which was perfectly cooked: succulent inside and nicely grilled on the outside. He tried to get a little of the rice mixture and the fried scallions along with it on his fork. He chewed. The explosion of the pungent Asian flavors against the plain rice and the contrast of the crispy greens with the almost creamy scallops and the meaty tuna--both fresh and canned--was fabulous.

"Oh, Gracie, this is wonderful, you made this up?" he asked, genuinely impressed. And as good a cook as Gracie was, that was saying something.

"I kind of got the idea from sushi, but I expanded on it," Gracie answered. "So what do you think about Yedid and Broadstreet?"

Jack shrugged and sipped his wine. "They might be involved. But I always thought he was--"

"Seeing Rita Licora, I know," Gracie chimed in, smiling. "But I stopped in and visited Rita before I came back home yesterday,"

Gracie informed him. "I invited her to join Club," she said, sounding pleased at her inspiration, which in fact, she was.

"What did she say?"

"She was thrilled," Gracie answered truthfully. "I told her that I was good friends with you and had just been in Northampton to meet a friend, and thought of her and decided to issue the invitation," Gracie explained.

Jack just nodded, and kept eating. He even liked the avocado, the way Gracie had prepared it. "No, I meant, what did Rita say about Broadstreet?" Jack corrected in between mouthfuls.

"I didn't ask her about him," Gracie replied in an admonishing tone. "But I'm inviting her to come to the Club Cookout at Farida Salama's," she finished. "I figure I can get her talking there, in a more relaxed atmosphere, and find out pretty quickly if she's seeing anybody. Or if she was seeing anybody."

"Sasha Yedid isn't going to be there, is she, by any chance?" Jack asked, knowing Gracie's methods.

Gracie shook her head. "She's not in Club and given the fact that she's Farida's ex sister in law, and Farida *is* in Club, no, I doubt it. But her name might come up, and it will be interesting to watch Rita Licora's reaction, don't you think?"

Chapter Fourteen

Thursday about noon, Gracie returned from a morning kickboxing class and coffee with her friend Anne to find a message on her answering machine: apparently, UPS Global had a package for her and wanted to make delivery arrangements.

Quickly, Gracie phoned her contractor Larry on his cell phone.

"It's here!" she crowed when he answered.

Larry, who at the moment was on top of a customer's roof putting down new shingles, gave the phone a puzzled look. Then he placed Gracie's voice. And he understood what she meant.

"The conservatory?" he asked. "You must have had it shipped express."

"Yes," Gracie admitted. "I thought if I got it here, then you could arrange your schedule with the least disruption and we could have it done more quickly, and with fewer issues," she explained. "UPS wants to know when to deliver it," Gracie finished delightedly, sounding like a little kid.

They spoke briefly and decided that Gracie could have the trucking firm deliver it the next day. It was all in crates and boxes and these could sit at the side of Gracie's home until Larry and his crew arrived to begin work. Larry would use Friday and the weekend to finish up this customer's roof and any other critical, pending work before beginning Gracie's job.

Anticipating the delivery, Larry had already been to Gracie's earlier in the week to remove the forsythia and rhododendron which grew along the side of the house where the conservatory would go, and to rough out the foundation for the new structure. The shrubs he'd re-planted at the bottom of Gracie's garden to make an extended hedgerow.

Gracie was delighted: starting the construction so soon meant the conservatory could be up and running in another few weeks, and would be in full glory by the time Labor Day rolled around with her usual House Party.

Grinning, she headed for the butler's pantry off her kitchen where she kept her cook books and recipe file. She started to pull a couple out with the thought of assembling a tentative menu even though it was early, when her mobile rang.

She hurried out, through the dining room and into the small alcove off the hallway which she called her 'office' and where she'd dropped her handbag with her mobile in it.

She answered breathlessly: it was Jack.

"Gracie, a girl was just found dead down in Lee," he said without preamble. "She's a secretary at Lee Lime, and she didn't show up for work this morning so one of her co-workers checked on her at lunch. Found her in her car."

"What was she doing in her car?" Gracie queried.

"I'm on my way there now, so I'm not sure, but maybe the girl was on her way to work: her shift started at 7 a.m. And she died before she could even start the car up."

Gracie frowned at the phone. "This makes three, doesn't it?" she said, low.

"Yup. Look, it didn't go out on the scanner yet, so here's the address--" and he gave her a number and street in Lee. "I'll have dispatch call it in, in about ten minutes, because I'm going to call for Dr. Spears," he added, and Gracie understood what he meant: she had a ten minute head start to get to the scene. For sure, Gil Butcher would be on his way, too, as soon as he heard the scanner call.

Gracie grabbed a clementine and a protein shake and dashed back out to her Jeep. She made the trip down to Lee in under 30 minutes and when she arrived, only Jack and a marked cruiser from Lee PD were in the rear car park of the tidy brick three story apartment building. She flashed her ID and tried not to get in the way.

The parking lot had numbered spaces corresponding to the apartments in the building; most of the action was clustered around the space marked 3F and Gracie observed a late model Toyota Avalon whose driver's side door had been jimmied open. She couldn't see too well because already there were several 'looky-loos' gaping at the tragedy, but it looked like the young woman had been removed from the car and put on the tarmac next to it. Gracie suspected local LEO's had attempted resuscitation, but to no avail. The woman's face had been covered by someone's jacket.

A shaken looking middle aged woman in low heels, a print skirt and a coordinating sweater stood off to one side, crying silently. Gracie wondered if this was the co-worker who had found the girl, and moved closer. Sympathetically, she offered the woman the small packet of tissues she kept in her handbag, and wordlessly, the woman accepted it and gave Gracie a tremulous smile.

"What happened here?" Gracie asked softly.

"That's Desirée," the woman replied. "Desirée Manning. She works with me. She didn't show up for work today and I--I was worried about her. I came over to check on her, on my lunch break, and--and--" she started crying afresh and Gracie thought that before the woman said much more she'd have to explain who she was and why she was there.

Gracie bit her lip. "I'm so sorry. Have they called the coroner?"

The woman nodded. "I think so."

Gracie stuck out her hand. "I'm Gracie Barufaldi. I write for the *Intelligencer*. I heard the call on the scanner and I happened to be nearby, so I came," she said earnestly. "This is awful--it's the third girl in this area who's been found dead, isn't it?" she added, hoping the woman wouldn't be put off by the revelation that she was chatting to a news reporter.

But it seemed not to have had much effect. Maybe it hadn't really registered: the woman was likely in shock.

"I'm Linda Cross. We both work at Lee Lime."

"And you said you were worried about Desirée?" Gracie asked gently. "Why was that? Was she often absent from work without calling?"

Cross shook her head. "No, that's just it: she would always call. But really, Desirée didn't take much time off. Until lately: she hadn't been feeling too well the last few weeks. Said it started as a stomach bug, but the last few days she'd had a really awful headache, too."

"So when she didn't come in today, and didn't call, you were concerned."

Cross nodded. "She's always called in the past." She sighed. "I don't know, call it the mother instinct, I just knew something was wrong, and I wanted to check on her. But I never expected to find--"

she gestured towards the prone figure on the tarmac and broke into tears afresh.

"I'm sorry, Ma'am? I'm going to have to take your statement, now," one of the local police officers said, approaching Cross and giving Gracie an inclusive look. "Your friend can come with you if you want," he added kindly.

"Oh, no, I'm not--" Gracie began, but at that moment the Medical Examiner's van pulled into the car park and Dr. Spears jumped out of the passenger seat and headed towards them.

Gracie saw Jack have a quick word with one of the other police officers and the next thing she knew, Linda Cross was in the cruiser giving a statement and the other officer was telling people to either go away or step well back, and surrounding the area with yellow crime scene tape.

Gracie took a few steps over to a cherry tree that was in full bloom, and leaving pink drifts all along the sidewalk and the cars. She just observed as Dr. Spears and his assistant did a cursory examination of Desirée, then loaded her onto a wheeled gurney and into his van. She snapped a quick photo which showed the cluster of people, the back of Dr. Spears, the van and part of Desirée's car, but not Desirée herself, and thought that it was discreet and tasteful while still showing the immediacy of the event.

Through all of this Jack was talking to Cross and to the two police officers. Gracie was just about to see if she could talk to him when Gil Butcher's old maroon Chevy Suburban hove into sight and pulled into a parking spot. The *Gazetteer* Editor got out, slammed the door, and walked purposefully up to the cruiser where Linda Cross was just being allowed to leave.

"What's going on here?" he asked, looking in turn at Jack and the two Lee PD officers.

"Lady found a body in a car," one of the policemen said tersely.

"Can't give you any details until we notify next of kin, of course," Jack said to Butcher, a bit more eloquently.

"How long's the body been dead? Male or female? Who found it?" Butcher asked in quick succession.

"Don't know the time of death yet, can't say if it's male or female and can't release the name of the person who found it, either. Not just yet. There'll be a news release, probably late today or tomorrow morning," Jack answered him.

Grimacing in frustration, Butcher looked away, then hurried over to the ME's van and snapped a quick shot of the back of the van with the covered, loaded stretcher on it.

That wasn't much of a photo, Gracie smirked to herself.

She noted the arrival of the Berkshire County Crime Scene Unit at this moment; they all piled out of their king cab truck and swarmed around Desirée's car, conferring with Jack and the local policemen.

Meanwhile, Linda Cross had returned and was heading in Gracie's direction. Both so Butcher wouldn't recognize her and out of sensitivity to Cross, Gracie went up to the woman and then turned them both away as she asked Cross if she had anyone she could call to be with her, and offered to stay until someone could come.

Cross, looking surprised yet grateful at Gracie's kindness, made a call to her supervisor at Lee Lime to tell them what happened, and then called her son who she said worked locally, to come and get her and bring her home.

The ME's van left. Butcher, who hadn't spotted Gracie and apparently hadn't noticed her Jeep parked at the far end of the lot, was still hanging around watching Jack , the CSU team, and the local police officers process the vehicle Desirée had been found in.

"Miss Cross?" Gracie began tentatively. Linda Cross had finished her phone calls and was just standing near the pink cherry tree with Gracie. Her face was blank.

She started at the sound of her name and looked at Gracie. Her eyes focused, and she smiled a little. "You've been very kind."

"It had to have been a terrible shock," Gracie said. "Miss Cross: I did tell you I'm Gracie Barufaldi, a news reporter for the *Intelligencer*?" she repeated slowly.

Linda Cross nodded. "Yes. I remember." She looked a bit puzzled.

"Well, would you mind if I used your name, and mentioned how you found Miss Manning, in my article on this--tragedy?" Gracie asked gently.

Linda Cross shook her head. "No, of course not. I have nothing to hide, I was just trying to help poor Desirée--"

"Yes, of course, and that's how I'll write it," Gracie reassured her, already mentally composing the article. "But I wanted to be certain it was okay with you, and be certain you remembered I was a reporter."

"Yes. You told me: almost right away, when you gave me the tissues," Linda Cross added with a grateful smile. She gazed across the parking lot where Gil Butcher was still badgering Jack and the CSU team and the police for more details. "He's one, too, isn't he?" she asked. "A reporter, I mean."

"Erm, yes: he's from the *Gazetteer*," Gracie said tersely. She wanted to say, 'don't talk to him, he'll screw it up,' but of course she couldn't. However, Cross seemed to read her mind.

"I don't think I want to talk to him," she murmured, eyes narrowed. Then her gaze brightened as a late model Ford pickup pulled into the lot. "Oh! My son's here, I'll be okay now. Thank you, Miss Bar--"

"Barufaldi."

"Got it. Thank you."

"You're welcome."

So that made three, Gracie thought to herself as she drove home. Of course she'd have to wait for the toxicology results before she could say definitively that Desirée Manning had died from antifreeze poisoning, just like the other two. But meanwhile, the similarities among the deceased impressed her.

All three young women had worked at fairly low-paying jobs: Manning was a secretary at Lee Lime, Ford had been a secretary at Stockbridge Auto Repair, and Sullivan had been an assistant produce manager at the Food Mart. She knew that Ford and Sullivan had been members of Sure Fit Gym: that had been the only connection she'd unearthed so far. But she wondered now if Manning had also been a member. She pulled out her phone and dialed Sure Fit; Jarrod answered on the second ring.

Gracie re-introduced herself but Jarrod remembered her and was happy to hear from her until Gracie told him the terrible news.

"It's just that it's another young woman from this area," Gracie said solicitously as she headed back to Pittsfield. "And she could've been Pattie Ford's sister, she looked enough like her," Manning had been ash blonde, petite and fit from what Gracie had seen.

"Can you tell me the name?" Jarrod asked, sounding intrigued to be part of the mystery.

"Well, I'm going to publish it later today because I talked to the woman who found the body," Gracie explained, silently reminding herself to contact Jack and let him know who she'd talked to and what she was planning to write. She knew he'd appreciate knowing. "So I guess I can say--it was Desirée Manning," she finished.

Jarrod gasped.

"You knew her?" Gracie asked quickly, thinking that she already knew what Jarrod was going to say.

"She was a member here," Jarrod replied, his voice a whisper.

Chapter Fifteen

"You've got a serial killer on your hands, I think, Jack," Dr. Spears' voice was weary but certain. He had just called Jack's office to give him the details on his autopsy of Desirée Manning; it was Friday morning.

"Cause of death was antifreeze poisoning?" Jack queried, stunned.

"Ethylene glycol, yes. Caused rapid and severe cerebral edema: the oxalate crystal deposits are unmistakable," he confirmed. "Did you notice the sores around the girl's mouth?" Dr. Spears asked then, and Jack had to admit he hadn't. "Well, no matter: she had them: they looked like cold sores but they're another symptom of ethylene glycol poisoning."

"But what was she doing in her car, Doc?" Jack asked, mystified. If he'd felt as sick as he'd learned antifreeze poisoning made you, the last thing he'd want to do was drive somewhere.

"Maybe she was going to work," Dr. Spears theorized. "Or she might have been driving herself to the hospital. We don't know. She passed out before she got the key in the ignition, and although she was dressed, it looked like she'd just thrown her clothes on not really caring how she looked, if you take my meaning."

Jack did: when he was ill, he put on whatever was comfortable and reasonably clean and didn't bother with the details.

"With the cerebral edema, she would have been quite dizzy and had an excruciating headache," Dr. Spears put in.

Jack talked for a few more moments to the County ME and then hung up. Gracie had done him the courtesy of telling him she'd talked to Linda Cross, the woman who had found Desirée Manning. She'd also told him she would be writing a story naming both women despite the fact that the name of the deceased hadn't yet been officially released, although the family had been informed. SoJack felt he should let Gracie know Manning's cause of death, and that the case was now part of a confirmed serial killer investigation. Gracie had also told him that Manning had also been a member of Sure Fit Gym, and for that bit of news, Jack had been very grateful.

He picked up the phone and speed dialed her.

Gracie was very appreciative of the information, and said she'd get a 'breaking news' article into the online *Intelligencer* by that afternoon. Jack said that by then, he would have sent a news release to the *Gazetteer* as well.

"Jack, have you gone through Sullivan's or Ford's things yet? Or gone to Manning's apartment?"

"Sullivan's stuff is all in storage I think," Jack replied. "We did go through her apartment, since that was where she was found, and it was therefore a crime scene. Ford's things are at her brother's house in his garage, but no one's looked through them since her apartment wasn't a crime scene because she was found at the gym. Manning's stuff is still in her apartment. Why?"

Gracie frowned. "I don't know: it just seems like if someone's targeting young attractive female members of Sure Fit, there might be another clue as to why among their belongings."

Jack made a doubtful hum.

"Were you planning on checking their stuff?" Gracie asked, a bit more pointedly.

Jack sighed. "It's on my list, but between the drug bust last week and--"

"No, no I'm not faulting you for not having done it yet, actually, I'm glad."

"Why?"

"Because I'd like to come along. You know, when you look through their stuff," Gracie answered. "Another pair of eyes," she put in persuasively. "There has to be a reason beyond the fact that all these girls were members of that gym for them to be murder victims."

Jack found himself nodding. "Agreed."

They arranged that Jack would contact the storage facility and request access, and call Ford's brother to see if he'd let them look at his sister's belongings. As for Manning, Jack would call next of kin to see if they would allow him to inspect her apartment. If everyone agreed, he'd set everything up for the following day and contact Gracie about where to meet.

Delighted, Gracie agreed. She then returned to moving furniture in her formal living room to make space for the construction which would start the following week. Once she'd cleared away chairs, tables, sofas and other items, she draped everything she could in old sheets and shower curtains saved for this and similar purposes, and laid a tarp over the carpet to cover as much of the area as she could.

Pumpkin helped by watching the activity from a windowsill, and then walking delicately across the tarp and sniffing along the draped furniture. When all had met with her approval, she left the room, tail high, and headed for the back porch and the sunshine.

Pattie Ford's brother George said they could look through his sister's things early Saturday, so Gracie and Jack found themselves at his double garage doors at 8:30 the following morning.

"I don't know what I'm going to do with all this stuff," George commented. "It's a good thing it's decent weather and I can keep my cars in the driveway." George and his wife lived in a nice suburban development. Their vehicles, temporarily ousted from the garage, did indeed occupy most of the short, paved drive to the side of the white ranch style house.

"You could give it to charity, maybe, or have a yard sale," Jack suggested.

George nodded. "My wife said the same thing. I guess I will, when I'm ready."

"This is the peak time for garage sales and yard sales," Jack put in helpfully.

George left them alone then, and Gracie and Jack began. It was an unofficial investigation: they had no warrants for any of the places they'd be that day, just permission from whomever had custody of the dead girls' belongings. Therefore, Jack felt, there was no real reason Gracie shouldn't be along to help. And after all, as she had said, 'another pair of eyes.' And one attuned, perhaps, to things he was not.

"Nice enough furniture," Jack commented. Pattie Ford had apparently bought out Ikea to furnish her apartment: everything was quite new, and fairly pricey.

"Mmmm..." Gracie was opening a large box marked 'linens.' "She liked bamboo towels," she commented a second later.

"Bamboo?" Jack echoed disbelievingly. Those didn't sound like towels he would want to use.

"Unh-huh...they spin the bamboo into a rayon like fiber and mix it with cotton. It's really soft and sucks up water like a sponge," Gracie said. "And she liked good sheets," she added a moment later. "There's a beige satin set here and a couple of 800 thread count Egyptian cotton sets, in lavender and pink."

Jack was looking through a small desk which apparently had been where Ford had kept all her bills, her checkbook and other items of that type. "She had HBO, Showtime and Cinemax on her satellite TV," he commented. "Paid her bills on time, from what I can see," he added, flicking through her checkbook. "I ran financials on her and Sullivan," he went on, reminding Gracie that he'd done that as a matter of course to see if he could uncover anything which could indicate a motive for murder. "Nothing was out of place, both had checking and savings accounts, and a couple of CDs and IRAs."

"They had CDs and IRAs?" Gracie queried, pausing in her examination of what had been Ford's dresser.

Jack nodded.

"How much?" Gracie asked quickly.

Jack shrugged then shook his head. "I don't recall specifically, but I think in the ten or twenty-thousand dollar range, why?"

Gracie frowned. "Just seems like a lot of money for secretaries and produce managers," she answered. "And George isn't rich, so it's not family money," she added, gesturing to the well-kept, pleasant, but quite standard two car garage and house.

They continued digging. After a few more minutes, Gracie stood up from the box of Ford's clothing she'd been looking through.

"Okay, I've seen enough."

Jack chuckled. "Really? What do you think?"

Gracie took a deep breath and shut the box. "I think Pattie Ford lived very well for someone on a secretary's salary. And she seemed to have two wardrobes, if you know what I mean: work clothes, and then what I guess were her going out clothes, or stuff she wore on the cruises she liked to take."

"So?"

"So, her work clothes weren't very interesting, but the going out and cruise clothes were on the expensive side," Gracie explained. "The labels included DKNY, diesel, Neiman Marcus, like that. She had a Kate Spade bag--" Gracie lifted a large beige leather satchel, "and a couple dozen really impractical and really expensive pair of shoes, including Jimmy Choos and Manolos."

Jack wondered what a Jimmy Choo was, or a Manolo for that matter. But Gracie sounded positive.

"And then there's the underwear," Gracie was continuing. "La Perla, very high end, all bright colors. And a couple of numbers from Victoria's Secret that are just the teensiest bit on the naughty side," she added, wrinkling her nose. "You know: bustiers and garter belts in satin?"

Jack didn't exactly know, but he could imagine. He nodded.

"Her skincare stuff is Kiehl's, again, not cheap. Her makeup's mostly Chanel, and her perfume is Baccarat 'Les Larmes Sacrées de Thebes'," she pointed to a crystal pyramid shaped bottle she'd removed temporarily from a carton marked 'dresser.' " $1700 for a quarter ounce."

Jack whistled. Wow. And he thought his mom's Chanel No. 5 was pricey.

"How could she afford this, and the premium TV, high speed internet, etc. etc. and the apartment she lived in, all on a secretary's salary?" Gracie queried, obviously intrigued.

Their next stop was the storage facility with Sullivan's belongings in it. The items would be secured until the case was closed, but since the Berkshire County DA's office didn't have an impound lot or a large evidence locker, they used a local storage facility in cases like this one.

Sullivan's furniture had been less pristine than Ford's, a mixture of antiques or hand me downs and newer acquisitions. Her sheets and towels had also not been quite as high end, at least according to Gracie, but she'd had a lot of them, all in good condition.

Sullivan's clothing carried labels from well known stores: Macy's and Lord and Taylor mostly, along with Christopher & Banks and NY & Co. She had work and casual clothes, and what

Gracie thought must be her 'clubbing' clothes which were mostly leather and denim featuring a lot of studs and chains.

She had used Angel perfume, fairly pricey but not in the Baccarat range. And her cosmetics were mostly Revlon.

But it was Sullivan's jewelry box that got Gracie's attention.

"You said Sullivan had some CDs and IRAs like Ford?" she asked Jack as she lifted the leather covered box out of its spot in the large carton marked 'personals' and turned the little key to open it.

"Yes, why?"

Gracie studied the contents of the jewelry box for a moment.

"Because this isn't costume jewelry," she answered a moment later. She pointed to a gold 'torque' style necklace. "That's real. Probably retails for about $2800 at today's prices," she added. "And this is a ruby," she commented, lifting a ring out and holding it to the light. "Wait--"

She dug in her handbag and in a moment or two produced a jeweler's loupe in a small velvet bag. "Sometimes this comes in handy," she murmured apologetically, and affixed the magnifier to her left eye. "Yes, a ruby, and a good one, with diamond baguettes," she said.

She plucked a pair of earrings out next: pearls, big ones, and real. Some diamond studs at about a carat each, pearl necklaces that were of varying colors and millimeters but all genuine, and a few more pieces Gracie spotted as paraiba tourmaline and tanzanite. And more diamonds, including a diamond watch.

"Looks like she liked the home shopping channels a lot," Gracie said, shutting the jewelry box. "She's got several thousand dollars worth of jewelry in here: what was on her when she was found? Where would that be?"

"In the evidence locker at the courthouse," Jack answered. At Gracie's quizzical look he explained that there was a small locked closet in the basement where items of manageable size were kept until the cases connected to them were solved.

"Did anyone examine Sullivan's insurance policies?" Gracie asked next. "I'll bet she had a rider on it to cover jewelry."

Jack didn't answer. He remembered noting that Sullivan had had renter's insurance: it had come up when he'd run her financials. But it had not seemed necessary to check into what the policy contained. Not until he'd really taken a good look at Sullivan's things.

He finished examining the rest of Sullivan's personal papers and files, then called Gracie over to look at one particular document.

"It's a receipt from K&G Furs," Gracie read, nodding her head as she recognized the name of a furrier in Springfield. She looked more closely. "Sullivan had just put her--full length mink coat?--" her tone was disbelieving, "in storage for the summer."

"What does a full length mink coat cost, d'you know?" Jack asked.

Gracie, who didn't wear fur, made a face. "I'm not sure, but I think upwards of thirty grand depending on the quality."

Jack nodded sagely. "So...not something she'd wear to unload the orange crates at the market, then," he deadpanned, and Gracie, despite the circumstances, chuckled as she shook her head in agreement.

Their next stop was Manning's apartment, but Gracie was lobbying hard to end their tour with a stop at the county courthouse's basement so she could check on Sullivan's handbag and jewelry and clothing, all in the evidence closet. Jack hadn't given her a definitive answer yet. He could examine items in the evidence locker, of course, but Gracie? Letting her see that was different from letting her come with him on these unofficial investigations and he didn't think it would be a wise move.

But he wasn't looking forward to explaining that to her.

Manning's family had left word with the apartment complex office, which was open on a Saturday, to allow Jack entry, so shortly they were inside, looking at what had recently been the dead girl's abode.

The furniture was unremarkable. Gracie's glance through the closet didn't provoke the excitement Ford's clothing had, and she told Jack that Manning's taste in fashion trended to the GAP, H&M, and Banana Republic although she did have several fancy cocktail type dresses. She wore Ombre Rose perfume and used L'Oréal cosmetics. Her handbag, which she apparently had been too ill to remember to bring with her to her car, since it was still on a table in her apartment, was a Louis Vuitton.

Gracie looked inside and made a small noise.

"What?"

"It's fake: a good fake, probably set her back a couple hundred bucks, but the real deal would be about $1500," Gracie assessed.

Jack momentarily wondered how she knew that but then decided he was just glad she did, and went on looking through Manning's small filing cabinet in which she kept her bills and bank statements.

Manning's jewelry box was small and contained only a few pieces which looked genuine enough but which weren't hugely valuable. It was Jack's rummaging through Manning's files that turned up several receipts and the key to a bank deposit box.

He whistled. "Whoa-ho, what do we have here?" he called Gracie over. "Look--"

She looked: several receipts from a well known merchant of gold pieces and coins. The amounts ranged from a few hundred dollars to the thousands.

"Looks like Manning didn't believe in the stock market or in banks," Jack commented.

"That's what's in the safe deposit box I'll bet," Gracie deduced. "We need to check that out."

"Down, girl!" Jack admonished. "The family obviously doesn't have any idea about this," he put in. "I ran Manning's financials and it looked pretty pedestrian to me, but of course, these didn't show up," he flourished the receipts. "I think on Monday I should contact her lawyer, or her family's lawyer, and see if she had a will, and go from there."

Gracie looked mildly disappointed, but she realized Jack was right. And it was a fair bet that the gold coin collection was what was in the deposit box.

Nothing else in Manning's apartment really captured their interest, so Jack and Gracie secured it, returned the key to the complex office, and were on their way back to Pittsfield shortly after noon.

Jack didn't let Gracie come with him to the evidence closet, but he did make a photo copy of the manifest which listed everything in the closet connected to Sally Sullivan. This he gave to her a little after one o'clock that day.

"A Coach bag?" Gracie asked, scanning the list. Jack nodded. "And what're all these 'white metal with clear stone ring' entries?" she queried.

Jack explained that when cataloging jewelry, police practice was to write, 'white metal' or 'yellow metal' and to just describe the color of the stone not hazard a guess as to what type of metal or stone it was.

"Oh..." Gracie studied the list again. "Well, if we can assume the jewelry she had on was of the same quality as the stuff in her jewelry box, that makes it a yellow gold diamond three stone ring, a yellow gold diamond pendant, more diamond earrings, and one, two, three bracelets with diamonds and rubies or just diamonds, again in yellow gold." She paused. "I'll bet her birthday was in July."

"Why?"

"Ruby is probably her birthstone," Gracie answered. "I'm starving: can we go to lunch?"

Chapter Sixteen

Over lunch, Jack and Gracie tried to sketch out profiles of the three antifreeze victims. The first one to be killed, over a month ago, was Sally Sullivan, 24, an assistant produce manager at a market in Stockbridge. She lived in a fairly nice apartment complex, drove a year old Honda Accord, and had, according to her family and friends, liked to go clubbing. She hadn't had a particular boyfriend, at least that her friends knew of. She'd been obsessed with fitness and her appearance and had belonged to the Sure Fit Gym in Stockbridge. She'd had a couple of CD's for $4000 each, and an IRA she apparently contributed to every year which stood at $8000. The anomalies in her financial profile were the fur coat and the expensive jewelry, which Jack and Gracie felt were out of reach on Sullivan's $32,000 a year income.

The second girl to be killed, just two weeks before, was Pattie Ford, 22, a secretary at Stockbridge Auto Repair. Her brother said she didn't have a steady boyfriend but seemed to go on a lot of casual dates. Ford's lifestyle was far above her $27,000 a year salary with high end linens, expensive clothes, shoes and perfume. She had gone on at least two luxury cruises a year, and been into fitness and yoga and a member of Sure Fit. She drove a new top of the line Acura which, according to her financials, she was leasing, and had a couple of small CD's for about $2500 each.

The third victim, Desirée Manning, 23, had been a secretary at Lee Lime. Her clothing, perfume, accessories and lifestyle fit fairly well with her $28,000 a year income but she obviously had acquired another source of income somewhere, since she had invested heavily in gold coins. She had not had much in her savings or checking account, but she'd owned her Toyota Avalon outright. Friends said that she frequented a couple of downtown Lee bars, but that she hadn't been dating anyone special. She, too, had been particular about her appearance and the condition of her body and had belonged to the Sure Fit Gym.

"I think someone's targeting young, attractive members of Sure Fit," Gracie said, taking a bite of the Reuben sandwich she'd ordered. It was one of her favorites at The Docket.

Jack stole one of her french fries and nodded. "I agree. But why?"

"Well, all three of them had money, more money than you might have thought: maybe that was a motive?" Gracie hazarded.

Jack made a face and bit into his venison burger. The Docket did it up on a whole wheat kaiser roll with crumbled blue cheese and a cranberry onion relish, and it was one of their most popular sandwiches. "I don't think so: if money'd been the motive, don't you think Sullivan's jewelry would have been taken? Or Manning's gold?"

"Mmmm...but it would have been hard to steal stuff from Ford, unless the killer wanted a closet full of designer duds and perfume," Gracie agreed.

Jack wiped his mouth and took a long swallow of his iced tea. "Motives for murder are money, revenge, love." He ticked them off on his fingers. "I don't think it was money. Even though, I agree, we have to find out where all the victims' money came from: I think that's a clue, but I don't think it's the motive. These women didn't have anything taken, and the places they worked are all clean, so it wasn't like they had discovered embezzling or were part of it or anything."

"OK."

"And I don't see how it could have been love: none of the victims had a boyfriend, even," Jack went on.

"Mmmm..."

"So, we're left with revenge. Who would want to get revenge on these girls, and why?" he asked rhetorically.

Gracie frowned and sipped her coffee. "I think we're missing something." She sighed. "I mean, the pieces of the puzzle are all there, but we're not putting them in the right spots."

That Sunday, Gracie tried a trick Jack had taught her a few years before when they'd worked their first case together: she made notations of important facts about the case on separate pieces of paper, and then experimented with different ways to connect them. She'd heard about other detectives doing this. Most used index cards or whiteboards. She used post it notes and the cleared off surface of her large cherry wood dining room table.

This day, she divided the table into two halves: one for the 'antifreeze murders' as she was mentally labeling them, and the other for the Garnier murder/Hampshire County JDC scheme.

She spent about an hour moving post its around in the hope of noticing a new connection between Sullivan, Ford and Manning, but all she ended up with were wrinkled post it notes and a slightly gummy table top she'd have to polish later. She felt somehow that if she could just figure out where the three victims' extra money had come from, she'd crack the case, but there had been no paper trail whatsoever, and no clues from the victims' families or friends.

The fact that all three had been members of Sure Fit Gym was also important, very important, Gracie felt. But she didn't know how. Maybe it was the way the killer found his or her victims? That seemed likely, Gracie thought, and wondered if Jack was going to question everyone who was a Sure Fit member. He might: that could be the only way, after all, to uncover the truth. As he was so fond of saying, sometimes good old fashioned police work was the best way to go.

As for the Juvenile Detention Center case, both Gracie and Jack felt sure that Mike Garnier had been murdered because of what he had found out or was close to finding out about that. But what was there to find out? And who would have murdered Mike for it?

Ignoring that last question for the moment, Gracie tried to organize what she'd learned about the JDC on her colorful post its.

As she saw it, the JDC 'caper' had two parts: the first scheme which surrounded the building of the center itself, and the second scheme which involved how the center was run.

In the first part, Itty Azar, the Hampshire County Commissioner might have thrown the bid for the construction on the JDC to his second cousin, Chacko Salama of Salama Construction. In return, Itty had received kickbacks which he secreted in an account under his wife's birth name.

Gracie suspected that Chacko Salama had cut some corners during the construction of the JDC but that was only a hunch. Also, his financials hadn't shown anything unusual, and the company's financials were clean, yet Chacko drove an extremely costly SUV, the Porsche Cayenne. She wrote, 'off shore account???'

in big letters on a post it and stuck it next to the one with Chacko's name on it.

The second part of the JDC scheme involved the day to day running of the center. The JDC had been turned over to a company called Epiphany, headed by Sasha Yedid. Yedid happened to be Chacko Salama's ex-wife and although they were divorced and had a child, Ishtar, no mention of child or spousal support was made in the divorce agreement. So Gracie suspected that some kind of payment or deal had been negotiated out of court.

Whether this was separate from, or was confined to, the kickbacks Yedid received over and above her $98,000 a year salary as JDC Director, Gracie didn't know. But Yedid had been receiving monthly payments to an account in her child's name since the opening of the JDC a couple of years before. And she lived the lifestyle of someone who made several times more per annum than she was supposed to be making.

In addition to Yedid, others who had to be involved in the day to day JDC scheme were very likely Mark Broadstreet, head of Juvenile Probation and possibly Yedid's boyfriend, and the Hampshire County Judge, Bob Elderson. Gracie hadn't investigated either one of them yet.

She went back to the $400 a day per inmate figure she'd read on the JDC website. She'd said then, and she said to herself now, that seemed like a lot of money. And that was a 'base' figure: additional or specialized treatments, counseling and the like were all added costs.

The county prison charged around $80 a day for its inmates, Gracie knew. Certainly, the JDC was not the county prison, but the disparity in cost of more than $300 a day seemed extreme to Gracie.

And the JDC was always full, or nearly full: county records showed that on average, 65 of the 70 beds were filled, with the lowest census at 62. Gracie knew that society was having a tough time of it and juvenile delinquency was on the rise. Also, the JDC accepted inmates from the surrounding counties, not just Hampshire County. But still, the occupancy rate seemed exceptionally high.

And what was it Sandy had told Mike which had started this whole thing? She felt that some of the kids in her cases had been sentenced to do time in the JDC against her recommendation. Gracie knew Sandy: that hadn't been an ego thing. Sandy had truly felt those kids didn't belong in the JDC. And it had been more than one or two in the course of a year: when they'd last talked about it, Sandy had told Gracie and Jack that something like ten of her cases in the last few months had been sent on to the JDC against her specific recommendations.

'It's like they just automatically assign the kids there, even if it's only for a short while,' Sandy had explained, frustrated.

OK, Gracie thought now, scribbling on post it notes and sticking them to her table. If money was the goal, and the only way to make money was to keep the JDC full or near capacity, that would require as many cases as possible be sentenced there. And who would be responsible for seeing that juveniles were sentenced to the JDC? Mark Broadstreet and Judge Elderson.

So, if Gracie's theory were right, they did their part and kept the JDC full. Undoubtedly once she ran their financials and did a little digging, she would uncover unexplained wealth somewhere, or mysterious payments that showed up like clockwork in their accounts.

Now, how was the JDC made into a cash cow? Epiphany was a for profit, so of course it had to pay its staff and make money. According to its financial statements, it did exactly that: it was healthy, but not ridiculously profitable. Epiphany was privately owned, too, by a company Gracie hadn't been able to find much on so far: Youth Solutions, or 'YS.' She'd have to do more digging.

If JDC were to turn the amount of profit Gracie was theorizing, it would have to inflate its rates to about double what they should be. Could it be as simple as that? If it really cost about $200 a day to keep an inmate at the JDC and yet the facility charged $400, there was the profit.

But who made sure that the JDC was the facility juveniles were sent to? Gracie frowned. Then she went back to another post it and added a new one. The Hampshire County Commissioners were the ones who signed the contract every year with juvenile probation service providers, namely the JDC. The Hampshire

County Commissioners meant Itty Azar. That explained the continuing deposits to his account.

So the center had been built by Salama Construction because Azar arranged for them to get the bid. He got a payoff for that. Meanwhile, the center was run by Epiphany, again arranged by Azar, who continued to get payoffs for that, too. Epiphany's Director and the Director of the JDC was Sasha Yedid, Chacko Salama's ex wife. She pocketed some of the profit the center made from the inflated prices charged to the county, which explained her very healthy bank account and lavish lifestyle. Chacko probably received some money every month, too, perhaps as hush money. It was a fair bet that Broadstreet and Elderson both received monthly payoffs so they would keep the JDC full, and the cash would keep flowing.

Gracie stood back and surveyed her paper covered table. It all made sense, at least, the half of the table where the post it notes concerned the JDC made sense. And she could see how, if Mike had been close to figuring this out, or maybe getting proof of it, someone would have wanted to silence him.

She sighed, and made a note to dig a little more into Chacko Salama, Mark Broadstreet and Judge Bob Elderson, and to see what she could find on 'Youth Solutions.'

Then she gathered up all the post its on one side of the table and went in search of the furniture polish and her dusting cloth.

"My head's going to explode," Gracie complained jokingly later that evening. Jack had called and she had explained to him how she'd spent her Sunday afternoon: with a jigsaw puzzle of mysteries.

He chuckled. "Yeah, but I think you've got a handle on the JDC case," he agreed, and said that her conclusions were pretty much the same as he'd come to. Jack mentioned that he'd contacted a couple other juvenile detention facilities in New England, and learned that their base rates were far below Hampshire County's JDC's rates. "I don't know how the JDC has convinced the county that it's the best option," Jack confided. "Seems to me that responsible county personnel would have checked the proposed charges against costs and services in comparable facilities nearby," he added.

"Well, maybe that's just it," Gracie offered. "They aren't responsible county personnel," she quoted.

Jack grunted an assent. "Let me know if you turn anything up on Broadstreet or Elderson," he added.

"Of course I will. But won't you be checking on them, too?" she asked, curious.

"Yes, I will," Jack drawled. "But I have a feeling our, erm, approaches are different, and you may uncover some things I don't," he admitted. "But that's not really why I called," Jack said then. Gracie, who had been curled on her sofa with Pumpkin asleep on her lap, and who had been about to switch on the TV, now put the remote down.

"Oh?" she asked encouragingly.

"Mmmmm...right." Jack paused. "D'you have any plans for the Fourth, Gracie?"

Gracie blinked. This was unexpected. "Well, no, not really," she admitted slowly. "Larry and the guys will be starting the conservatory this week, but the weather forecast is for rain, so they won't be finished by next weekend. I imagine I'll still have half my house torn apart and workers tramping around," she added, sounding a bit glum. "Why?"

On his end of the phone, Jack took a breath. "Well, on the Saturday my Mom and Dad are having a barbecue, and I'd like to invite you to come with me," he said quietly.

"You trying to piss off your Mother or something?" Gracie quipped. Jack's mother didn't especially like her it seemed, and when Gracie and Jack had been dating, Marilyn Draper had not been thrilled by her son's choice. Jack had told Gracie that it was just that his mother felt upstaged by Gracie, not that she didn't like her. Gracie, however, thought Marilyn should be mature enough to be happy her son was involved with an accomplished woman and not see it as some sort of contest.

Jack laughed out loud. "No, no, Gracie, I'm not. But they invited me, and, well, I'd like to spend the afternoon with you. That is, if you're available, and you'd like to."

Gracie thought quickly: they had been getting along very well since her return from England, working on the antifreeze murder case and investigating Mike's death together and sharing their ideas and insights. She didn't know that she wanted to start dating Jack again, though: somehow it almost seemed better when they just stayed friends. But she couldn't deny the physical attraction that was between them. It was as strong as it ever had been.

And then, of course, there was David, back in England. Gracie felt that chapter hadn't been finished just yet and while she was not romantically involved with David, the potential for that was there if she chose to pursue it, she thought. But she didn't want to get involved again with Jack if she were going to become involved with David. She'd learned before that wasn't a wise course of action.

"I'd love to go with you, Jack," Gracie said suddenly, feeling like she was over-thinking the situation. It was a fault of hers, she knew. All Jack was doing was asking her to go with him to a family cookout. It wasn't a date. She knew his parents and had met his sister and her family. And doubtless there would be other people there. It wasn't like he was asking her to marry him.

"Great!" Jack had replied, just a bit surprised at Gracie's alacrity. He was telling her now that his sister Laura and her husband Dave and their two toddlers and the new baby would all be there, as would a couple of his parents' friends. "Judges and their wives," Jack had said, making the combination sound extremely boring.

"Should I bring anything?" Gracie asked. Her living room might be a mess with the construction but her kitchen was up and running and she loved to cook.

"I think my Mother has the menu planned out," Jack replied tactfully.

"Ah, yes, so better not or she'll think I'm trying to steal her glory," Gracie deduced correctly, but she didn't sound angry.

"I'm glad you understand," Jack told Gracie.

Gracie sighed. "I do." If for nothing else but Jack's sake, she'd be sensitive to his Mother's feelings. Even if she did think the older woman was being silly.

Chapter Seventeen

Jack called in the services of a young Police profiler from the Lenox PD, Carla Sommers, to help with the interviews down at Sure Fit. As it turned out, Carla was a member there, too, so she was a natural for helping to check out the nearly 200 members of the gym.

Jack and Carla had worked together before on a case involving the murder of a rock star which had taken place at Berkshire County's own Tanglewood Concert Series. Carla was intuitive, had a degree in psychology, and was a trained profiler whose talent for sizing up people was uncanny. Jack's strong suit was his interrogation technique; together he and Carla made a very efficient and effective team.

Lenox PD's chief MacLellan was happy to 'loan' Carla out once again to the Berkshire County DA's office--for of course, the request had to come from Popovitch. But when Jack had mentioned bringing Carla in to help with the 'antifreeze murders' Popovitch had given in immediately, probably because it would mean less work for him, even if it meant more county money spent. Of course, Berkshire County would pay Officer Sommers for her time spent working on their behalf.

By Wednesday, Jack and Carla had made quite a bit of progress, with nearly all the members at Sure Fit, and all of the staff, finished. Wednesday afternoon, Gracie had called Jack on his mobile and asked if he wanted to come to dinner. "I've got some news," she had said breathlessly.

Jack had agreed, and had mentioned that he and Carla would be finishing up at Sure Fit about five, so would seven o'clock be okay?

Gracie had said yes, of course, but had invited Carla to come to dinner, too. The two had met the year before when Carla had been helping Jack solve the rock star's murder, and Gracie had liked her very much.

Carla, after initially protesting that she didn't want to intrude, agreed and said she would be happy to come, and to see Gracie again.

So just after 7 pm, Jack rang Gracie's old fashioned door bell and moments later Gracie opened the door to him, Carla and of course, Woof.

"What a beautiful house!" Carla exclaimed, taking in the parquet floor and creamy white walls of the foyer. To her right the pocket doors to Gracie's Oak Room were open with the room invitingly on display just beyond. Cleverly counter sunk ceiling spot lights as well as Tiffany style lamps illuminated the space against the evening gloom: as Gracie had predicted, the week had been rainy, with this day no exception.

"She'll give you the fifty cent tour with historical footnotes if you're nice," Jack joked as he and Carla shed their waterproof windbreakers.

Gracie had the good sense to laugh: she supposed she did wax a bit enthusiastic about her house.

"What's this?" Jack asked, tapping an obviously temporary, spring-loaded bifold door in the living room archway.

"Larry wanted to block off the entire living room, just in case Pumpkin got over-inquisitive," Gracie explained. "I'm not sure why, since the opening for the French doors was the first thing he finished, and the doors are installed, so it's not like she or anything else can get in or out."

"Yeah, but it probably makes it easier for him, if he and his guys come and go through the French doors--" Jack answered. "Can we see?" He turned to Carla. "Gracie's having a conservatory--what you and I would call a sunroom--put in," he explained.

Carla grinned. "I'd love to see, Gracie," she encouraged and Gracie, not needing much prodding, unfastened the temporary door and led them inside.

The formal living room's furniture was still draped and pushed away from the area where the new French doors had been installed, and there was some painting and finishing work to be done around the two thermal glass 'triple glazed' multi-paned doors. But Jack and Carla could see the framework of the conservatory beyond. Larry and his crew had begun Monday morning, just barely able to pour the foundation and anchor the four corners of the frame before the rain had come. Tenting the construction area in heavy tarps, the crew had assembled the frame along the four uprights on that first day, but hadn't been able to do more.

Tuesday, Larry had installed the sub-floor and heating ducts and the wrap around hip high moisture barrier walls. These would be insulated and faced with interior drywall inside, and with slate colored brick outside.

The conservatory would be all glass from about hip height up, with a little cupola on the top, also glass. But the rain, which was supposed to break the following day, had meant all the work had run very slowly, and none of the glass had been installed yet.

"Larry's crew is putting the glass panes in tomorrow," Gracie explained. "I think they'll run the electricity in Friday," Gracie explained. "And they'll install the walls and the hot tub as soon as that's done," she added, pointing to a hollowed out space in the sub floor where the hot tub would go.

"What are you going to have for a floor?" Carla queried.

"Tile," Gracie replied. "I found a source for some really beautiful mosaic stuff," she added, obviously delighted at the prospect of her conservatory. "And the walls will be tile, too, on top of the drywall. Thank goodness one of Larry's guys is really expert at laying the stuff or I'd be in trouble with my design." She paused. "There will be shelves along there that Larry'll build in," Gracie added, pointing again. "And they still have to put in the steps at the far door," she explained, adding that they would also lay a path from the conservatory's back door to join up with the other paths in her gardens that surrounded the house.

"It'll be beautiful, I'm sure," Carla said warmly and Gracie smiled at her.

"On Labor Day weekend I'm having a 'conservatory warming:' a big party and a cookout and stuff--I'll send you an invitation. Bring your swimsuit and you can test out the hot tub!" she offered happily, and Carla enthusiastically said she would love to do that.

Everyone trooped into the kitchen then, and Gracie told them to have a seat at her big barn board table. Over drinks, Jack and Carla told Gracie about the past two days interviewing everyone at Sure Fit Gym, and Gracie continued her dinner preparations while she listened.

"So it sounds like you didn't really turn up anyone suspicious," she said when they had concluded their summary.

"No." Carla sounded disappointed.

"The guys sure liked Sally, Pattie and Desirée though," Jack put in, taking a sip of the pinot grigio Gracie had uncorked.

"Funny, Jarrod said something similar to me when I was there," Gracie murmured.

"Well, all three girls were very pretty, and very fit and took care of themselves," Carla observed. "It's no wonder that the men at Sure Fit--and elsewhere, too, I should think--took a second look," she commented. "The only hunch I got was with Kim Foley," Carla continued. She'd told Jack about this 'feeling' but she hadn't had anything to back it up, and Jack hadn't given it too much credence, although he knew Carla's profiling skills were exceptional.

"The co-owner?" Gracie asked, surprised. She was assembling a large, very green salad in a big glass bowl. Now, apparently finished with that, she handed Jack placemats, napkins and cutlery and he set the table quickly and put the large salad bowl to one side. Gracie handed him dinner plates and salad plates, then she moved over to her indoor grill.

"Yeah--she seemed, I don't know, kind of fanatic about the whole thing," Carla said uncomfortably. She couldn't explain it any better than that. Something was 'off' with Kim Foley but she didn't know what.

"Well, Jarrod told me Kim's very religious," Gracie put in helpfully. She took several different types of vegetables which had been marinating in a shallow pan and plopped them on the grill: thinly sliced eggplant, peppers, courgettes, and portobello mushrooms.

Carla was nodding. "I know, he told me that too. And that's kind of what bothers me." She shrugged. "I guess maybe I'm letting my own opinion of organized religion get in the way," she added.

Gracie shrugged. "I'm not a regular church goer, either, Carla, and none of us can help it if our own feelings sometimes color our perceptions. That's why we work together, because usually we can filter out what doesn't make sense and keep what does if we team up," she finished, shooting a quick smile at Jack.

"She did seem a bit zealous," Jack agreed slowly. "That whole thing with god's mission to make our bodies temples and so on."

"It's in the Bible," Gracie interjected, flipping the vegetables with long-handled tongs.

"Yeah, okay, but maybe Foley carries it a bit too far?" Jack suggested. "Wow, that smells incredible," he added.

Gracie smiled.

"Still, even if Foley's some kind of religious fanatic who sees fitness as her sacred mission in life, it doesn't tie in to the murders very well," Carla replied.

"No: each of the dead girls was pretty much an embodiment of the fit lifestyle," Gracie agreed. "They were beautiful, they were in the best shape they could be, and they worked at staying that way."

Discussion of the murders was suspended for dinner time by mutual unspoken agreement. Gracie placed the grilled vegetables on a large platter then drizzled them with spiced olive oil and red apple infused balsamic vinegar. Then she transferred sautéed quinoa to another platter and scattered chopped parsley over it. In a big bowl, Gracie served a chunky tomato sauce with caramelized onions from a pot on her range top.

"You remembered I'm a vegan," Carla commented, touched that Gracie would have recalled such a detail.

"Yes, I did: but I don't eat a lot of meat so it wasn't too much of a stretch. I do use dairy, so I had to watch for that. But I managed," she said with a cheeky grin. "It's even gluten free!" she added. "Dig in."

The meal, as almost always, was delicious. Jack, who didn't remember encountering quinoa before, discovered he quite enjoyed it: especially smothered in the delicious tomato sauce. And Carla gobbled up everything.

"It's not too often I get a home cooked meal like this," she admitted, explaining that her family was still pretty much meat based when it came to their diet. "For family dinner I get the vegetables," she concluded, making a wry face. "And I don't go to all this trouble for myself."

"I'm really glad you enjoyed it," Gracie said as Carla and Jack helped her clear the table. "I'm sending the leftovers home with you," she added in a no-nonsense voice, putting the quinoa, the tomato sauce and the few remaining grilled vegetables in plastic containers as she spoke. Her tone indicated that arguing would be a waste of time.

"Thanks, Gracie."

"My pleasure."

Everyone wanted coffee, so Gracie fired up the proper appliance, and got busy plating desert: fresh strawberries in pretty crystal bowls. On the table she put a small dish of vanilla raw sugar and a little pitcher of creamy custard.

"Made with almond milk," Gracie said of the custard, and, delighted, Carla indulged.

While they sipped on their coffee, Jack wanted to ask Gracie what 'news' she had, and wondered why she'd been so reticent. That was unlike her. Finally, when Carla excused herself for a few minutes after all the cups and plates had been cleared away, Jack decided he had to find out.

"I wasn't sure if I should say anything in front of Carla, since this is hardly an official investigation," Gracie murmured. They were standing in front of her sink as she finished rinsing and Jack finished drying the last of the coffee mugs. "Judge Elderson's got quite a hefty bank balance, but not enough to account for what I figure his payoffs must be," she said quickly. "And Broadstreet's financials didn't raise any red flags. So I started investigating that 'Youth Solutions' company. Seems they're incorporated in New Hampshire--"

"Probably because of the favorable tax climate there," Jack put in.

"Right. But they don't seem to exist except on paper," Gracie explained. "I think they're a 'shell' company. And they're owned by a company called 'C.S. Limited.'"

"CS Limited?" Jack echoed.

Gracie nodded her head. She heard the door to the downstairs bathroom open, so she talked fast. "Yes, C.S. Limited. I think maybe 'CS' for 'Chacko Salama.' And CS Limited is registered in the Cayman Islands," she added.

Jack hardly had time to digest this last fact before Carla returned to the kitchen and asked Gracie for a tour of her house.

Gracie, happy to oblige, began immediately with an explanation of the recent renovation to the kitchen. She showed Carla the butler's pantry which connected to the dining room and also had kept an original feature of the house, an exterior doorway that led to the gardens. "It's handy if I want to bring in flowers, or produce, and wash them off here," Gracie explained of the door, and gestured to the small sink in the butler's pantry.

Carla nodded, intrigued.

Next, Gracie showed Carla the little closet area off the alcove in the hall. In the 1860s, the closet, which was accessed through a panel behind what looked like a carved wood column, and which ran inside the outer wall of the living room, had housed runaway slaves.

"So this house was part of the Underground Railroad?" Carla asked.

Gracie nodded. "Yes, it was," she confirmed, adding that according to the house construction records she'd been able to find, the addition which encompassed the formal living room had been completed in the 1850s. "Before the war. But I wonder if that double wall with the closet space wasn't purpose built," Gracie finished. "It doesn't seem to have any other use, and the Underground Railroad use is documented," she added, referencing papers she'd found in the county's Historical Society.

She continued with the tour, explaining that the Oak Room had been created out of two smaller rooms which had been added on to the base house. The original dwelling, built in 1697, had only really consisted of what was now the front foyer and her office alcove space. "They had a cook house out back, and a privy, back then," Gracie explained. "The first addition, in about 1730, were the two smaller rooms on the west side. Later they enclosed the kitchen and added the dining room. That was about 1780. Then subsequent owners put in the second floor, about 1820. In the 1850s the formal living room and that odd double wall was added, and the people who owned it after that put in more bedrooms, above the living room, on the second floor, about 1920."

By now Gracie, Jack and Carla had climbed the stairs and Gracie showed off the three guest rooms, the large bathroom, the linen closet and small attic, and finally her bedroom suite consisting of full bath, dressing room and bedroom. Pumpkin and Woof were happily sleeping almost nose to nose atop Gracie's iris-patterned duvet and didn't wake up when Gracie switched on the lights. In the corner, the floor clock with the hand painted irises began to chime 10 pm.

"I can't believe it's that late already!" Carla exclaimed.

"Time flies when you're having fun," Jack quipped, and smiled over at Gracie. He whistled for Woof, who came awake instantly at the summons and clambered off the bed and down the stairs. Jack and Carla took their leave then, with profuse thanks from Carla and a low directive from Jack for Gracie to call him when she found CS Limited.

"I will, but it may take some doing," Gracie replied as Woof and Carla got settled in Jack's truck. "I've never traced an off shore account before."

Jack gave her a wry grin. "Yeah, but you can do it," he replied confidently.

"You know, I've been thinking," Jack said as he drove back to his place, where Carla had left her car. "I know we'd need a warrant to do it, but I think we need to search Sure Fit again."

Carla frowned. "Wasn't it searched when Ford's body was found there?"

Jack nodded. "Yes. But I don't know if everything was checked: at the time, we weren't sure of cause of death and I don't think, once we had the COD, that we considered that the gym might have been the place of ingestion," he explained.

Carla made an 'ah hah!' sort of noise and said, "there's a juice bar at Sure Fit."

"Yup," Jack confirmed.

"You think someone at the gym is poisoning these women at the juice bar?" Carla asked.

"Seems possible, doesn't it?" Jack countered, and Carla nodded. "But I can't get a warrant on a hunch," Jack added, deflated.

"No, you're right: we'd need probable cause, and so far we haven't turned anything like that up in the interviews," Carla agreed. She thought for a minute. "And even if that was how the murderer poisoned his victims, it's probably all cleaned up by now."

Jack nodded. "Right. And I don't remember antifreeze even being found on the premises. And even if it had been, it could have been there in case someone's vehicle needed it," he added.

"Well," Carla sighed. "We'll finish up tomorrow: we have, what, five more people to see?" she asked, and Jack confirmed that. "And then we'll go from there."

Chapter Eighteen

Like most investigations, the one into the deaths of the three young women took time, effort, and what Jack called 'good old fashioned detective work.' Gracie called it slogging. Or research. Either way, it was painstaking and involved talking to endless witnesses or suspects and spending hours combing relevant--and sometimes not so relevant--documents.

But both had learned the value of such an approach. It was all about the details, and Jack was certain that if you looked under every rock, checked in every corner and questioned every statement, eventually you'd find something.

The five members of Sure Fit Gym interviewed on Thursday were as seemingly blameless as the rest had been. However, Thursday afternoon as Carla and Jack sat back and looked at the gym members as a whole, an interesting pattern began to develop. None of the male members had admitted to dating any of the three dead girls, but eight of them had admitted to 'buying them a drink' at a local bar, the Toll Gate Pub, just south of Stockbridge.

Although the patronization of the Toll Gate Pub might have been a coincidence, Jack and Carla didn't really believe in coincidences. So Friday night found them both--in civilian clothes--at the Pub, to see what they could find out. They had also called Gracie, to invite her to come with them on their 'fact finding undercover mission' as Carla had phrased it. She had agreed, but had explained that she thought it would be best if they pretended not to know each other when they got there.

Mystified as to why, but agreeing, Jack and Carla arrived about 8 pm, got drinks and secured a table next to a handy floor plant into which they could dump their alcohol. Although they wanted to appear as though they were indulging, both intended to stay completely sober, and not just because both were carrying concealed weapons.

The Toll Gate Pub was a fairly upscale bar and restaurant with a distinctly Irish flair: the walls were painted green and graced with prints and photos of castles and fields of sheep. A shillelagh hung over the mirrored back of the bar and there were shamrocks in abundance even though St. Patrick's Day had long passed. The clientele was mostly 30's and 40's, some couples in the restaurant section of the place, and singles at the bar. The two areas were separated by a 'wall' of French doors not unlike the ones Gracie had just had installed at her house. The Toll Gate's doors were highly varnished oak like the rest of the interior woodwork; their many panes allowed people to see the bar from the restaurant and vice versa. A couple of the doors stood ajar, allowing some of the noise to mingle as well.

Gracie arrived about 8:30 pm and made straight for the bar, where she hopped on a seat, gave the barkeep a big smile, and ordered a rum and coke.

"A rum and coke?" Jack whispered to Carla. "She hates rum and coke. Loves rum, hates coke. All soda, really. What the heck?" His surprise at Gracie's choice of beverage increased when Gracie removed her outer wrap: a big, fluffy cream colored pashmina shawl. She was wearing beige suede leggings--they were too tight to be called trousers and looked as though they'd been painted on-- and a cream colored lacy halter top which tied with slender spaghetti straps. Her shoes were cream as well, with very high heels.

Jack nearly choked on his drink.

Gracie's 'look' was completed with large diamond stud earrings and, now that he looked more closely, rather dramatic makeup. He was used to seeing Gracie with her 'work' makeup: a little concealer, a little blush, some mascara and lipstick. But tonight Gracie had added dark eyeshadow, eyeliner, and a bit of glitter scattered here and there. She looked classy but easy, Jack thought and said as much to Carla.

Carla gave him a slow smile. "She's a smart girl, that Gracie: I think I know what theory she's testing."

Jack looked a question, and then looked back at Gracie, who was sipping at her drink and smiling at a young guy sitting a few seats down from her. Then she started chatting with the bartender, who appeared quite taken with her. He was in his mid 20's, Jack would guess.

"Okay, what theory is she testing?" Jack asked Carla.

"Remember the kind of clothing Sally, Pattie and Desirée had? The fancy stuff for going out?" Carla prodded.

Jack nodded and he suddenly saw where Gracie was going with her outfit. "The three girls might have been--erm--escorts, shall we call it?" he suggested, and Carla nodded.

"The thought had crossed my mind, when those guys said they'd seen all three girls here, and bought them drinks. Maybe they had done more than that," Carla said.

"We'll talk to them again," Jack murmured, low. "Do you think one of them could be--"

Carla smiled at him as though he'd told a funny story and nodded. "Stop looking so intense, Jack," she whispered. "Yes, I think one of them could be the murderer, and could have used the juice bar at Sure Fit to do his dirty work," Carla summarized, still smiling as though discussing the pleasantest of subjects.

Jack took a deep breath. "Well, I guess we should order something," he advised, although food was the last thing on his mind.

"This is a great place, first time I've come," Gracie was telling the bartender, whose name was Hal.

"You live around here?" he asked.

Gracie shook her curls, conscious of the waft of perfume the motion created, and smiling more widely. "Not too far," she answered obliquely. "I just moved from, erm, Schenectady," she extemporized.

"How'd you find us?" Hal asked, curious.

"A friend of mine recommended it," Gracie answered, still vague. "She used to come here."

Hal frowned. "Used to? What happened?"

Gracie affected sudden sorrow, and looked down. Then she looked back up at Hal. From her jeweled handbag that Jack knew was a Judith Lieber only because his mother had one, too, she withdrew a photograph and showed it to the bartender.

"This is me and Dez--Desirée," Gracie whispered, her voice thick with emotion.

The photo was of a smiling Desirée Manning and an equally happy Gracie, their heads together like the best of friends. Gracie had photoshopped her own image into the photo of Desirée which had been part of the police file and with which Jack had supplied her. She had also photoshopped in a background of a casino floor.

"We used to love going to the casinos," Gracie confessed, still grief-stricken and now managing to call up enough tears to make her eyes glisten.

"I know her," Hal said, looking at the photo. "She hasn't been in for a while. Last time she was here, oh, three weeks ago I think now, she said she hadn't been feeling well, and thought she had a stomach bug," he offered helpfully. "She's your friend?"

Gracie nodded. "She was." She paused, and stared directly at the bartender. "She's dead."

Hal's reaction was one of shock: he nearly dropped the glass he was drying and his face went very pale.

"Dead?" he echoed. "When? How?"

"Just last week--" Gracie choked out, then made a show of pulling herself together. "I moved here because she said it was such a great area," she murmured, touching a tissue delicately to the inside margin of both eyes while Hal regarded her in stunned silence. "She and I got to be really good friends and I was relying on her to show--show me around, help me out, you know, when you move to a new place?" Gracie asked, making her voice sound vulnerable and a bit lost.

Hal, completely engaged, nodded.

Gracie sighed, wondering how far she could push being a gullible young 20-something. Well, the lighting was indirect: she'd go for it. "I just finished at Schenectady Secretarial, and Dez was going to help me find a job. I used my savings to get an apartment over in the same complex she lived in," Gracie went on, trying to sound pathetic but not ridiculous. "And she said there was a great gym near here she worked out at and they had a spa...she even told me she'd found a great hairdresser and manicurist," Gracie finished, gesturing to her curls. "These cost a mint, and most hair stylists can't make them look natural," she said to Hal confidingly.

Hal looked Gracie over. "That's a perm?" he asked. "Geez, it looks so real," he replied.

Gracie felt that she and Hal had bonded sufficiently for her to ask a more probing question. Frankly, she didn't think Hal could be all that bright: he apparently hadn't heard of Desirée Manning's death, and it had been in the news, as had the deaths of Ford and Sullivan, and the theory that the three deaths were somehow connected. But Hal either didn't watch the news or he hadn't made the connection between patrons of his bar and the dead women.

"So, Hal: did Dez always come in by herself when she came here?" she asked a minute later. Hal had refreshed her rum and coke 'on the house' and Gracie was wondering if she dared have a second drink. She didn't want to get drunk. She also wondered if Hal might be the murderer: it wouldn't be hard to have some antifreeze in one of the many bottles behind the bar and sneak it into the drinks of his victims. She'd watched him make both her drinks: Meyer's Dark rum from the familiar bottle, and Coke from a labelled dispenser. So she thought she was probably safe. But she really didn't want the second drink.

"Most times. A couple times she was with another girl, said she knew her from that gym, maybe the same one she told you about," Hal said helpfully.

Gracie nodded. "I don't even know the name of it," she said, sounding distraught at being unable to find an outlet for physical fitness.

"Oh, it was Sure Fit, over on Commerce Street," Hal replied brightly. "I can give you directions if you want."

Gracie looked at Hal as though he were the Second Coming. "Oh, could you Hal? That would be so wonderful!" she gushed.

Hal busily got himself a pad and pen and started writing directions to Sure Fit down for her.

"Good god, she's got him eating out of the palm of her hand," Carla murmured, impressed. They had ordered a platter of tempura style fried veggies and were nibbling as they pretended to talk to each other, but really were surreptitiously watching Gracie's performance.

"Yeah, she's good at that," Jack commented, not able to resist a smile. He didn't like what Gracie was up to, and didn't like it even more that she hadn't told him what she was planning, but he had to admit, she was good. And he knew from experience that she hadn't told him her intentions because he would have objected and they only would have argued.

Too late for that now.

"I wonder if she'll get any information out of him?" Jack said a moment later.

Carla wiped her mouth and stood. "Well, I'll find out soon. Going to the ladies'," she added, and grabbed her handbag, smiled at Jack, and proceeded down the aisle towards the back where the restrooms were.

Jack glanced over at the bar. Gracie was standing by her seat--on which she'd left her pashmina draped--also preparing to go to the ladies' room.

"Hal, I have to go to the little girls' room," Gracie had said a few seconds before. "Will you hold my seat for me?" she'd asked sweetly, draping her pashmina over the back of the bar chair but holding her handbag and her drink.

"Sure--you don't have to take your drink, though," Hal had answered.

"Oh, I trust YOU, but I've heard of too many guys who slip a roofie in a girl's drink when the barkeep's not looking," Gracie had returned ingenuously. She had shaken her head for emphasis. "I don't want that kind of trouble. I'll be right back," she had insisted, and with another smile, she'd moved away.

Gracie and Carla met in the ladies' room, which was fortunately deserted except for them.

"Here--" Gracie said, producing a zip lock bag from her jeweled evening purse and pouring a little of her drink into it. "Have this tested? I don't think there's any antifreeze in it, but you can never tell." She handed the bag to a startled Carla.

"Have you found out anything?" Carla asked then, recovering herself and tucking the baggie into her purse. It made a nice complement to her gun, badge and wallet.

"Not really," Gracie replied, pouring more of her drink down the sink and then adding water so it looked much as it had before. "The bartender's name is Hal, and he recognized this," she produced the photoshopped image of Desirée and herself and showed Carla.

"Wow, that's great!" Carla crowed, both for the info and for the cleverness with the picture. "He knew her?"

"Said she used to come in but hasn't for a few weeks, said she wasn't feeling well, thought she had a stomach bug or something," Gracie replied. She checked her look in the mirror. "He also said she usually came alone but sometimes came with another of the girls from Sure Fit," she added. She applied more lipstick, and Carla watched.

"Your get up practically gave Jack heart failure," she joked, giving Gracie a look.

"Yeah? Well, he's not used to seeing me--like this," she amended quickly. "It's not too much?" Gracie asked Carla.

Carla shook her head. "I think it's perfect."

Gracie sighed. "Well, I'm going back out there and see what else Hal will tell me. Maybe nothing, maybe something, but at least we can see if his drinks are spiked."

"We'll be watching you," Carla assured her.

"Yeah," Gracie gave her a cheeky grin. "You guys make a cute couple," she joked as she left.

Carla made a face and laughed.

Chapter Nineteen

Gracie returned to the bar and took up her conversation with Hal, and sipped at her much watered down drink. When Hal offered to 'set her up with a fresh one,' Gracie refused.

"I can't drink that much: two's my limit or I start getting a little, well," she hesitated coyly. "My judgement becomes impaired," she said finally, sounding exactly like someone on the verge of giddiness trying to sound very serious.

Hal nodded. "I know what you mean, and I respect that," Hal said earnestly. "What's your name, anyway?" he asked. They'd been talking away for over an hour now, it was time he could refer to her by something other than 'Miss' or 'you.'

"Verena Davenport," Gracie replied promptly, giving her cousin's name. "But people just call me Vee," she added, smiling again. Her cheeks were starting to get sore.

"Well, okay, Vee it is," Hal returned happily. "You know--" he leaned over the bar towards Gracie and lowered his voice. "There were a couple of guys who used to meet Dez here--and I think some other gals from Sure Fit--and buy her a couple of drinks."

"Oh?" Gracie gave Hal a sort of mildly curious look and waited.

"I mean, they might be able to tell you more about Dez than I can," Hal backpedalled quickly once he saw that 'Vee' had no idea what he was talking about.

Gracie nodded. "Unh huh, I guess." Her tone still indicated that she had no clue what Hal meant.

Hal hesitated. "And, uh, if Dez was going to introduce you to people and show you around and help you get a job and stuff, maybe she would have wanted you to meet these guys?" he suggested. Again, he looked hopeful that 'Vee' would read between the lines and again, Gracie affected a profound lack of understanding.

As Jack always said, for a very bright woman, Gracie did dense really well.

Gracie decided to let the light dawn slowly. "Oooooooohhhh," she breathed finally. It was a long, drawn out syllable with more shades of meaning than most paragraphs. She gave Hal a look of comprehension, then nodded once, twice. "Yes. Yes, Dez did mention something about that," she said, and then covered her lips with her hand as though she'd blurted out something she shouldn't have. "I mean, she said you could meet some really nice guys here, who would buy you a drink, or even stand you to a meal," Gracie hinted.

Hal was grinning at her like a teacher smiling on a favored but dull witted student who had finally worked out a math problem. "Exactly," he affirmed. "But I don't see them here tonight. Well, it's still early," he reassured Gracie and made a motion with his hand as if to suggest that it was just the shank of the evening. Then he moved off to take another customer's order.

Gracie looked around: The Toll Gate had filled up considerably in the time she'd been here, she realized. There was hardly a vacant seat at the bar and even most of the tables were full. Jack and Carla still pretended to be on a first date, nibbling at their tempura platter and surreptitiously dumping their drinks into the potted palm that flanked their table.

Hal returned to Gracie's spot at the bar once he'd finished his ministrations to the other customers.

"Will you let me know if one of them comes in, and maybe introduce me?" Gracie whispered to Hal as she picked up the thread of their conversation where they'd left off.

Hal looked suddenly self important and quite pleased, and said he would do exactly that.

"Well, that was a risky business," Jack chastised Gracie a couple of hours later. They had all met back at Jack's trailer where Carla had left her vehicle, and which was on Gracie's way home, once they had all left the Toll Gate Pub.

"How so?" Gracie retorted, tossing the pashmina she'd wrapped herself in on a chair and squatting down to say hello to Woof. Generally, that kept him from jumping up and putting his paws on her shoulders in greeting. Although the lace halter wasn't exactly her style, she might possibly wear it again, and there was no way she wanted dog prints on her suede leggings, which she definitely wanted to wear again.

"That guy," Carla put in, wanting to defuse the situation she thought she could sense brewing. "He might have wanted to do more than buy you a drink," she explained.

"Yeah, he might have. But at least for tonight I think he would have accepted a 'no' even if he was used to hearing 'yes.' And we don't know that he would have done anything more than just be friendly," Gracie replied in her own defense.

"I don't know: he looked like he was getting pretty friendly," Jack said darkly.

The 'guy' they were referring to was one of the men Hal had told Gracie had been pals with Dez and possibly the other girls Dez knew from the gym. By the name of Alan, he was reasonably attractive, about five foot ten with sandy brown hair, brown eyes and since he was a Sure Fit regular, a toned body. He was also married, as he'd confessed to Gracie in her role as 'Vee' once he'd shown up about 10 pm. But in words Gracie could have scripted for him they were so trite, 'his wife didn't understand him' and he had looked hopefully at her.

Gracie, wanting to get whatever information she could but not wanting to become involved herself, had smiled at Alan and talked about how difficult it was sometimes to find a sympathetic ear.

Alan had eaten it up, offered to buy Gracie another drink, which she declined, and then asked her if instead, he could buy her dinner another evening, since it was already so late.

Gracie had bitten her lip, genuinely at a loss and stalling for time. She had never expected the 'undercover fact finding mission' to progress this quickly. Then inspiration had come to her.

'Well, Alan,' she had begun, her voice low but very sweet. 'I'd really like that, I mean, to have dinner with you.' She had sighed. 'But I would have to insist on finding a way to, erm, pay you back?' Gracie had suggested, her voice lilting between shy and flirtatious.

Alan had waited a beat, and then reached out a hand to cover Gracie's. She noticed the man's palm atop hers was moist, and only with difficulty kept herself from pulling away or making a face. Yikes, even if the profit was good, she thought to herself, this was a crappy way to earn money.

'I'm sure we can think up a way for you to repay me, Vee,' Alan had whispered, and leaned in to kiss her cheek.

Gracie had kept smiling.

Alan had uncovered her hand and was busily consulting a slim smart phone. 'How about next Tuesday?' he had asked, and Gracie, too happy to have achieved her goal and have the end in sight to really care, had agreed with alacrity.

Now, Jack, Carla and Gracie were reviewing what they'd learned at the Toll Gate Pub.

"Well, I think you'd better talk to that Alan guy again," Gracie said sternly. "And any of those other men who said they bought girls from the gym drinks at that Pub."

"D'you think Hal's in on it?" Carla asked, noticing the air still crackling between Gracie and Jack.

Gracie shrugged. "I don't know. I don't think he's a pimp or anything," she assessed frankly. "He may not be aware of exactly what is going on, either," she went on. "I think it's most likely that he just thinks the guys are being nice to the girls, and if they hook up, well, they hook up."

"So you don't think he knows that money changed hands?" Jack put in, somewhat calmer. After all, he and Carla had been right there. And, as Gracie had pointed out, on a first meeting the guy would probably have taken 'no' for an answer if the question had been asked. As it had turned out, though, he'd taken it slow and planned for another evening with 'Vee'. And Gracie was fine.

She had also been armed he saw now, as she opened her jeweled clutch bag to get her iPhone, so she could make notes on it. A little silver .22 was nestled next to a few bills, a lipstick and the phone.

"And just what did you think you were going to do with that?" Jack asked, angry again. He pointed to the gun.

Gracie shrugged. "A girl's got to have protection," she answered cheekily. "I didn't know where the evening was going to end up, or how well you and Carla would be able to cover me."

It was a reasonable point and Jack knew he was just over reacting, as he almost always did, at the thought of Gracie coming to harm. He calmed himself down with almost visible effort.

"Well, anyway, no, I don't think Hal knows that Dez and possibly Sullivan and Ford, were taking money from their, erm, 'male friends,'" Gracie finished, fiddling with the notebook function on her phone.

"Not that we've proven that," Carla cautioned. She was relieved that the tension between Jack and Gracie appeared to be dissipating.

"No, but we've got a pretty clear indication of it," Jack agreed.

"So...you don't want me to keep my date with Alan next Tuesday and get proof absolute?" Gracie asked, only half joking. She would have done it, as long as Jack and maybe Carla had been nearby to break up the assignation at the right moment. But mostly she asked the question to get a rise out of Jack.

And she did.

Jack's jaw clenched and Gracie thought to herself that she was a wicked girl to tease him so.

"No," he replied tightly, glaring at her. "We have enough to go on."

"You're sure?" Gracie queried, genuinely curious. She noticed that Carla was staying out of the debate.

Jack nodded. "Enough to question all of those guys again, and Hal, too."

Saturday morning Gracie slept in and only woke when the sound of power tools from the construction zone on the ground floor penetrated her dreams. Quickly, the events of the evening before returned to her and she groaned, shook her head, and passed one hand over her face as though to rub it into full consciousness.

She adjusted herself against the pillows and squinted at her bedroom: it was a sunny day beyond the wooden shutters that kept the room shadowed. Probably time for her to be up and about: there was gardening to be done, and of course the conservatory project to check on.

She reached over and stroked Pumpkin, who was curled up in her usual spot on the other side of the bed. The cat miaowed shortly in response, then turned so Gracie could stroke her other side.

In the corner, the iris clock chimed the half hour and Gracie finally faced reality: 9:30 a.m.! That was respectably late, she thought, so enough. Gracie stretched luxuriously, then moved the covers off and got quickly out of bed. Pumpkin gave her a lazy look which said, 'I don't have to get up yet, do I?' and returned to slumber.

A few minutes later Gracie had wriggled into her full length lavender terrycloth robe and opened the shutters and casement windows in her bedroom. Then she went downstairs to start the coffee as well as her day.

While the coffee was brewing, she threw together ingredients for strawberry scones and plopped the batter into two circular scone pans. She put them into her convection oven to bake and brought a large mug of coffee over to her laptop, switched it on, and quickly entered her email program. There were several emails from various people but the one which stood out above the rest was one from David.

Smiling, Gracie opened and scanned it. Then she relaxed into a wide grin. David told her he'd been promoted to Detective Sergeant 'much to the consternation of DS Bowman' he put in cheekily. DS Bowman had, until his promotion, outranked him. Now they were equals, and it was no secret DS Bowman had resented David's rapid rise to the top and their superiors' encouragement.

'So a celebration is in order, and Saturday your cousin Verena's friend Tamara and I, and Verena, and a few blokes from the station and I think some of Verena's friends are all going out to the Windjammer. I wish you were still here, to join us.'

Gracie read and re-read that last sentence. Then the oven timer dinged, and she went to get the scones and put on another pot of coffee.

"Morning, guys," she said a few moments later. She had run upstairs and changed into a peach colored track suit and sneakers. Then she had, indeed, made a fresh, full pot of coffee and she now arrived at the newly constructed conservatory bearing a tray with several mugs of dark fragrant liquid, spoons, raw sugar and half and half, and a plate of warm scones and butter.

Everybody was delighted to see her, not only because she brought coffee and goodies but because the project she'd hired them for was finally going well and they were eager to show off their work. They quickly swarmed around her, helping themselves to the coffee and scones and then pointing out various aspects of the work they had done.

Gracie was really pleased to note that the hot tub was in place and had been tested. Now, it was covered, not only to keep dust and debris out, but to keep the warmth in. The custom cover Gracie would keep on the tub when not in use was in turn covered by a large tarp.

Larry's tile man Mel was about half finished with laying the tiles on the floor. He'd probably have that finished, and the walls, in another day or so. All the electricals and heat ducts were in, the molding around the doors was up and the concrete steps were being put in place at the back door of the conservatory.

"So it's nearly done!" Gracie crowed.

"It's come together really quickly," Larry admitted. "Once the rain stopped," he added with a grin.

Originally, he had said one week, minimum, for the job, but it looked like they'd come in under that. Often somewhat pessimistic, he had cautioned Gracie that the project might not even be finished until mid July. However, he'd received no emergency calls from people whose septic tank had blocked or whose roof had collapsed, and so had been able to devote all of his and his crew's time to the conservatory.

Larry also told Gracie that the unit she had ordered from the specialty company in England was very well constructed and had been a breeze to assemble.

"It's really sturdy," Larry noted, munching on a scone. "I put in all the rebar and reinforcements, like we discussed, but this baby isn't going anywhere," he tapped one triple glazed glass panel fondly. "Or if it does, we have worse things to worry about, if you know what I mean," he joked.

"Like worldwide devastation or the Second Coming?" Gracie quipped and Larry nodded.

"I'll move the dirt back in as soon as those steps set up, and then what do you want, grass seed or flower beds?" he asked Gracie, knowing the answer.

"Oh, flower beds of course!" Gracie said immediately. "There's compost to--"

"Yeah, I know, we'll put some compost and peat in and then tidy it all up so it's ready for you to plant whatever you want," Larry chuckled good naturedly. He knew Gracie, and had known she would not be able to resist the chance to get new flower beds dug as a side benefit to installing the conservatory.

So, she thought to herself, the whole thing should be done by the middle of the month. That gave her six weeks to furnish the interior with the orchids, cycads and ferns she'd been intending to buy, and to plant the outside, perhaps just with annuals this year.

She'd already decided to have her Labor Day house party as usual, and had started crafting the menu, but it was wonderful that the new conservatory would be up and running for that event, and that it could be, as she had told Carla, a 'conservatory warming.'

Later that morning, Gracie sent a congratulatory email back to David and told him to say hello to everyone for her and to have a wonderful time at the Windjammer. She did not directly address David's 'wish you were here' comment, and gave only a fleeting thought to his statement that he and Tamara and some friends were all going out. It sounded, and it probably was, completely innocent.

But Gracie had learned to listen to her 'little voice' as she called it and now she found herself thinking that David and Tamara might make a good couple. Of course, neither had said anything even remotely connected to that to Gracie in any of the several emails they'd exchanged since she'd left England.

But she wasn't going to fool herself into believing that a relationship could survive across an ocean. Oh, she knew it could be done. But she also knew that it was far more likely for David to begin to fancy someone who lived locally, much as he might have been attracted to Gracie. Or she to him.

And she had been attracted to him: he reminded her, in a way, of Jack when Jack was a few years younger and still on the police force. And she and David had certainly got on well.

But, she admitted to herself later that weekend as she watched Larry and his crew work on the conservatory and made his tile man Mel teach her how to lay the beautiful Mediterranean tiles she'd selected, she wouldn't be surprised if David and Tamara got together. And frankly, she would wish them well.

Chapter Twenty

Gracie called Rita Licora the following week and asked if she would be able to meet some time to go over a few things concerning the Pittsfield Junior League. Rita, who had been so delighted that Gracie had invited her to join Club, laughingly told her that she'd meet her 'anywhere, anytime.'

At first Gracie had thought of suggesting lunch somewhere in Northampton; its proximity to several colleges and ski resorts meant there was a great choice of restaurants in the village. But by the time Gracie made the call, she'd had a better idea. She explained her thought process to Rita.

"Usually we have a prospective member Tea, for several women who want to join, at the start of each Club year," she told Rita. "But technically Club is finished for this year--although you can come to the Barbecue and then be inducted at the September meeting--and I'd hate to make you wait for a Tea to learn all about Club."

Rita made encouraging noises on the other end of the phone.

"So I'd like to give you the powerpoint presentation that I've developed for the Tea, and also have the time to give you an overview of all the Club committees," Gracie continued. "Kind of like a Tea just for you, only how about dinner instead?"

While all of this made sense, Gracie's real purpose was to get Rita to talk about Mark Broadstreet and anything shady which might be going on in Hampshire County. She didn't think she could readily do that in a public place, and so had decided to try to get Rita to come out to her house for dinner. To make it look less suspicious, Gracie was inviting two of her closest friends from Club, Anne and Jean, to dinner too. Since they were both on the Membership Committee with Gracie, it made sense.

Rita seemed thrilled at the attention Gracie and her friends were willing to give her and agreed to come out to Gracie's on Wednesday of that week, for dinner. After telling Gracie that she pretty much ate what people put in front of her, Rita thanked her and they hung up. Anne and Jean had both already told Gracie they were available on Wednesday, so now all Gracie had to do was plan the menu and strategize a little with Anne and Jean about what she wanted to find out.

This would mean, she realized, letting them in on her suspicions with regard to Hampshire County, at least to some degree. But she trusted both Anne and Jean implicitly, and so decided that she'd read them in when they arrived ahead of Rita on Wednesday.

Jack and Carla were busy this week with the male clients from Sure Fit who had known the three dead women. Although Gracie was in the courthouse on Tuesday getting her usual updates, she didn't see either Jack or Carla around, and Mille told her in an excited whisper that they were 'down in interrogation' meaning the sheriff's office, which had a small interview space with a one way mirror and an attached observation room.

Popovitch, of course, was also nowhere to be found, but Millie didn't offer to reveal his whereabouts. She either didn't know, or knew Gracie didn't care.

Gracie was sure Jack and Carla were questioning the Sure Fit suspects and she was eager to hear from Jack how that was coming along.

On Wednesday, Larry and his crew finished work on the conservatory, a couple days ahead of schedule. Mel cautioned Gracie to allow the tile to 'set up' for another 24 hours before she got it wet or started dragging things across it. Gracie nodded enthusiastically, and spent the afternoon putting the furniture in her formal living room back in its proper place and giving everything a once over with her duster and hoover. She was eager to start getting plants for the conservatory, but she would wait to start on that project. Meanwhile, she could get some annuals for the new outside beds. And this was July Fourth Weekend: Saturday was Jack's parents' cookout, she mustn't forget.

Anne and Jean were suitably impressed with the conservatory when they arrived, even though it was still empty. Then they sat with Gracie on her screened porch to discuss Rita Licora, her prospective membership in Club, and what Gracie wanted to try to find out from her that evening.

Briefly, Gracie explained what she and Jack thought might be going on in Hampshire County. She also told her friends what

Rita's connection to Mark Broadstreet was--or had been, at any rate. And then she told them that in addition to familiarizing Rita with Club that evening, she also wanted to do a little prodding to see if she would say anything about Broadstreet or the JDC or anything else untoward that might be going on. Since she was County Detective, Rita would be in a likely position to know about any underhandedness, or at least have a suspicion.

"Well, if she's broken up with Broadstreet, she'll probably want to talk about that," Jean assessed knowingly. "Especially if he dumped her." She sipped at the 'summer splash' Gracie had given her upon arrival: elderflower liqueur splashed in prosecco. Tasty. And not too dry: sometimes Jean, who preferred semi sweet wines, had trouble with the very dry wines Gracie usually preferred.

"And if he's going out with someone else and he hasn't broken up with Rita, and she finds out, she'll really want to talk," Anne chimed in. "I'll let you figure out how to tell her you saw him out with--what was her name?"

"Sasha Yedid."

"She's not in Club, is she?" Anne asked.

"No," Gracie replied. "That's Farida Salama. Sasha used to be her sister in law," Gracie added, watching both friends digest this bit of news. "She was married to Chako Salama, Farida's husband Koshy's brother."

"Hmmm...curiouser and curiouser," Anne murmured. "And I won't ask how you know that." She sipped her drink, too, and nibbled on a cracker loaded with a delicious chunky creamy dip Gracie had put out.

"Public record, nothing sneaky, just a little research," Gracie replied. She paused. "So--you guys don't mind kind of guiding the conversation towards Mark Broadstreet and Hampshire County and the JDC?" Gracie asked.

Both Anne and Jean shook their heads, Jean's long chestnut brown hair swinging against her shoulders and Anne's spiky bob swishing. "Nope. It's good we know your agenda, Gracie," Jean replied. "And as far as I'm concerned, I'm always happy to help you in your investigations, you know that."

Gracie nodded. A year or so before, Jean had come to her with concerns about federal mail tampering and missing money at the county jail, and Gracie along with Jack had helped uncover the crime and put a stop to it.

"Now, what's in this dip?" Anne asked, changing the subject and helping herself to another cracker.

"It's called 'chat 'n' chew'," Gracie replied with a smile. "It's based on that vegetable soup mix and sour cream, only I use an organic version of the soup mix, half cream cheese and half sour cream, and I add a can of drained water chestnuts, some drained chopped frozen spinach, and fresh chives," she explained.

Gracie's antique doorbell sounded.

"That's Rita!" Gracie announced, and left the porch to welcome her guest.

By the end of dinner, the four young women had discovered that they all very much liked each other. And Jean and Anne agreed with Gracie that witty, clever Rita with her short wiry auburn hair, enthusiastic energy, and big green eyes would be a great addition to Club.

Rita, who lived in the village of Goshen in Hampshire County, just a short drive east on Route 9, had relocated a couple of years before from her previous post as County Detective in rural Coos County, NH. Since settling in Hampshire County she had focused almost exclusively on her job and although she'd met a few people, she was eagerly anticipating the social entrée being in Club would give her.

As to why she'd moved south from the very northern part of New Hampshire, she confided to Jean, Gracie and Anne that her goal was to be the County Detective in a bigger, more metropolitan county some day, and that Hampshire County with its proximity to both Springfield and Worcester, not to mention Boston, was a step in the right direction.

She was impressed with Jean's career as a Corrections Officer and wistful when Anne discussed her growing brood of children.

"I'd like to get married and have kids someday," Rita said, spooning up the last of the strawberry granita Gracie had served for dessert. They'd enjoyed a big Mediterranean style antipasto salad and Greek spiced chicken kebabs over brown rice, which Gracie had served with a yoghurt based sauce.

The bottle of wine Rita had brought had also been well received; even though she'd had a wine ready to open with dinner, Gracie decided they would drink the bottle from the Follies a Deux wineries Rita had brought. They had not been disappointed, except when the bottle had been emptied.

"Surely you're seeing someone?" Jean asked now, quite naturally.

Rita made a face at her empty granita dish. "I was."

Her tone didn't invite further inquiry, so Anne just said encouragingly, "and you will again, Rita, don't worry," and with that Gracie suggested they get refills on their coffee and move into the Oak Room where she'd set up the power point Club presentation.

After the program, which only lasted about twelve minutes, Rita had a lot of questions and seemed mostly concerned with how she could participate in Club programs and help them raise money to disburse to area charities.

"I had no idea the PJL gave that kind of money away," Rita told Gracie, Jean and Anne. The figure from the year before for Club's charitable giving of $25,000 had floored her.

"We're really proud of being able to raise so much," Anne replied, smiling.

"And as you could see from the list of beneficiaries, not all the charities are in Berkshire County. Some are in Hampshire, and Hampden even," Jean put in, naming the two closest counties in Massachusetts.

Rita was busy looking over the committee list, and she asked about the upcoming Barbecue.

"That's purely social," Gracie assured her. "Each year a different member has a summer event, like a barbecue or a pool party or whatever, and club members come with their husbands or boyfriends or significant others, or with girlfriends--often prospective members, like you!"

"The children stay home, and it's just a great evening out for members and guests," Anne chimed in.

"Last year, didn't you have it here, Gracie?" Jean asked, knowing full well that Gracie had, but going somewhere with her question.

So Gracie nodded in the affirmative.

Jean grinned. "We had a great time: Gracie has this spring fed pond just over the hill in that meadow out there, and we were all swimming and floating around in that. And then, the food: amazing! Even the guys had fun."

"You were dating Chet something, weren't you?" Anne asked conversationally of Jean.

Jean nodded, then looked brightly at Rita. "You probably know him: Chet Sullivan?"

"Oh, yeah, out in Worcester County," Rita replied. "You dated him?"

"For a few months. Now I'm dating a guy I knew in High School if you can believe it!" Jean replied, and she briefly explained to Rita about Tom's reappearance in her life.

Rita was nodding, thinking. "Don't tell Chet, but it's his job I want," she told her new friends. She was grinning, but she was serious.

Gracie, Jean and Anne all agreed that Worcester County would be the type of place Rita would do well in.

"Well, maybe Chet will move on and there'll be an opening," Anne put in with a smile.

"You didn't happen to break his heart or anything, so he'll want to leave the state?" Rita asked Jean hopefully.

Jean chuckled. "No, it wasn't quite that wrenching," she said of their breakup. "I'm not the heartbreaker in the crowd: that's Gracie," she added mischievously.

"Heart breaker?" Gracie echoed, quite dumbfounded. She never thought of herself that way.

"She was dating this hunk last year: I mean, a totally gorgeous man, and rich, too," Jean explained, giving Gracie a cheeky smile. "And then just when he was about to propose--"

"I thought he did propose?" Anne interjected.

Everyone looked at Gracie. "Well, erm, that's what the discussion was about, but he didn't actually get to the 'will you marry me' down on one knee bit," she clarified, just a little uncomfortable.

"Well, anyway, just at that point, Gracie broke up with him," Jean finished.

"What happened?" Rita couldn't help herself asking. She looked eagerly at Gracie, eager to hear the details.

Gracie sighed. "Well, first: I don't know if I exactly 'broke his heart,'" she made a face, and shot Jean a look. "He didn't really understand or know me. Not deep down."

"Where it counts," Anne chimed in.

When Gracie had explained her breakup with Ben to Anne and Jean, they had both thought she'd made the right decision.

"I got the feeling that Ben only loved me inasmuch as I fit in with his Master Plan," Gracie now explained to Rita.

"Ah," Rita nodded sagely. Then: "Well, at least he didn't cheat on you."

Gracie shook her head. "No, he didn't." She paused. Well, in for a penny..."You sound like you've had a bad experience, Rita," she said softy.

Rita made a face. "I don't like to dwell on it," she said flatly. "It's over, so I should just put it behind me."

"Mmmm..." Anne nodded. "But it could help to talk about it," she nudged, ever so gently. She sipped at her coffee.

Rita took a moment, then started to tell them about how she'd met Mark Broadstreet shortly after she had started her job as Hampshire County Detective.

"He was charming, he was funny, and we always had a good time together," she said. "We took lots of mini trips, too, to places like Boston and the Cape, and New York City, even Montreal once," Rita continued, sounding wistful. "I thought he was it. And I thought he felt the same."

Anne frowned, concerned. "So why did you break up with him?"

"Was he cheating on you?" Jean asked quickly, seizing on the remark Rita had made a few minutes before.

Rita nodded. "About a year ago he started seeing Sasha Yedid. She heads Epiphany, the outfit that runs the Juvenile Detention Center." She sighed. "I suppose it was inevitable, I mean, they work so closely together. And Sasha's very--exotic," she finished, sounding quite resigned but also what Gracie would call 'bummed.'

"But surely if you and Mark were so good together, he didn't just suddenly decide one day he wanted to date Sasha?" Gracie asked ingenuously.

Rita shook her head. "No, of course not. I think--I think Sasha had actually been working on him for a long time, you know, hoping to lure him away from me," she confided.

Jean, Anne and Gracie all listened, rapt, especially because of Gracie's 'hidden agenda:' this was the kind of information that could be invaluable.

"And it seemed that Mark, I don't know, he somehow changed." Rita frowned. "All of a sudden, it seemed he wanted more, of everything. He bought a fancy car," she began, ticking things off on her fingers.

Gracie noticed Rita's freckled hands were manicured, but the nails were not varnished. And she recalled the Jaguar XKE whose license plate she'd traced to Broadstreet, and nodded.

"It's a vintage Jaguar," Rita went on. "Can you imagine anything less practical? Of course he also got a top of the line Chevy truck," she added, grimacing.

"Wow," Anne murmured.

"And he bought himself some really expensive new clothes-- the kind that are so expensive, they don't even look expensive?" she asked, looking hopefully at her new friends that they would understand. "Suddenly shopped at Neiman Marcus and Armani."

Gracie knew exactly what she meant: her black cashmere coat had cost the earth, but to anyone unfamiliar with the finer things, it just looked like a black cloth coat. Or Sasha Yedid's Chanel suit, she remembered suddenly: it just looked like a suit, kind of plain, actually, unless you knew Chanel and knew what to look for. Off hand, she couldn't recall exactly what Mark Broadstreet had been wearing the day she'd seen him with Sasha at lunch. But then again, Gracie's eye was more attuned to women's haberdashery than men's.

"And then he told me he'd met someone else," Rita concluded. "It didn't take much to get him to tell me who," she added wryly. "He was almost proud of it."

"So you think his newly conspicuous consumption was tied to him starting to see Sasha Yedid?" Gracie asked.

Rita nodded. "It seems to be. She's a -- flashy -- sort of person, anyway," she added hesitantly. "And Mark told me she 'suited' him better than I did." Rita paused and Jean 'tut-tutted' quietly into her coffee mug. "She's got lots of money: I think she must have got it in the divorce," Rita hazarded, and Gracie decided that this would not be the time to correct her impression. "Along with Epiphany."

"Epiphany?" Gracie queried, fast. She hoped, not too fast.

Rita shrugged. "Mark told me once, when he was singing Sasha's praises, that she'd started the company from scratch when she and her ex husband got divorced, and that he'd helped her fund it as part of the settlement," she answered.

Hmmm, Gracie thought: close to what she had suspected...

"So anyway, Sasha likes showing off her money," Rita continued, "and it seemed, at least to me, that Mark started to act that way, too once he got interested in her."

"Didn't you ever wonder how he could afford a car like that, or the clothes?" Jean asked.

Rita leaned back on Gracie's soft leather sofa and sighed. "I did. I even asked him about it when he bought the Jag. He said an aunt had died and left him a little money."

"But you didn't believe him," Anne assessed quickly.

Rita shrugged. "I didn't know. I suppose it's possible. I'd heard Mark talk about his family, though, and he'd never mentioned an aunt, much less a rich aunt! But the Mark I knew, or thought I knew--the 'old' Mark--would have invested most of any kind of inheritance, and maybe spent a little on a nice trip somewhere: we'd been talking about wanting to go to Disneyworld, and maybe the Kennedy Space Center," Rita added quietly. "He'd never been that interested in cars or cashmere socks before."

Gracie waited a moment, then decided she might as well ask Rita what she wanted to know: there might not ever be a better time. And if she knew nothing, well, Gracie would just pursue other lines of inquiry. There were plenty of those.

"Rita--" she began, leaning towards her guest from the love seat she'd perched on after the powerpoint program was finished. "Have you ever thought there was something, oh, I don't know, odd going on over at that Juvenile Detention Center?" Gracie asked, her tone curious but not accusing.

Rita, who had been reliving memories and staring down at Gracie's coffee table, looked up, and met Gracie's gaze.

"Well, it's always full to capacity, and it has been, almost from day one," she answered immediately. "I suppose that makes sense, since everyone said how much we needed a JDC out here." She paused, and Gracie could almost see her linking the two disparate areas of information in her mind. "But now that you mention it, Mark's 'windfall' from his aunt came a couple of months after the center opened," Rita went on, sounding like she'd just realized something. "But I don't see how the two could be connected," she finished dismissively a second later. She shook her head.

Gracie, Anne and Jean all waited.

"Unless, of course, there *was* no aunt," Rita murmured a few moments after.

Chapter Twenty-one

Thursday, Gracie left a message for Jack with Millie, and a voice mail message on his mobile. She didn't hear from him until that evening, and when he called, he sounded like it was the last thing in the world he wanted to be doing.

"Well, grumpy guts, thanks for calling back!" Gracie retorted when she heard Jack's 'ok, Gracie, it's Jack, what do you want?' to her 'Hello!'

"I'm not grumpy," he argued.

"Yes you are: I can even see you: you're making that face where your mouth turns down and your lips get all thin and you're frowning," Gracie chastised him.

"Look Gracie, regardless of what kind of face I'm making, I'm calling you as you asked. So what do you want?" Jack said again, testy.

"Oooh, snippy, snippy," Gracie didn't relent. "Look Jack, call me back when you're in a better mood, okay?"

"No--Gracie--don't hang up," Jack said loudly into the telephone.

He was home, finally, after the fourth grueling day of fruitless questioning. He and Carla had both thrown in the towel that afternoon after they'd spoken to the last guy who had claimed to have known Ford, Sullivan or Manning from Sure Fit Gym. They had spent hours in the interrogation room both singly and as a team since Monday. And still, they knew nothing.

Jack had come home, given Woof a brief constitutional, and decided to return Gracie's call while he downed the first of what he thought would be more than a couple of beers that evening. He remembered his Dad coming home from court on some days and pouring himself a large scotch; Jack had always thought it an affectation, but now he realized there were some days when you just needed a little help relaxing and putting everything behind you. Especially if you weren't happy about what had gone on.

"It's just that it's been a hell of a week and I'm not feeling very happy peppy, if you know what I mean," Jack admitted grudgingly. "So, what's up?" he asked, trying to sound a bit more interested.

Actually, if it got his mind off the apparent dead end in the antifreeze murder case, he'd welcome it.

"I'm sorry you've had such a crappy week. Want to tell me about it?" Gracie asked, immediately switching from spiky to soothing.

"Maybe later. You were saying?" Jack prodded, and then Gracie proceeded to tell him all about her dinner with Rita Licora and Rita's information on Mark Broadstreet.

Jack was intrigued.

"So she thinks that Broadstreet might be involved in something along with Sasha Yedid and the JDC, huh?" he asked when Gracie had finished.

"Yes, and she might be calling you if she finds anything concrete out," Gracie replied. "Of course, she can't exactly go snooping around, it would look suspicious. I didn't say anything about Mike and our, erm, theory linking his death to what he may or may not have uncovered with regard to the JDC. But I don't want her to put herself in danger."

"Of course not," Jack agreed. But, as he and Gracie had discussed before, everything as far as the JDC's financials on record looked like it was on the up and up, so they had no hard evidence to start any kind of real investigation with. And although he'd never heard anything negative about Rita Licora, he somewhat doubted her ability to suddenly unearth concrete evidence, particularly when Mike hadn't been able to. "Have you made any progress with the Cayman Islands accounts?" he asked next.

Gracie ruefully admitted that she hadn't. "I guess that's why people go there: it's hard to trace," she told Jack. "But I haven't given up."

"Just be careful," Jack cautioned, and Gracie told him she would be, although mentally she was rolling her eyes. He was such a worrier.

Friday morning, Gracie went to her local garden center and chose several types of annuals to plant in the new beds Larry's crew had dug around the perimeter of the conservatory. As she'd told her contractor, she'd just put in seasonal plants this year, and then in the autumn decide on shrubs or perennials for that area.

She'd always liked lobelia, and she was pleased to discover her favorite variety, Crystal Palace, which was a deep indigo blue. She thought New Guinea impatiens in that flaming orange color would also do well with the moderate sun exposure they'd get in the new beds. And she chose a new variety of marigold, called 'snoflake' because it was a pure creamy white, to offset the indigo and the orange.

Several forsythia bushes had been removed to make room for the conservatory, and Gracie thought she might replace two of these, one on either side of the conservatory's back steps. She also was thinking about Japanese painted ferns and other ferns which liked an eastern exposure, for permanent plantings. And she planned to transplant some of the celandine from the northeast corner: it spread very quickly, and would make a lovely ground cover by the following spring if she transplanted it now.

Friday afternoon, since the forecast was for rain overnight, Gracie did the transplanting she wanted to do, but left the annuals for another time, setting them outside in a wheelbarrow tucked against the side of the garden shed. She wanted to decide on her outfit for the cookout at Jack's parents' house the next day, and also give herself a manicure and pedicure so she wouldn't look as though she'd been grubbing about in the dirt all day. Which, pretty much, she had.

While she treated herself to a deep bubble bath and a glass of pinot grigio, Gracie thought about the rest of her conversation the night before with Jack. He'd explained that he and Carla had finished talking to everyone at Sure Fit who they thought could possibly have a connection to the three dead girls, and had come up empty.

Now, Jack had said, it was back to square one. Although Sure Fit was definitely a part of the puzzle, it didn't appear to be the place where the murderer had chosen or poisoned his victims. It was, however, the place where the three women had met some, if not all, of their clients: during questioning, it had developed fairly quickly that Ford, Sullivan and Manning had all taken cash and/or gifts as payment for spending time with and having sex with different men.

All of the men who confessed to paying the girls for their 'company'--and there could be others in addition to the guys from Sure Fit--agreed to cooperate with law enforcement in exchange for immunity from prosecution. And as Jack had told Gracie wryly during their conversation, the men had all seemed pretty sure they'd never use call girls, escorts or hookers again, since being considered murder suspects had made quite an impression on them.

So, Gracie thought now sinking up to her chin in fragrant bubbles, all three dead women had had entry level jobs that didn't pay too well. All had been very particular--one could say obsessed--about their appearance, and had belonged to the same gym. And all had done a little escort work on the side to supplement their income.

Who would want to kill them? Not their clients: Jack and Carla had eliminated them. What about, Gracie thought, other escorts in the area? Were there any? There had to be. Had Sullivan, Ford and Manning been working independently or had they been working for someone? Maybe that someone had killed them? Or maybe they'd been working on their own and another--for lack of a better word, Gracie would use the term 'Madam'--had killed them because they were cutting into her territory?

All possibilities. She'd have to see if Jack had thought of this tack, and urge him to check into escort activity in the Stockbridge and Lee area. She was sure they'd have time to talk at his parents' cookout.

The manicure and pedicure were quickly accomplished, and Gracie chose a pale ivory polish which looked almost clear and set off the beginnings of her 'gardening tan' nicely. Once her nails were dry Gracie looked through her clothes closets to see what struck her fancy for the next day's event.

The outfit she settled on was a pair of white capri trousers teamed with a navy and white striped cotton twin set. The top was sleeveless and scoop necked, and both the cardigan and the top were trimmed in narrow navy braid, the former accented with gold buttons. Gracie peered more closely at the buttons and snickered to herself when she saw the intertwined capital 'C' which signified the twin-set as Chanel.

She tried to remember when and where she'd bought it, and thought it must have been when she'd gone down to Washington one Christmas, with Ben: all the upscale shops at Tyson's Corners had been showing their cruise and resort wear and she'd bought a number of things.

The capri trousers, however, were from a local discount merchandise shop.

Gracie decided on white open-toed sandals, and double checked that everything she would need was in the white quilted leather Chanel bag she used in summer. She'd wear a chunky link gold necklace and matching earrings and bracelet with the capris and twin set, she decided. Mostly, she wore plain studs and just a wristwatch, so it was nice to be able to take some of her more impressive jewelry out from time to time.

After her toilette and dinner, Gracie sat down at her laptop again, determined to find a way to access the Banque de Cayman's client list. After about a half hour pursuing the same routes she'd tried before, and having the same lack of success she'd had before, Gracie decided to change her approach.

"If you do what you have always done," she muttered to herself, "you'll get what you've always got."

Pretending to be a client of the bank already, she typed in a name: Mark Broadstreet.

Up popped a password screen. Of course.

Ok, time for another program, which she accessed and set in motion. By the time Gracie had got herself a cup of tea and returned to the laptop, the password encryption program had worked its magic, and Mark Broadstreet's Cayman Island bank account details were winking at her from her laptop's screen.

Gasping, Gracie quickly printed out every document she could find. Then she repeated her actions with a different name: Chacko Salama's dummy corporation that owned Epiphany, 'Youth Solutions'. After a few minutes, the program again succeeded and once more, Gracie printed out everything she unearthed.

She then ran Chacko Salama himself, and began to see a pattern: withdrawals from the Youth Solutions/YS account matched deposits into Chacko's and Broadstreet's accounts.

There was one more name she wanted to try. In addition to Chacko Salama and Broadstreet, Gracie suspected that the Hampshire County President Judge, Bob Elderson, was in on the JDC scheme. Unlike Sasha Yedid and Itty Azar, whose bank accounts she'd found stateside under what they had apparently thought were cleverly disguised names, Gracie hadn't found any money trail in the States for Chacko, Broadstreet or Elderson.

Now she'd found Broadstreet's, Chacko's and Youth Solution's accounts in the Caymans. After a few more minutes, during which Gracie washed out her tea mug and replenished the water and food in Pumpkin's bowls, Gracie heard the happy 'ping' from her laptop and returned to her alcove study to find that Judge Robert P. Elderson did, indeed, have a Cayman Islands account. And it, like Broadstreet's and Chacko's, had received regular monthly deposits from the YS account.

Quickly, Gracie printed out everything, and also saved all the information on Chacko and YS, Broadstreet and Elderson to a handily empty thumb drive. She'd give that to Jack the next day.

She was tempted to call him right now, and tell him what she'd found. He had sounded like he could use some good news when they'd talked the evening before, and she knew that today had been a 'catch up' day for him to deal with the mounting stack of other work that had piled up while he and Carla had been tackling the antifreeze interrogations.

Of course, what Gracie had found wasn't conclusive. All it meant was that a bunch of people connected to the JDC in various ways had rather a lot of money, some of it in offshore accounts. While that might be suspicious, aside from the fact that the offshore account holders weren't paying income tax on that money, it wasn't criminal.

She recalled that Yedid's and Azar's tax returns had included the interest from fairly large CD's as income. The CD's, Gracie had found out, were the substantial holdings in Ishtar Yedid's name and in Ruth Romano Azar's name, respectively. So as far as the tax picture went for them, they were playing by the rules.

And now that she'd found the account number for YS she could probably link the deposits to Yedid's and Azar's accounts to YS too.

The YS account showed almost daily deposits, in cash, like clockwork. Because the deposits were cash wire transfers there was no way to know where the money had originated, although Gracie was pretty sure it was from the JDC. The wire transfers were all from the same 'financial services' office--the kind of place between a liquor store and a bar--that also, according to their usual ads, cashed third party checks and made loans at usurious rates.

But there was still a piece missing: how did the JDC, and by extension, Youth Solutions, make all that 'extra' money with which it paid Broadstreet, Yedid, Azar, Elderson and Chacko? And who, exactly, was the one responsible for collecting the cash and making the deposits into the YS account?

It would help if she could somehow get case files on kids who'd gone through the probation department in Hampshire County, and compare them to files on kids who'd gone through the probation department, say, in her own county, Gracie thought. Maybe she could find enough similar cases where the juvenile from Hampshire County had been sent to the JDC but the juvenile from Berkshire County hadn't, to justify an investigation.

Getting juvenile records from Berkshire County probably wouldn't be too hard: Jack had a good working relationship with the entire Probation Department both adult and juvenile, and could probably obtain the files she would need.

But Hampshire County was a whole other situation. While Rita Licora was the obvious choice, Gracie knew what had happened to Mike, felt in her gut it was connected to the questions he'd started to ask about the whole JDC arrangement, and didn't want anyone else to put themselves in danger trying to investigate it.

She'd have to talk to Jack about that, and see what he thought. Maybe there was some way he could get the records himself. Or, failing that, maybe there was some way Rita could get them without anyone knowing.

Chapter Twenty-two

The promised rain materialized: there was a tremendous thunderstorm overnight that made Pumpkin burrow under the summer duvet Gracie had on her bed, and snuggle close. But by Saturday at one pm when Jack came to collect Gracie and drop off Woof, the sun was shining and everything looked bright and scrubbed clean.

"You look summery," Jack said, smiling. It was a beautiful day and he was going to spend it with Gracie. For the next few hours, at least, he would try to put the frustrations of his job behind him.

"Thank you," Gracie beamed. She gestured to a good sized bouquet of flowers wrapped in paper from the Cheshire Florist, Budz. "These are for your mother," she said quietly.

Jack's smile widened. Flowers would be perfect, and of course, Gracie had thought of it. And although he was no connoisseur of flowers, the bouquet looked like it contained several blossoms his mother particularly favored.

On the drive down to Pittsfield--Jack had insisted upon picking Gracie up and driving her home, using the excuse of leaving Woof at her spacious house with the handy porch and his buddy Pumpkin--Gracie excitedly told him about the discovery she'd made accessing the Cayman Island bank's accounts.

Jack was extremely happy, and just the tiniest bit concerned.

"There's no way that Cayman Island bank can trace anything back to you, is there?" he asked, rounding the corner towards the County Courthouse. His parents lived just past it, on a beautiful residential side street replete with gracious older homes, good sized lots, and venerable elms lining the sidewalks.

"You mean, know I hacked in and got access to a few accounts?" Gracie asked. She shook her head. "I doubt it. And even if they do, before I even went to their website I went through a special ISP router that bounces my trail all over the world through different servers, via satellites."

Jack shot a skeptical look at her. He'd heard about programs like the one she was referencing. They made it extremely difficult to trace activity back to a particular ISP, but he still worried.

"How did you figure out which bank it was?" Jack asked, curious.

"Well, I didn't really: I used some new deductive logic software when I did the search for the names. It turned up the bank on Grand Cayman, Banque du Cayman," Gracie replied matter of factly.

Jack sighed. "Well, it's good you found all of that. Did you make hard copies?"

Gracie grinned. "Of course: they're in my safe."

Jack hadn't known she had a safe. He wondered where it was.

"And I put everything on a thumb drive for you, too," Gracie added, slipping the tiny piece of hardware which was, indeed, no bigger than a person's thumb, into Jack's trouser pocket.

"Oh!" The touch had surprised him. "Thanks, that's good."

Gracie murmured something about having to find the link between the JDC and the bank account held by Youth Solutions, but added that she hoped they could talk later.

"We'll find time," Jack assured her. He parked his truck next to his sister's Nissan SUV, helped Gracie out, and they walked around to the back gate: they could hear the sounds of a cookout party just getting started from the garden beyond.

"Gracie, you know Amanda and Harley Wickwire," Jack's father Elton Draper said a few minutes later. He was introducing Gracie around to his friends, 'other judges and their wives' as Jack had said. Jack's dad was on the bench of the Massachusetts Superior Court. Most of his social contacts came from his work, which explained his son's disclaimer to Gracie.

Gracie shook hands with the couple and recalled that they lived in Vermont, near the state border with Massachusetts, and that Amanda was on the Tanglewood Board along with Jack's mother, Marilyn.

"And this is Potsie Farmer and you know his wife Catherine," chimed in Marilyn, who had exclaimed over the bouquet Gracie had brought and had rushed off to put them in a vase. Now, she'd returned, and indicated another older couple who both shook Gracie's hand. Then Marilyn leaned over and pecked Gracie on the cheek.

Gracie looked startled. Jack's mother, to the best of her recollection, might have given her a stiff hug or two in the few years she and Jack had been on-again-off-again dating, but she'd never kissed her.

"Those flowers are lovely, Gracie: I put them right in the center of the dining room table where I'll set up dessert, so everyone can enjoy them," she said warmly.

"I'm happy you like them, Marilyn," Gracie replied sweetly, wondering if Jack's mother had perhaps had more than a couple of the mimosas she was pouring out from a large glass pitcher.

"Catherine's the Board President of the Greylock Manor Preservation Society," Marilyn explained. "Which of course you know," she added. Gracie had been admitted to the Greylock Manor Board the previous year.

Gracie smiled at the petite, frosted blonde haired woman. All of Marilyn's friends were on the boards of something important, just as most of her husband's friends were judges. Gracie supposed there was nothing wrong with that, but she did think it made for a rather narrow sort of social life.

That was one of the things she liked so much about Club: although it was certainly socially prominent, membership in the past few years had become more varied, and you could make all sorts of friends there. Then again, Gracie didn't exactly limit herself to Club: some of her closest friends were not members, and in fact lived at quite some distance. Joey and Tyler, the restaurateurs, lived in Boston, where Gracie was from, and Susan, her research biologist pal who was deeply into the indie art scene in the Village, lived in New York City.

She brought herself back to the present. Elton Draper was introducing her to the third couple he and Marilyn had invited for the cookout: Lawrence 'call me Larry' and Frances 'call me Frannie' Stevens. Larry was a judge, like Jack's dad, on the Superior Court bench. He was short and feisty and reminded Gracie of a terrier: not a bad quality in a Judge, she supposed.

Judge Wickwire, Gracie knew, was on the Vermont Superior Court bench, and Judge Farmer--his real name couldn't be 'Potsie' could it, Gracie thought and was relieved to later find out it was

Gerald--was on the Massachusetts Third Circuit bench, which encompassed most of Massachusetts west of Springfield.

Frannie was in Marilyn's quilting group, and also on the Board of Mount Holyoke College. She herself was an alumna of the prestigious women's university, and held a degree in Art History. She seemed like an exceptionally sweet woman, Gracie thought, and she took an immediate liking to her.

Of course, Jack's sister Laura and her husband Dave were there, along with their three children. The Stevenses hadn't brought their children: Frannie explained to Gracie while showing her snapshots on her phone, that their offspring were variously on vacation in Arizona, at home having their own party in upstate New York, and away finishing their first year at Annapolis. Gracie was impressed.

The Farmers had brought their only son, Phil, and his fiancée Lainie, who stayed for drinks and then went on to another party somewhere else.

And mercifully as far as Jack was concerned, the Wickwires had not brought their daughter Tammy. His mother had, quite disastrously, tried to fix him up with Tammy a couple of years before when he and Gracie had stopped dating for a while. Although he brought himself to inquire politely as to her welfare-- he was told by a smiling Amanda that Tammy was finishing up her first year teaching second grade and would be heading off to friends in Montreal for the summer--that was the end of his interest.

Jack's dad was expertly handling the grill by the time everyone was settled with more mimosas on the Drapers' prettily decorated patio. Marilyn's red white and blue bunting reminded Gracie that she hadn't even got her Flag out to display, much less decorate, she'd been so absorbed in her investigative work, and in her new conservatory.

"You'll have to come see the conservatory, some time," she told Marilyn with a smile as she confessed her preoccupation.

"I'd really like that, Gracie," Marilyn replied, and she sounded sincere. "And you still have two days of the long weekend to hang your Flag," she consoled her with a smile.

"It sounds really beautiful," Catherine agreed of the conservatory, and Amanda nodded.

"Aren't greenhouses, or conservatories as you call them, terribly expensive?" Frannie asked solicitously.

Gracie nodded. "It wasn't cheap, particularly since I had it shipped over from England," she revealed.

"Oh, my!" Frannie exclaimed.

"But they make the best ones, you see, so it was worth it. My contractor was even impressed with the quality of construction!" She sighed. "And when my parents died, more than a decade ago now--"

Murmurs of sympathy all around.

"They did leave me with enough money to make these types of improvements to my home," Gracie explained vaguely.

She'd always been taught, and she was sure Marilyn would agree, that talking about money was bad form. But mentioning it as she had, in the context of her orphan-hood, was all right. And it made sense: anyone with a brain could figure out that writing for the *Intelligencer* wouldn't allow her to live quite the way she did, so there had to be money somewhere else. Giving a sensible explanation without going into detail was just the logical thing to do, and it tended to forestall more intrusive questions.

"Well, it's a very smart investment," Marilyn chimed in, nodding. "You know, when Jack dug that ornamental pond for me, I just wanted it because, well, I wanted it," she said then.

"It's lovely!" Gracie exclaimed.

"And your koi are huge!" Catherine put in.

"Yes, now that we've broken Laura and Dave's oldest of trying to fish them out, they're growing nicely," Marilyn said with a laugh. "But I also found out that it increases the value of the property, to have a 'water feature'. That's what the real estate people call it!" she declared merrily, and everyone laughed.

"Larry always says that property is a sound investment," Frannie offered. "And every time he buys me a piece of jewelry, he says the same thing!" She blushed. A blue eyed red head, she blushed a lot. "Says he can't hang ten acres around my neck!" she giggled good naturedly.

Catherine nodded enthusiastically. "He's right: gold has doubled in value in the past couple of years, and so have most stones."

"Diamonds really are a girl's best friend, then," murmured Amanda, looking appreciatively at the large solitaire in her wedding set, the smaller stones in her eternity band, and the beautiful three stone ring her husband had bought her on the recent occasion of their Silver Anniversary.

Gracie just nodded, thinking of the three women from Sure Fit who had invested in furs and jewelry and gold, and also thinking about the contrast between the two groups of women discussing the same type of investments.

Dinner was quite tasty: Marilyn had marinated chicken breasts, and stuffed hamburgers with herbs and cheese so the meats all had high flavor. Her potato salad was, arguably, about the best Gracie had ever had next to her neighbor Anna's and possibly her own, and the accompanying green salad was crispy and refreshing. She complimented Marilyn on the food, and Marilyn looked genuinely pleased.

"Jack!" Gracie hissed at one point late in the afternoon when everyone had more or less finished eating and was milling around involved in various occupations. Dessert and coffee would be coming in a little while.

Jack, who had been on his way from the downstairs powder room back out to the patio, turned as Gracie waylaid him in the hall.

"Hi Gracie," he said, smiling. "Everything all right?" he asked.

Gracie nodded. "Yes, exceptionally so," she replied. "Your mother is being amazingly nice to me: what gives?"

Jack cleared his throat. "Why does anything have to 'give'?" he queried, just a bit defensive.

Gracie gave him a grin. "Because when you and I broke up last fall I thought your mother was going to give a party, that's why," she replied cheekily.

Jack made a face. "Oh, it wasn't that bad, Gracie," he admonished her. Then he sighed. "But when I told her I was bringing you today, I did ask her if she could please, for my sake, just be nice. I explained that we're able to still be good friends despite everything that's happened, and so I asked her if she couldn't do the same."

"Well, I think it worked," Gracie answered, relieved. Having Jack's mother dislike her had been annoying, even if it hadn't been problematical. She was glad if they were past it.

"You bringing the flowers helped: it was an unsolicited gesture of truce," Jack explained. "Mom even asked me if I'd suggested you bring them and when I said no, you'd done it all on your own, I think that went a long way with her."

A bunch of flowers.

Amazing.

Gracie shrugged. "Well, anyway, do we have time now to talk about the case?" she asked eagerly. She wanted to see what course of action Jack thought might be best to pursue.

"Sure--" Jack led her into his parents' large, sunny living room and they sat down on the love seat. Without much preamble, Gracie launched into her idea about comparing juvenile cases in Berkshire and Hampshire counties to see if they could spot inconsistencies or irregularities which might justify an investigation.

Jack listened intently. When Gracie had finished, he nodded. "I think we can do something with that, Gracie, but I don't think involving Rita Licora is the way to go: having the county detective involved would put Broadstreet and the rest of them on alert immediately, put them on the defensive."

"I agree," Gracie said. "But then, how--"

"I think I'll have a talk with Tara Torrissi, the most senior Probation Officer in our county. She's the Deputy for the Department too, and could probably get files from Broadstreet's office without much trouble, particularly if she told him she needed them for, oh, I don't know, some grant or something she could be applying for."

"Why not ask the Probation Director?" Gracie asked, curious.

Jack shrugged. "Who, Lance Melling?" he asked, then made an uncertain, uncomfortable sort of face and shook his head. "Don't much care for the guy. Never have. He's okay, but there's something, I don't know—squirrely about him."

Gracie raised her eyebrows and then chuckled. "Well, I think that's a great approach, Jack. But you like this Torrissi?" she queried.

"Oh, yes: she's on the level," he replied. "Good at her job, too."

"Well, then I think that's perfect!" Gracie said, and impulsively hugged him. "I never would have thought of that!"

Jack reluctantly let Gracie go after the hug. In truth, he'd been so surprised by it, he hadn't even had time to react to or appreciate it. And now it seemed too soon to let her go.

One of Jack's nephews ran in at this point to tell them dessert was being served, so together they moved towards the dining room where Marilyn had set up coffee, tea and three amazing looking desserts.

"This is a Boston Cream Pie cake, Gracie," Marilyn said with a twinkle in her eye.

Gracie was still confounded by Jack's mother's friendliness, but she smiled widely and said that Boston Cream Pie was a favorite.

The other offerings were a blueberry lemon trifle and strawberry rhubarb pie with ice cream.

"Oh, god, I want some of all of them!" Gracie groaned, and reached for a plate.

Chapter Twenty-three

"Well, you can't just buy your way onto a Board!" Marilyn pronounced in high dudgeon. They had all had dessert and coffee; the men had gone out to the patio to smoke cigars and drink port, although Jack would confine himself to the port since he had just recently quit smoking and didn't want to backslide. And the women had seated themselves in the living room with liqueurs. The grandchildren had all been put to bed upstairs, and Jack's sister Laura was enjoying a rare evening of adult company and conversation.

Marilyn's comment had been engendered by Catherine's revelation that a Barbara Elderson had recently sent a letter of inquiry to the Greylock Manor Preservation Board, asking to become a member.

"And you don't just send a letter, either," Catherine now commented, with spirit.

Amanda Wickwire nodded. "No, indeed." She turned to Marilyn. "You had to put me up for Board membership at Tanglewood, didn't you?" she asked, to make her point, and Marilyn nodded.

"It's the same in the Junior League," Gracie put in, invoking the official name of 'Club' for this august assembly. "A member has to recommend you for membership."

"I think it's that way in most places," Laura offered, "like country clubs and such," and Frannie nodded her agreement.

Gracie's ears had pricked up at the name 'Barbara Elderson'. Until then she'd been sort of drifting in and out of the conversation, sipping at a glass of limoncello mixed with club soda.

"Yes, and to mention making a 'donation' in a letter requesting membership, well, it sounds like bribery to me," Frannie said, shaking her head. "It's not like it's a country club with membership fees, after all."

"Who is this Barbara Elderson, anyway?" Gracie asked, deeply interested in the reply.

"She's married to Judge Robert Elderson, in Hampshire County," Catherine told Gracie. "By itself, if she's involved in volunteer work or in any clubs like yours, Gracie, the Junior

League, I mean, or the Senior Women's Club in her case, that would be enough along with a recommendation from someone already on the Board at Greylock."

"Maybe she doesn't know anyone on the Board?" Amanda asked.

Catherine shrugged. "You could always just find out who is on the Board, and then call one of them, expressing your interest in the Board's mission, but not outright asking to be considered for membership."

"Yes, most people, getting a call like that, know what the caller is after," Marilyn agreed. "They'd do a little discreet inquiry about the person, and then, if it all seemed, well, 'kosher,' as they say, the Board would invite the person to attend a meeting and be considered for membership."

Gracie thought that Jack's mother had probably received her share of calls like that, being on Tanglewood's prestigious Board.

So, Barbara Elderson was married to Judge Elderson, and had offered money to get on the Board at Greylock. Interesting. Gracie wondered why she wanted to be on the Board. Maybe just for the social status it carried with it? Some people were like that.

Or maybe she had a deep interest in preserving and protecting Greylock Manor and Mount Greylock? Possible, though Gracie had never heard the woman's name before, and certainly had not thought her associated even casually with the Manor or the State Forest that encompassed the mountain and the historic home.

Maybe she'd just discovered its pristine beauty and its extensive stand of ancient forest hemlocks? Maybe she had an interest in architecture and wanted to preserve historic houses? But if either of those had been the case, Gracie would have thought she would have run into the woman somewhere, at Greylock Manor's fund raisers or other functions, if nowhere else.

"Not to be tacky," Gracie put in, "but how much did she offer to--erm--contribute?" she asked Catherine. She supposed, as a Greylock Manor Board member, she had a right to ask, at least.

"Fifty-thousand dollars," Catherine whispered after only the briefest of hesitations.

188

"What?" Marilyn sounded scandalized again. "Where's she going to get that kind of money, in cash?" she asked. She knew what a county Judge made: it wasn't pocket change, but it didn't allow for gratuitous donations in that amount.

Catherine just raised her eyebrows and sipped at her sparkling water.

"Well, this may have nothing to do with anything," Frannie began, smiling disarmingly, "but when you said the name," she nodded to Catherine, "it sounded familiar. I just remembered, Larry told me a couple of months ago that at the Judges' conference, he'd got to talking with Judge Elderson. He was bragging about the way his new Mercedes sports car had handled in the snow."

Gracie swallowed. "Elderson drives an SL Roadster," she offered without explaining how she knew that. Oddly enough, no one asked. "It retails for about $100,000."

Everyone looked at her in stunned silence.

"Maybe he's leasing it?" Amanda suggested.

"Maybe they got an inheritance?" Frannie put in.

"Maybe they won the lottery!" Marilyn said in a tone that dripped scornful sarcasm.

So, Gracie thought: Marilyn considered the Eldersons' flush lifestyle a bit suspicious too, didn't she.

Frannie shrugged. "Maybe. But it all does seem--excessive, doesn't it?"

Everyone nodded.

Gracie bit her lip, and drained her glass.

By about 9:30 pm Jack and Gracie took their leave, Jack explaining that Woof would need a 'constitutional' after being in the house all afternoon and evening. That was true, of course, but the party was winding down, anyway.

"That was really pleasant," Gracie began as Jack drove north on Route 8. She told him of the conversation about the Eldersons, too.

"So it was an informative event as well as an entertaining one," Jack assessed with a smile. "I'm glad, Gracie."

"Your mother kissed me again when we were saying goodbye," Gracie told him. "It's a little unnerving, her *volte face*."

Jack laughed. "Well, maybe she's finally begun to see what I see in you," he said quietly.

Gracie didn't know what to say to that so she said nothing.

What, exactly, did Jack see in her? They had always respected each other and admired each other's work. They worked well together, and from that had developed a friendship. They liked enough similar things to make a basis for shared interests, and enough different things to keep it exciting. Gracie felt that Jack always challenged her to be her best professionally and ethically, too, and that was very appealing to her.

As for Jack, what he saw in Gracie and had always seen in her was his future. Even though they had broken up, then got back together, and now had broken up again, he had never stopped loving her. But he didn't know if Gracie was ready yet to settle down: certainly last year she hadn't been. She didn't seem very different now, but they had been getting along exceptionally well of late, and Jack wondered if, now that Ben Holmes was history, Gracie was finding herself drawn again to him. He didn't know exactly why she'd broken it off with Holmes, though, and he didn't want to be anybody's 'sloppy seconds.' Of course, maybe he wasn't that, since he had dated Gracie first. Maybe it had been Ben who had been the experiment, and now Gracie had realized where her heart truly was?

They pulled in her driveway and both of them jumped out of Jack's truck and made a beeline for the front door: they could hear Woof barking already. After quick hellos, Jack took Woof outside, and came back in a few minutes later. Woof trotted over to his water bowl and began drinking noisily.

"Well, I guess I should be going," Jack said, although now that Woof had been taken care of, there really was no rush.

Gracie said as much and told him he had to at least come admire her conservatory, which he'd only seen from the outside, while it was still under construction.

He dutifully followed her through the formal living room, which was now all dusted and tidy. She opened the double French doors and they stepped into the conservatory. It was a clear night and the waxing gibbous moon was high in the eastern sky and shining right in through the glass ceiling of the conservatory.

Jack was impressed, but he asked the usual factual questions about the strength of the walls and ceiling, which he considered it almost his responsibility to do. Gracie told him that special heating elements, similar to those on rear window car defrosters, helped melt snow on the roof of the conservatory and that all the glass was triple glazed for stability and strength. The roof was quite steeply pitched as well, and the glass there was specially coated to encourage any snow that might fall on it to slide off. There were also steel rebars in concrete all around the frame.

"So as Larry said, if this blows over, we have worse things to worry about," she quoted, and smiled.

"So what's going in here?" Jack asked conversationally. "Nice tile."

"Thanks! Oh, probably orchids, and cycads and some ferns," Gracie answered casually. "I'll have to go shopping for them next week, or at least start. I think I'll do a lot of my buying on line."

Jack nodded.

"And then, of course, there's this--" she reached over and pushed a button on the wall. A thermally padded, fitted cover slid back into a little slot to reveal the hot tub. The flick of another button brought the tub to life, bubbling invitingly.

"Wow, that's right, you always said you wanted a hot tub in your greenhouse. Conservatory. Whatever," Jack said. "Have you christened it yet?" he asked.

Gracie shook her head. "Not yet." She hesitated, then pushed the buttons to turn the tub off and re-install the cover. "One of these days soon I will," she assured Jack.

He pushed the image of Gracie in her hot tub, her hair spiraling down from a top knot and the bubbles lapping at her bare shoulders out of his mind. God, he wished she didn't get to him so easily, or that his reaction to her wasn't so predictable.

She talked him into staying, inviting him to see what was on TV, and Jack, who wasn't ready to go home in any case, decided he'd stay for a little while longer.

They spent the next couple of hours watching a special on the History Channel about the origins of July Fourth, and not talking about either the antifreeze murder case or the JDC case. It was a relief to take a respite from both, and Jack knew that sometimes by stepping away from a problem, a solution presented itself.

Woof and Pumpkin were snuggling together on the other end of Gracie's long leather sofa, but finally at about midnight when Gracie's clocks all started to chime, bong, hoot, chirp and cuckoo, he said he and Woof would be going home.

"Well, thank you for a lovely day, Jack," Gracie said, meaning it.

"Yeah, I had fun and I'm glad you did," Jack answered. They were standing in Gracie's foyer, Woof sitting at Jack's feet and Pumpkin sitting at Gracie's, as though they were saying their goodbyes, too.

"Listen, if you and Woof want to come by tomorrow or Monday and swim in the pond or run in the meadow, feel free," Gracie offered.

"Nothing I like more than a good run in the meadow," Jack returned jokingly and Gracie punched him playfully on the arm.

"You know what I mean: Woof, not you! The pond should be warm enough for floating," she added temptingly.

Jack just nodded. The image of Gracie in the spring fed pond--and him along side her--started to form in his head, and he pushed it away.

"Well, good night, Gracie," he said then, and grinned as he often did when he echoed George Burns.

"Good night, Jack."

Neither one was certain who had leaned in first, but in a moment, Jack's lips were on Gracie's. It was a soft, gentle, and quick kiss and he pulled away so he could look into her eyes properly after a couple of seconds.

His eyes were deep, deep blue, Gracie thought, like a vast ocean pool she'd like to swim in.

Jack could smell Gracie's perfume and feel her heart beating against his as he held her. He didn't want to move, and she didn't make a move, either, just looked at him. Jack suddenly realized that it was an exceptionally warm evening, and wondered why he hadn't noticed that before.

Another moment went by, and then Gracie's lips were on Jack's again. She deepened the kiss, and he responded, making a small groaning sort of noise deep in the back of his throat and winding his arms around her, fisting one hand in her hair.

They pulled apart again, both of them breathing hard, like they'd just run all the way up from the meadow.

Pumpkin and Woof looked at each other.

"I have to go now," Jack whispered in a strangled sort of voice.

Gracie nodded, and stepped back. "I'll see you soon," she whispered, half query, half statement.

Jack nodded, and motioned to Woof, who followed him out Gracie's front door and down her walk.

Gracie scooped Pumpkin up in her arms and stood in the doorway, watching as Jack and Woof got in the truck, and drove away with a brief wave from Jack.

When she shut the front door, she was smiling into Pumpkin's long orange fur.

Chapter Twenty-four

Gracie was up to her elbows in dirt the next afternoon when she heard a car come up her drive. A door slammed, and faintly she heard footsteps tap up her front walk. The front doorbell rang. Then footsteps tapped around the side of the house towards the conservatory, where she was putting in the lobelia, impatiens and marigolds she'd bought. She'd already dug up and re-transplanted the celandine and two forsythia bushes, and it was from behind one of these that she appeared now, standing and brushing the dirt from her hands.

"Jack! Woof!" she exclaimed happily. She and the wolf dog exchanged their usual greeting. She turned to Jack, but he didn't move so Gracie didn't think a kiss was the right thing to do, for whatever reason.

Maybe he was angry? He didn't look angry, and the night before he hadn't acted angry. Maybe he was confused? Could be. Or upset? Could be. The kiss had surprised her, even though she knew she'd had a full share in its creation. And the feelings it had awakened within her had given her a night of vivid dreams and not especially restful sleep. If Jack's reaction had been similar...

"You want to go for a swim?" she asked the wolf dog, who looked at her intelligently and let out a small 'woof.'

"Guess we better take him, eh?" Jack drawled.

He had purposely held back from kissing Gracie 'hello' even though it had felt like the natural thing to do, and even though he had badly wanted to do it. He'd spent the majority of the night tossing and turning and thinking and wondering and had decided that he and Gracie needed to talk after the direction their relationship had appeared to be taking on the previous evening.

Now, Woof ran on ahead as they started to walk down the newly laid slate path. It connected to older stone paths which ran throughout Gracie's garden. Today's route took them through her walled garden where she grew herbs, around to the back of the house to a more open garden plan with several beds of greens, vegetables and flowers. Wooden tipi-shaped trellises flaunted healthy looking bean vines that scampered around and up, and morning glories curled alongside them, their flowers still buds. Ornamental grasses provided unique accents.

They passed Gracie's sundial in the center of the garden, and headed out the back gate and up a dirt path towards the spring fed pond and the meadow beyond.

As they walked, Jack took her hand.

"My hands are dirty," Gracie murmured, but she didn't pull away.

Jack glanced at the hand clasped in his. "Filthy," he agreed, but didn't let go.

They reached the small incline which hid the pond from view and walked a little further along. Now, with the ten acres of water sparkling before him, Woof increased his speed and ran all the way to the pond's edge, jumping in it through a break in the cattails.

"There he goes!" Gracie laughed, shading her eyes as she watched the wolf dog. It had got quite warm that afternoon, and very sunny, and of course she hadn't brought her sunglasses.

"Gracie," Jack said. He was still holding her hand, but now he turned her towards him.

"Mmmm?" She looked up at him, squinting.

"What was that last night? That kiss?" Jack asked, just a little bit abruptly. But his tone was not unkind.

Gracie swallowed. "A kiss," she answered.

"But what did it mean? To you," Jack amended.

Gracie looked down for a moment, to rest her eyes from the glare as much as anything else. Then she looked up. God, his eyes were beautiful!

"Jack, I love you. I always have," Gracie said simply.

Jack looked stunned. Perhaps by her frankness? "But--then what was that with Ben Holmes last year?" he asked.

Gracie smiled a little sadly. She sighed. "I loved Ben a lot."

It hurt Jack to hear that, but he said nothing.

"But I never felt about him the way I feel about you," she went on. "He had a lot of great qualities, and he was a good man," she said earnestly. "Like you, in many ways. But he didn't really know me, didn't want to, not when it came down to it, so it wasn't something more time would solve: he never really 'got' me. And although I enjoyed being with him, I always felt there was something missing." She paused, and looked out towards Woof again, who was happily chasing a couple of ducks, who flew away, and some bullfrogs at the edge of the pond, who burrowed into the mud and disappeared. Gracie hoped Woof didn't encounter a snapping turtle.

Jack still waited, silent. He'd wondered, of course, why Gracie and Ben had broken up. Perhaps she was about to tell him.

Gracie sighed again. "What was missing was what I prize so much with you: your unconditional love. You love me the way I am: not the way you wish I were, or the way you think you can cajole or manipulate me to be," she said, sounding disappointed at what must have been Holmes' behavior, and looking right into Jack's eyes. "Even though that means we fight a lot because you disapprove--"

"I don't--" Jack began.

"You do," Gracie forged ahead, insistent. " You disapprove of some of the things I do, or rather, the way I do some things: I guess that's more accurate. And that's okay: your opinion matters to me, Jack, and you usually make a good point, even if I do feel you're too cautious some time, too protective of me."

"It's only because I love you so much, Gracie," Jack said, low.

Gracie hugged him close, and then looked up at him again. "I'm so sorry I hurt you by being with Ben. I could be coy and say he beguiled me, but the fact is I just wasn't ready then to admit how deeply I cared for you."

Jack was still looking at her. "And are you ready now?" he asked, his voice very soft. He stroked the side of her face, which had a slight smear of garden soil on it, and cupped her cheek in his hand. "I adore you, Gracie. I love you more than I've ever loved anyone in my life. And you're right: I love you just the way you are, as annoying and stubborn as that can be sometimes." He smiled and ran his fingers through her hair. "I wouldn't change a thing. And I'll never stop feeling that way: I'll love you forever. If you don't want that, I'll let you go, but I can't share you--"

Gracie reached up to touch his face as he was touching hers. "It's not that I don't want that, Jack," Gracie began. "And it's not that

I didn't enjoy that kiss," she added with a sweet smile. "But—right now—I'm just not looking for, well, for more. Not now."

Jack swallowed, hard.

"But when I do—want—more," Gracie continued. "It will be with you."

Chapter Twenty-five

When Woof had tired of swimming, Jack and Gracie brought him back to Gracie's house where he could dry out in the sunshine on her screened porch, and they could have a glass of iced tea. They discussed the cases they were working on, and Jack told Gracie he planned to call Tara Torrissi, the Berkshire Probation Deputy, on Tuesday and see if she would be willing to go along with the ruse he'd concocted to get the files from Mark Broadstreet. He felt pretty sure she would.

Additionally, Gracie reminded him that the cash wire transfers to the YS Cayman Islands account had always been done from the same 'fast money check cashing' hole-in-the-wall in Springfield. The name on the transfers had been 'Bob Smith' which was about as obvious an alias as you could get. Gracie suspected that because the transfers were done in cash, and always at the same office, the clerk handling the transaction was getting paid something to look the other way when 'Bob Smith' came to do business and failed to show ID.

Jack said he would make a call to one of his favorite instructors down at Quantico, where he'd gone through FBI training. The man was a senior field agent now, and would probably farm the case out to the regional FBI office, but Jack valued his opinion. Since it looked like there was fraud, money laundering and possibly other crimes with a wide scope being perpetrated, he thought the FBI would be interested in hearing about what was going on.

So Tuesday, Jack put in a call to Brady Fitzpatrick and, delighted to find him at his desk rather than in the field, Jack briefed him on what he thought might be happening with regard to the JDC.

Fitzpatrick listened carefully, even though Jack was sure he had a dozen people, calls and reports all vying for his attention. But that was one of the things Jack had appreciated most in Fitzpatrick, and something he tried to emulate: his talent for listening.

When Jack had finished, Brady told him the FBI would certainly come into the case if he, as lead, requested it. However, he suggested that before formally making that request, Jack complete the comparative analysis of juvenile cases from Berkshire and Hampshire Counties to see if more cases than was appropriate were being sent to the Detention Center. Then, Fitzpatrick said, everything could be done at once: the Probation Office, the JDC and the money laundering/ Cayman Islands bank.

Jack's next call was to Tara Torrissi, who was in his office almost before he'd hung up from his call asking to meet with her, and who instantly agreed to go along with the scheme he'd devised.

"The hot topic in detention right now is reducing recidivism through occupational training and education," she said. The pert brunette wore beige dress trousers and the county's Probation Department short-sleeved henley shirt in a pretty shade of goldenrod. "The grant could be for that, through, oh, I'll think up some suitably obscure foundation, but it's a fair bet that if he doesn't have to do any work on the grant application, Broadstreet won't try to get any information on it, beyond what I tell him," she told Jack cheerily.

Tuesday afternoon, Tara excitedly told Mark Broadstreet about the grant opportunity for a two-county study and funding for a shared OT program to decrease recidivism. He agreed quite willingly to give her copies of all the Probation Department's files for the past six months; it was all computerized, he told her happily, so he could just pop everything onto a thumb drive and give it to her.

Gracie, meanwhile, was making her 'rounds' for the newspaper and thinking about Sullivan, Ford and Manning.

She'd have to go back to the basics. She knew what: murder. She knew where: the various places the victims had been found. They were all different, but the victims had the Toll Gate Pub and the Sure Fit Gym in common so those locales were key. She knew how: antifreeze poisoning. What was missing was why--and that would lead her to the other missing piece: the 'who.'

She'd shared her idea with Jack about questioning other prostitutes or pimps or madams in the Stockbridge area, and while he had thought the idea had some merit he had confessed to her that he had no time to begin that kind of blind canvassing. He wouldn't even know where to start, he'd told her, and in some respects Gracie had been happy to hear that.

So Tuesday evening Gracie made it her business to return to the Toll Gate Pub and see if she could at least get some leads or names for Jack to follow up on. Carla had gone back to her duties with the Lenox PD, so Gracie didn't think she'd be available to help with this line of inquiry, either. And Jack, after spending most of the rest of the holiday weekend with her, helping to plant annuals and offering his uninformed but well meant opinions on orchids for the conservatory, had returned to work. He had already told her he expected to be at his desk until late that evening. And, he'd said, he had do several loads of wash once he got back to his place.

Tuesday, Gracie rummaged in her clothes closet and dresser drawers until she came up with an outfit that she supposed could pass for the flashy girl 'Vee' she intended to once again impersonate at the pub: white trousers teamed with a red camisole and see-through sheer red top, and red heels. And by 9 pm Tuesday, she was once again perched on a stool at the Toll Gate Pub's bar, and chatting away breezily to Hal.

"Did you go out with that guy, then?" Hal asked her at one point. He meant Alan, one of the men from Sure Fit that Jack and Carla had grilled the week before, and the one who had met Gracie at the bar.

Gracie shrugged, and twisted a curl on one forefinger. "Nope, that fell through," she said vaguely. She sighed. "Hal--do you know of anyone around here who might, erm, know some nice guys who are looking for -- a date?" she finished, ladling on the insouciance.

Hall polished and re-polished a glass, thinking hard. Finally, he said he didn't really know about anyone like that, and why did 'Vee' want to know?

Gracie answered that after what had happened to her friend Desirée, and to Dez' other friends, she just felt she needed a little protection and that it would be difficult for her to know which 'boyfriends' were okay and which might not be.

Hal nodded, understanding.

"Well, as far as that goes, Vee, I'd never introduce you to anyone I didn't know and think was a nice guy," he offered, and Gracie looked gratefully at him from beneath the false lashes she'd stuck on. It was like looking through a spider's legs. "But I can see why you might be worried about dating guys who knew your friend." He lowered his voice. "You think Dez and those girls were killed by one of their boyfriends?" he asked her in a whisper. Thank goodness Tuesday nights were so slow: that gave him plenty of time to talk to 'Vee.'

Gracie nodded. "I think they might have been. And it scares me," she whispered.

Hal polished and polished and Gracie thought that soon he'd polish a hole in that glass.

"I can see that. For my part, I'm really glad none of the papers mentioned the pub in connection to the three dead women. Would've been bad for business," Hal told Gracie.

Gracie nodded. "Do you have any ideas about who might have killed them?" she asked innocently. She was sure Carla and Jack had asked him something similar when they'd questioned him, but she wasn't a cop. As a matter of fact right now she was as far away from 'cop' as you could get.

Hal leaned over the bar. "Well, Vee, I'll tell you. I think maybe it was someone who wanted to punish those girls, if you know what I mean."

Gracie nodded.

"That's why it's good you're being so careful," he added, commending her in a big brotherly sort of way.

"Because it could have been one of the boyfriends?" Gracie prompted.

Hal's voice dropped even lower. "I suppose, but...you know what I read on line this morning?" he asked her in a conspiratorial hiss. Gracie shook her head. "The *Intelligencer* on line said that several 'area men' had confessed to being involved with the three dead girls in a kind of a, well, call girl sort of arrangement."

Hal looked impressed with the information he was sharing, and so, therefore, did Gracie.

"Really? Call girls? That's what Dez was doing?" she asked in a whisper that matched her confidant's.

Hal shrugged. "Apparently. According to these guys, anyway, but why would they say that if it wasn't true?"

Gracie nodded and ignored his failure to use the subjunctive. 'Vee' wouldn't know a subjunctive if she fell over one. "So--do you think one of them 'punished' the girls?" she whispered anxiously.

Hal shook his head. "Like I said, I guess he could have, but it doesn't seem to make sense to me. I think those guys liked the girls," he went on.

"So they wouldn't have thought about 'punishing' them," Gracie concluded, trying to make it look like the realization had required a bit of effort.

"Right."

"So who would?" Gracie asked again. "Other, uhm, 'call girls' in the area? For pinching their turf?" she asked, mixing metaphors gleefully.

Hal shook his head. "Nah, like I said, I don't really know of much activity like that around here. And even if it does exist, it's probably somewhere besides right here," and he tapped the bar with two fingers of one hand for emphasis. "If you know what I mean."

Gracie did. He was telling her that the Toll Gate Pub hadn't had any other call girls, hookers or anything of that sort besides Dez and her chums, at least as far as he knew. So therefore, it was unlikely that there had been any sort of rivalry that could have led to the girls' murders. At least from other girls in that line of work.

So, who? Gracie wondered again. She had left the Toll Gate about 10:30pm, telling Hal that she was going to think long and hard about staying in the area after everything that had happened, and that maybe she'd just go back home to Schenectady.

He had told her he would miss her and if she did decide to leave, to come and say goodbye and her rum and coke would be on him.

Gracie had smiled and told him she would do that, and left. She thought about the case and the burning question of who would want to murder those three girls, all the way home, but no answer came to her.

Once home, she called Jack and told him what she'd been up to that evening and asked how his had gone. He told her of his conversations with Tara and with Brady Fitzpatrick of the FBI and while he wasn't thrilled with her going off alone to the Toll Gate Pub he supposed it could have been worse. She was only talking to Hal, after all, not trying to flush out a potential murderer.

Gracie read for a while and then went to bed, Pumpkin curled at her side.

The phone rang at midnight and Gracie jumped out of bed like a shot. She must have only been asleep for fifteen minutes.

"Gracie--it's David," came a voice she knew but was too surprised to place for a second or two.

"David? Is everything okay?" Quickly, she did the math and realized that it was only 5 a.m. where he was. She knew he was an early riser, but...and for him to ring her rather than email was unusual.

"Aye," came his answer. "But I've got to talk to you, Gracie, and I don't want to do it in an email," he explained. "This seemed like the best time: you're not asleep, are ye?" he queried.

"No, no," Gracie assured him. She realized that a month before she might have tantalized him by saying she was in bed, and letting him picture her that way. But now, she had no desire to do that. By rights, she should have called or emailed him long ago to straighten everything out, but it had never seemed a good moment.

Haltingly, David now explained to Gracie that since she'd left, he'd been spending quite a lot of time with Tamara, Verena's friend and the nursery school teacher on Sanderling Island.

Gracie listened, and smiled to herself. She had been anticipating exactly that, hadn't she? Why hadn't she told David she had no expectations where he was concerned?

David told her it had started when they had all gone out to celebrate his promotion, and while there had only been a couple of coffee dates since then, he and Tamara both wanted to take their friendship to the next level. However, both had been concerned once David had confessed his earlier feelings for Gracie and he had felt, although Tamara had offered to call, that it was his place to discuss everything with their American friend.

"David: I think that's great," Gracie said honestly. "As we said back in April, a long distance relationship is very difficult."

"Aye."

"And I like Tamara a lot," she added. "I think it's better, for both of us, that we be involved with people who live where we do. Who can be there for us, don't you?" Gracie asked David, who agreed.

Then Gracie explained that as he and Tamara had been becoming close, she and Jack had also been getting closer once more. David seemed happy to hear that, possibly because he'd always suspected Gracie really loved Jack, and possibly because knowing she did made him feel less guilty.

The conversation ended more cordially than most such conversations do: Gracie remembered her parting from Ben, and even past partings from Jack, and was grateful that she and David were so friendly, especially since they'd surely run into one another when Gracie visited her family and friends in England in the future.

And, she thought to herself as she re-adjusted the pillows and switched off the light, preparing once again for sleep, maybe it was easier because nothing too involved had really happened between her and David. So, although they still liked each other, the rest of the emotions they had felt had been nascent, and were now quite easily set aside.

Chapter Twenty-six

Thursday afternoon, Gracie returned to Sure Fit and asked Kim and Jarrod if she could take Kim's Kundalini Yoga class at 4 pm. "My chakras all out of whack with all the planting I've been doing," she explained, "and the chi's not flowing right."

Since the gym had a per session policy as well as monthly and yearly memberships, Kim and Jarrod were only too happy to have Gracie join the class. As she paid, she chatted to them about her new conservatory and the plants she'd re-landscaped around it, and asked how everything at the gym had been going.

"Really well, Gracie, thanks for asking," Kim and Jarrod said. They also both thanked her for not mentioning the gym in any of her articles except as the place that Pattie Ford had been found.

"Well, I think the girls all frequented a local watering hole, too, the Toll Gate Pub?" Gracie answered, smiling, "but I didn't mention that place, either. I don't think either locale has a connection to the murders, and neither do the police, so what would be the point?" Gracie outright lied, but smiled as Kim led her back to the locker room so she could change for class.

As Gracie and Carla had pre-arranged, the Lenox Police Officer also arrived at the gym, where she was a member, and took Kim's Kundalini Yoga class. Carla pretended she didn't know Gracie, as they had also pre-arranged when Gracie had phoned her Wednesday with what she called a 'lunatic idea.'

As the yoga room slowly filled up, Gracie chatted to Kim about her new conservatory and then again about the murders.

"So do you have any theories as to who it might be?" Kim asked, interested.

Gracie sighed. "Well, I think it's someone who knew the girls fairly well," she said, then she motioned Kim closer with one finger. "They all had sugar daddies for boyfriends, if you know what I mean," she whispered conspiratorially.

"No! Really?" Kim seemed surprised, and a little put off.

It was the reaction Gracie had hoped for, and it confirmed a hunch she had had the night before as she had been drifting to sleep the second time.

"That's what I heard down at the pub," Gracie said. "I think maybe the murderer was one of their, uh, johns."

"Ooooooh," Kim breathed.

"Which is a shame," Gracie went on, sounding more matter of fact. "Because after all, how're you supposed to manage on your own, especially at first?" She sighed eloquently. "I've had rich boyfriends, too," she added, her tone implying that the arrangement in her case had been similar to the arrangements the three dead girls had had. "It's just a case of supply and demand. And it would be a shame if one of those girls' customers turned on them because of the very thing they were soliciting from them, don't you think?"

Kim looked momentarily confused at Gracie's theory. Then: "but surely, you don't approve of--soliciting?" she asked, picking up on the term Gracie had intentionally used.

Gracie made a face. "Well, I don't know: like I said, it's supply and demand. We pay people for their faces, their brain power, their voices, their skill with their hands: why not for their skill with their bodies in sex?" she queried.

Kim had no time to answer as the timer to begin class pinged and she had to move away, but her face was a mix of confusion and disappointment and something else Gracie couldn't quite pinpoint. Perhaps anger?

After class, Gracie complimented Kim on her talent as an instructor and swiftly changed back into her jeans and top. Carla dawdled in the locker room. Then Gracie asked Kim if she could have one of her famous smoothies from the juice bar.

"I've got a hot date later tonight," Gracie said cheekily, grinning at the gym owner. "I'm sure he'll buy me a fancy dinner and if I'm good, I might get a pair of earrings out of it, too," she paused. "But I feel like I'd like a little something just now after that wonderful class," she added, and sat at the bar.

"Sure," Kim said politely enough, but her cheeriness had gone. "Any special flavor?"

Gracie shrugged. "Well, I like just about everything, as long as it's sweet," she replied.

Kim nodded. "I've got to re-stock the juice bar anyway: I'll get you some mango from the freezer and do you up something really nice," she told Gracie.

A few minutes later--Gracie used the time to text Jack and tell him where she was and with whom--Kim returned with containers of different types of fruit in her hands. These she put into the small fridge, and then she began assembling Gracie's smoothie. She used a couple of different types of fruit purée, and Gracie noticed that she emptied both small containers and rinsed them out in the juice bar's small sink when she was done.

Kim handed her the glass full of the lightly pink-tinged creamy liquid, and smiled, and said she could pay Jarrod for the smoothie on her way out of the gym.

Gracie pretended to take a sip, a trick she'd seen on NCIS.

"Oh, that's great! Delicious!" she commented, moving to take another sip, and Kim, satisfied that her customer was taken care of, turned to another woman who wanted to have a celery and carrot drink made.

Celery and carrot? Yuk, Gracie thought. The whole vegetables, okay, but juiced?

She mentally shuddered, then pretended her phone had vibrated, jumped off her chair, and spilled her drink all in one motion. The drink soaked her jeans and splattered her top, and there was very little left of it in the glass, which had upended on the counter. Lucky, it hadn't broken.

"Oh, damn!" Gracie said, gazing in dismay at herself.

"Here, let me wipe that up for you," Kim said. "I'll make you another one," she offered. "No charge.'

"Oh, I'm such a klutz," Gracie moaned. "But no, Kim, thanks, I just realized the time, and I have to run. I'm going to be late as it is and now I've got to shower as well as change," she gestured to her wet, stained clothing and sticky exposed skin.

Kim pressed her once more to take a new smoothie, but Gracie stood firm.

"Well, then, next time," Kim said, smiling. "You will come back, won't you?"

Gracie nodded enthusiastically and told another lie. This was getting to be a habit. "Yes, of course I will, Kim: that yoga class was wonderful. I'll come again Monday, if that's okay: I got a schedule from Jarrod. And I think I'll join at the start of next month," she added convincingly.

Kim nodded. "I'm glad to hear you say that."

Gracie got to her Jeep and texted Carla that she was leaving and everything had gone as she had hoped. Then she drove straight to Jack's house, as she had texted him she would.

"Evidence bags?" she asked as he opened his front door.

"Got 'em," he replied. "No, Woof," he chastised the dog, who was ready to give Gracie his usual greeting.

"In a minute, puppy," Gracie cooed, and made a beeline for Jack's bathroom. With the door half open--to preserve chain of evidence, Gracie told Jack in a no nonsense sort of voice--she stripped out of her wet jeans and top and handed them to him. He secured them in the evidence bags she'd asked him to bring home for that express purpose.

Then Gracie showered quickly to remove any residue of the smoothie from her skin, and dressed in the shorts and T shirt she'd stowed in the bottom of her gym bag.

"When can you send those out for testing?" she asked breathlessly, returning to Jack's living room after she was dressed.

Jack handed her a glass of her favorite, V-8 juice, with a thick wedge of lemon.

Gracie grinned. "Thanks!"

"I'll send them out tomorrow. We should have results Monday morning," he answered. Then he gave her a critical look. "You really think they'll find antifreeze in it?" he asked, referring to the drink remnants on Gracie's clothing.

She shrugged. "I don't know. But I told you my theory, and I told it to Carla, and she thought it could be. So we tried it."

Jack sighed. "I'm really glad you had Carla there," he said. "Just in case."

Gracie smiled at him. "Maybe your caution is rubbing off on me, at least a little bit," she admitted. "And it's a really good thing that Kim doesn't know me," she added with a sniff. "The way I acted and the stuff I said was totally out of character!"

Tara had told Jack that morning that from her preliminary review of the Hampshire County Juvenile cases, something 'hinky' was definitely going on. Nearly 100% of the juveniles who came through the office ended up being sentenced to at least a few months in the JDC.

'That's not normal,' Tara had said certainly. 'Statistically, it's way out of the park.'

Jack had immediately contacted Brady Fitzpatrick with Tara's information, and just that afternoon, around the time he was receiving Gracie's text about her trip to Sure Fit with Carla, Fitzpatrick had called him.

'There a decent hotel in Pittsfield?' he'd asked, his Maryland twang pronounced.

'There's a Hilton: that's pretty decent: why?' Jack had queried.

He could hear his old instructor's chuckle on the other end of the phone. 'Being a senior field agent has its privileges,' he had commented cryptically. Then he'd told Jack that on Monday two agents from the Boston FBI office would be coming out to see Jack about the whole JDC/Juvenile Probation/Cayman Islands affair. 'We'll be there about noon: order lunch in,' he'd told Jack, who had agreed.

'We?' he'd echoed as the pronoun registered.

Brady had chuckled again. 'Yeah, Jack: I'm coming along on this one. Sounds too interesting to pass up. And besides, it'll be good to see you again, maybe lure you back down here.'

Jack had been delighted that Brady was coming, and a bit proud that his old instructor thought a case of his was worthy of his time. He recounted all of this to Gracie on Thursday evening as she sipped her V-8.

"Wow, Jack, that's great," Gracie agreed. "I can't wait to meet him, I've heard you talk about him," she said of Brady Fitzpatrick. "But be sure not to forget about the test results on my jeans in all the excitement of the FBI coming," she admonished.

"I won't," Jack promised. "Hey, look: you want to stay for dinner?" he asked, as though the thought had just occurred to him. The truth was, he'd planned to ask Gracie to stay, and to that end had stopped at the market on his way home and bought some organic boneless skinless chicken thighs and the makings of an abundant salad.

Gracie grinned. "Sure. What'cha making?"

Jack told her to never mind that, and he poured her a glass of dry riesling and sat her on the sofa with Woof and the TV remote.

"I'll let you know when it's ready," he told her. "You're not the only one who can cook, you know!"

Jack's 'coq au riesling' was very tasty, and Gracie asked him where he'd got the recipe. He admitted to having seen one of the television chefs make a similar dish one morning on her program.

"You watch cooking shows?" Gracie queried, suspicious.

Jack shrugged. "It was on. I was getting ready to go for a run," he answered.

The chicken and wine and salad finished, Gracie helped Jack clean up and then they took Woof out for a long walk around the two acres Jack owned next to his trailer.

"So now, we wait?" Gracie said, meaning wait for the results in the JDC and the antifreeze murder cases.

"Yes," Jack replied, nodding. "Looks like everything might get resolved early next week," he added. "Then I can maybe get back to the files pending on my desk."

Gracie made a sympathetic noise. "Have you told Poppinfresh that the FBI's coming, yet?" she asked, knowing the DA disliked anyone from outside the county having the least involvement in any of his cases. Even though he, himself, was hardly involved. He'd go ballistic at the thought of a federal agency stepping in.

Jack made a face and shook his head. "I'll tell him tomorrow. And if he's out of the office and doesn't pick up his voice messages, oh well," he added cavalierly.

Gracie giggled. Then she looked up at the sky. "It's a beautiful night," she murmured. The moon wasn't up yet but the stars were bright and a lingering wash of violet from the sunset still remained in the west.

Jack agreed.

Chapter Twenty-seven

Rita Licora was very happy. When her boss, Hampshire County DA Don Jenkins, called her into his office Monday just after lunch, she broke into a wide grin despite the fact that three imposing looking FBI agents and her Berkshire County counterpart were in Jenkins' office.

She wasn't surprised, either, when the FBI guy named Fitzpatrick outlined what they'd uncovered, and what they were going to do.

Mark Broadstreet was going down! Not only hadn't there been an aunt who'd died and left him an inheritance, if the FBI and Jack Draper were right--and Rita thought they were-- Broadstreet had been colluding with Sasha Yedid, Judge Robert Elderson and Commissioner Itty Azar to funnel as many juveniles as they could to the JDC. From what Fitzpatrick said, they were going to execute a federal warrant on the JDC offices and expected to find two sets of books which would reveal significant profits.

What they didn't know yet was how those profits were being laundered and sent to a Cayman Islands bank account, or who was responsible for that, but they were fairly sure that Yedid was involved and thought that Chacko Salama might be the other connection. But as Fitzpatrick said, they would find out.

Giving her and Jenkins a heads up on the op was just a courtesy since they were now handling the case, but Rita went along to represent local law enforcement when one of the FBI agents from the Boston field office confronted Broadstreet in his office, showed him their warrant, and marched him out in handcuffs. All files from the Juvenile Probation Office were also seized and sent to the Pittsfield Hilton where the FBI had set up a temporary command post.

As this was taking place, Jenkins was having the Northampton Police Chief arrest Judge Elderson in his chambers.

The FBI had organized it so that all the suspects were seized at more or less the same time, and thus no warnings could be given.

The State Police were picking up Chacko Salama, who happened to be in his office at Salama Construction headquarters.

Another team of troopers was dispatched to arrest Commissioner Itty Azar at his home. And two FBI agents along with Detective Draper went out to the JDC to seize their records and bring in Sasha Yedid.

By 3 pm, Chacko, Yedid, Elderson and Broadstreet were all in custody in the Berkshire County Sheriff's office; because of the possible corruption in Hampshire County, the FBI had chosen to use Berkshire County's facilities and to borrow Berkshire County personnel: that meant Jack, as well as the Sheriff and a couple of deputies. Popovitch, conveniently and perhaps thankfully, was not around.

There was also the small fact that it was the Berkshire County Detective who'd broken the case.

Jack was in his office, catching up on his messages during a spare five minutes when Millie handed him a fax that had just arrived from the independent lab he'd sent Gracie's clothing out to. The test results were positive for ethylene glycol: according to the gas chromatograph, the concentration was 600 mg/L, a heavy dose that would have probably made Gracie quite ill—ill enough to make her miss her alleged 'hot date' that evening— although it wouldn't have killed her right away.

Before he left to re-join Fitzpatrick and the rest of the FBI and local team down in the Sheriff's office where the suspects were being held, Jack put in a quick call to the Lenox PD which had jurisdiction in Stockbridge, and asked if Kim Foley from Sure Fit could be brought up to Pittsfield: she was now a prime suspect in the murders of the three young women. Lenox PD said they'd be only too happy to do that and Jack wondered how Sheriff Shermayne would fit everyone in the few holding cells at their disposal. Well, if need be, they could always put someone across the street, in the Pittsfield PD's two small cells.

As Jack entered the Sheriff's office, Fitzpatrick was just closing his cell phone.

"Itty Azar's skipped town," he said to Jack. "The staties are on his tail, though: wife told them he was on his way to the Springfield Airport."

That was where Jack had taken his flying lessons and earned his Pilot's license. When he had time now, he often rented his favorite Cessna and went for a spin. Therefore, knew the airport and its personnel well.

Quickly he explained this to Fitzpatrick and offered to call and have Azar's flight grounded; Fitzpatrick, smiling at his protégé's fast thinking, gave Jack a thumbs up.

Then it was back to questioning the suspects in the Sheriff's custody; they had been separated, and Fitzpatrick and his team had put Broadstreet in the interrogation room first.

It had been several years since Jack had watched his mentor Brady Fitzpatrick do what he did so well: interrogate a suspect. Now, Jack observed from behind the two way mirror as Fitzpatrick sauntered into the small room where Broadstreet sat in the hard wooden chair at the plain metal table.

Saying nothing, Fitzpatrick placed a foot high stack of files on the table's edge, flipped a second wooden chair around so that its back was towards the suspect, and straddled it.

Fitzpatrick folded his arms across the chair's back and looked at Broadstreet.

"I didn't do anything: I don't know why I'm here," Broadstreet said in a voice that sounded calm but was underpinned with tremors. The man was still in his work clothes: navy silk trousers and a short sleeved silk dress shirt. The shirt was light blue and set off Broadstreet's eyes, and coordinated with his white, navy and gold tie that had a pattern of small stirrups throughout. Broadstreet's wavy brown hair had a few threads of silver in it and his eyes crinkled at the corners, but over all he was a good looking man in his early 40's who kept himself in good shape. Jack noticed that Broadstreet's nails were manicured, and he couldn't help smirking.

"You're here because you're the head of Juvenile Probation for Hampshire County, and there have been some irregularities with regard to the kids you've been sending to the JDC," Fitzpatrick answered mildly. He fixed Broadstreet with an expectant stare.

"Irregularities?" Broadstreet queried.

Good, Jack thought: he hadn't asked for a lawyer. Hopefully, Fitzpatrick could keep him off guard enough, and Broadstreet's ego was big enough, that he would think he could bluff his way out of anything incriminating.

Fitzpatrick raised eyebrows that were nearly all grey now, and reached over for a folder from his stack. He opened it and read: "Jessie Saunders, age 14, charged with running away from home and stealing three candy bars and an energy drink from the mini mart in Four Corners," he read flatly. "Sentenced to six months minimum at the JDC."

Broadstreet said nothing.

Fitzpatrick read from a second file he pulled: "Ralph Frumenty, age 15, charged with buying a controlled substance on school grounds. Sentenced to a year at the JDC."

"We take drug charges very seriously," Broadstreet interjected sanctimoniously.

Fitzpatrick gave a slight snort of derision and checked another page in another file. "Says here the boy's mother's got degenerative disk disease in her spine; he was buying oxycontin for her because she doesn't have health insurance and she couldn't afford to buy her pain medication at the pharmacy more than once every two or three months." He flipped the file shut with perhaps more force than was necessary, and moved on to another manila folder.

"Bernadette Strong, age 14, charged with underage drinking. Sentenced to a year in the JDC," Fitzpatrick read.

"Again, we take alcohol abuse and underage drinking very seriously," Broadstreet repeated, but less firmly than before.

Fitzpatrick nodded as though he understood but he read more from Strong's file: "and according to information I have, she was given the alcohol by her step father who then tried to rape her," he reminded Broadstreet.

"We have very good counsellors at the JDC," Broadstreet countered, but Jack thought he was starting to become uneasy: his eyes kept darting to the stack of files and a sheen of sweat had broken out on his upper lip. "That girl needed therapy after what had happened."

"Mmmmmm..." Again Fitzpatrick nodded, but again he flipped the file shut. Then he glared at Broadstreet. "And isn't it true that the stepfather walked?" he asked in a biting deadpan.

Broadstreet shrugged. "I had nothing to do with that."

"You did," Fitzpatrick corrected him. "You forced Bernadette Strong to withdraw her criminal complaint, so all the DA was left with was a charge of indecent exposure. Since it was a first offense, he was given a probationary sentence.'

"I had nothing--" Broadstreet began, but Fitzpatrick shut him up by grabbing another folder and reading, his voice loud this time, strident.

"Ronnie Burgholder, 16, charged with shoplifting, sentenced to nine months at the JDC," he read. Then he grabbed more files in quick succession, flipping open to the OTN on the top page and reading in the same aggressively loud voice the children's names, their ages, their crimes and their sentences which were all incarceration at the JDC for various periods of time. After six more files, Fitzpatrick stopped.

"Shall I go on, Mr. Broadstreet?" he asked, his voice dropping to a deceptively quiet tone.

Broadstreet was silent.

"We've checked these files," Fitzpatrick continued, and he gestured to the stack which still was nearly a foot high. "We've compared them to similar cases elsewhere and we know these sentences were outrageously harsh." He shook his head. "These kids didn't deserve the JDC, and you know it."

"But I didn't sentence them, that was Judge Elderson!" Broadstreet blurted, sounding panicked.

Oho, thought Jack: here we go. He hadn't thought Broadstreet would give up his co-conspirators and in particular the Judge, quite so easily. Then again, he thought, cowards often were the type to get involved in schemes like this.

"So you're telling me that these kids going to juvie was all Judge Elderson's idea?" Fitzpatrick asked quietly. "Didn't you recommend the JDC to him, in each case?" he queried, affecting confusion but knowing exactly what Broadstreet had done.

"Well, yes," Broadstreet admitted, "but--"

"But what, Mark?" Fitzpatrick asked softly. "You going to tell me the Judge doesn't have to take your recommendation? I know that. But why'd you do it? Why'd you recommend these kids for the JDC?"

Broadstreet's glance now flew around the room, like a bird trapped and desperately looking for an open window. His eyes alighted on the stack of files, then flew to Fitzpatrick's face, which was somehow both knowing and non judgmental at the same time.

"It was the Judge, I'm telling you, it was Elderson!"

"You saying he forced you to make those recommendations?" Fitzpatrick asked, disbelieving. "He doesn't need your recommendation," he told Broadstreet, and sat back, giving his quarry a long look.

Fitzpatrick got up from his chair and walked around so that he was behind Broadstreet, who turned and tried to look at his inquisitor. Since his wrists were still cuffed and attached to a metal ring on the table for that purpose, he had difficulty doing this.

Fitzpatrick bent down to whisper just behind Broadstreet's left ear.

"Elderson's just a supporting actor in this play," he whispered. "You're the star: you and your leading lady," he went on. "Whose idea was it, hers or yours, Mark?"

"I don't know what you mean," Broadstreet insisted.

Ah, so chivalry was not dead, Jack thought, observing.

"I mean," Fitzpatrick continued on, still whispering. "Your girlfriend, Sasha Yedid, the head of Epiphany and the Director of the JDC," he explained.

Broadstreet, who didn't know that Yedid had also been arrested and was sitting at that moment in a holding cell not fifty feet from him, blanched.

"Was this something the two of you cooked up together?" Fitzpatrick asked. "Maybe between the sheets one evening, thinking about all the money you could make if you cooked the books at the JDC and kept every bed over there filled?" Fitzpatrick went on, his voice silkily convincing.

He switched sides so he was now whispering in Broadstreet's other ear.

"She's a high maintenance lady, isn't she, Mark: Sasha, I mean. Not that other girl you used to date, Rita? Nah..." Fitzpatrick huffed in Broadstreet's ear. "You moved up when you traded her in for Ms. Yedid, didn't you, Mark? But Sasha took a lot of money to keep happy, didn't she: dinners out at three star restaurants, expensive jewelry, trips to the islands or Europe even. Hard to afford all that on--what is it a Juvenile Probation Director makes a year, about $80K?" Fitzpatrick asked.

Broadstreet didn't move but his eyes shifted from side to side.

"So who thought it up, Mark: the scheme to send every kid who came through your office to the JDC and skim the profits off the top? Was it you? Mark? Must've been," Fitzpatrick concluded after a moment. He straightened up, and walked around so he faced Broadstreet across the table, but remained standing. He looked at the Juvenile Probation director in a surprised sort of way. "I wouldn't have thought you were that smart, Mark, to tell you the truth," he said in a voice tinged with 'aw gee shucks' and just hinting of Fitzpatrick's Oklahoma upbringing.

Broadstreet shook his head in a panic. "I'm not!" he blurted. "It wasn't my idea! It was all Sasha's, she and Chacko set up the whole thing!" he said, desperate.

Jack, observing, sighed. It seemed chivalry was dead, after all.

Chapter Twenty-eight

Gracie was a very busy woman that week. News of the multiple arrests in the JDC case was announced by Popovitch, who hurried back to his office, once he'd learned from Jack that Broadstreet was talking and that everyone involved would likely go down in quick succession.

Popovitch tried to make it sound like he had been in on the entire investigation including the FBI's involvement, but of course Gracie knew that it had all been Jack.

When she wrote her article--the first of three, as it turned out--she didn't even mention Popovitch's name.

Butcher from the *Gazetteer*, on the other hand, included in his article a long and somewhat rambling interview with Popovitch which, since the DA knew nothing about the case, spoke in generalities and theories rather than particulars and wasn't very interesting.

Gracie talked to Fitzpatrick, who hated giving interviews but relented in Gracie's case. He wouldn't speak with Butcher, who told him he wanted to get the 'FBI perspective,' having got the DA's.

"If you talked to Mr. Popovitch, then you couldn't get anything more out of me," Fitzpatrick told Butcher.

Broadstreet made a statement to Gracie which painted Yedid as the mastermind of the whole JDC scheme, along with her ex husband, Chacko Salama. He told Gracie that Elderson was brought in because of course they needed a Judge who would guarantee that every kid was sent to the JDC. And, he said, the commissioner Itty Azar was included in the deal because they needed for the JDC to be renewed as the only contracted facility used for juvenile delinquents, and for Epiphany to continue to operate it, and those decisions were the commissioners'.

Gracie's first article dealt with the arrests made and with the case against the five people involved: Broadstreet, Yedid, Elderson, Chacko and Azar. Her follow up piece, which just squeaked in under the print deadline for Friday's edition of the *Intelligencer,* explained the fact that Yedid was Salama's ex wife and that the company they called 'Epiphany' had been set up by Chacko Salama for Sasha Yedid as part of their divorce deal.

It had never been included in the official court documents, but through her research into the state's business formation and licensing records, Gracie had discovered that Epiphany was created by Chacko for Sasha. She also discovered that Chacko had colluded with Azar, his second cousin, to be awarded the contract to build Hampshire County's new JDC and to name Epiphany as the company to run it. Gracie included these facts in her article.

The set up ensured Chacko's ex wife's position and income, and also gave Chacko a nice profit on the construction.

Gracie's perusal of the JDC's construction memos also revealed that sub standard materials had been used, although the county had been billed for code-compliant items. Chacko had pocketed a considerable amount of cash from that little scheme as well. Gracie ended up writing a fast sidebar covering this aspect of the story and by the time Friday evening rolled around felt she had truly earned her money that week.

While the fallout from the *Intelligencer* articles, which covered almost all of page one and most of page three, was still raining down, Fitzpatrick and the rest of his team--and he included Jack--continued to interview everyone involved in the JDC scheme to get particulars and so assign appropriate charges.

Itty Azar had been taken into custody at Springfield Airport when Jack's phone call to the Airport Manager had grounded his plane. Azar had run, his short, stubby legs pumping as he'd headed for the men's room where he'd tried to hide in a janitor's closet, but he'd been located and brought back to Berkshire County where he'd undergone questioning.

Jack had been in charge of that interview and had been sickened when Azar had immediately begun to give excuses for his behavior, his anger and bitterness spewing out as he told Jack that he'd been squirreling away the money he'd got from the JDC scheme so that he could escape his life--and his wife.

'All she does is suck me dry,' he had snarled of his wife, who had told law enforcement that her husband had left their home that morning announcing that he'd had enough and that he was leaving her for, as he had put it, 'the life he deserved.'

'This wasn't what I signed on for!' Azar had screamed to Jack in self-justification. His dull, steel-wool hair was too long in the back and rubbed on his dirty shirt collar. 'With the medications, the special equipment: I had to have my whole house re-done inside so she could reach stuff from her wheelchair!' he had declared derisively, as though that were an unreasonable demand, and he expected Jack to understand.

Jack had looked at him impassively. But that little detail explained where Azar had first met Chacko Salama, who had handled the renovation, and how some of the parts of the JDC scheme had been put together.

'And then, she wanted to go to Adult Day Care: do you know how much those programs cost?' Azar had continued incredulously. 'And the health insurance we get through the county is crap: it wouldn't pay for even half of it. And my salary sucks, so I couldn't afford it. Where did she think I was going to get the money?' Apparently that was how he'd justified using the county courthouse as his wife's daycare center.

He had wiped his sweaty forehead with one chubby hand and shaken his head. Itty Azar was round: chunky rather than chubby and packed rather than blubbery, but with a round face and waistline and bulbous blue eyes that regarded the world as though it owed him a living. 'I had to do something,' he had told Jack.

'He told me all I did was slow him down,' Ruth Azar had told the police when they'd asked her where her husband had gone. She'd been crying, and the hand that tried to wipe her tears away had shaken so badly she'd only succeeded in smearing her tears across her face.

'The JDC is as good as any place else,' Azar had said later in the interview with Jack. 'Throwing them the business by placing kids there wasn't a crime. And as for Salama Construction, again, they're as good as anyone else around, maybe better, so giving them the bid wasn't a bad thing to do: all these stupid rules and regulations!' he had declared. "Sometimes they don't make any sense and you have to go around them."

Trying not to look as amazed as he was at the Hampshire County Commissioner's complete disregard for the concept of ethics, never mind his oath of office, Jack had turned Azar over to the FBI as well as to Rita Licora and Don Jenkins, who had charged

Azar with a host of crimes beginning with conspiracy and ending with abuse of his office. Cruelty to a dependent person, theft of county services, abandonment, and attempted flight were included, too.

Broadstreet, Yedid, Elderson and Chacko Salama were charged with conspiracy and various crimes including improper use of a county facility, improper use of an office, abuse of power and fraud. Salama and Yedid were also charged with embezzlement and money laundering since the FBI had discovered through their interrogation of everyone concerned that Yedid had been the one to keep two sets of books for the JDC and to hand over the considerable profit--in cash--to Chacko. He then had run it through the shell company 'Youth Solutions' and split it up as everyone involved had agreed: Sasha and Broadstreet each got 25% , Elderson and Azar each got 20% and Chacko himself got the last ten percent.

Azar deposited most of his money in the account which ironically bore his long suffering and ill used wife's birth name, 'Ruth Romano.' He had also opened a new account in Grand Cayman in the past few months and had been funneling money into that in preparation for his departure. When he'd been arrested at the airport, Azar had had several hundred thousand dollars from the cleaned out Romano account on his person as well as a single one way ticket to Grand Cayman.

Elderson had spent a lot of his money: the new Mercedes, golfing trips to St. Andrews in Scotland and other revered courses across the US and in Europe, especially the South of France and Dubai. What remained was socked away in a savings account at a bank on Jersey, one of the Channel Islands between Great Britain and France.

Chacko's money was all in his Grand Cayman account; it contained profits from the JDC as well as a string of deposits going back several years from jobs he'd run for Salama Construction where he'd double-billed, billed for goods not used, or overcharged. Over three million dollars was in the Cayman account in Chacko's name.

Yedid's profit from the JDC scheme was in an account in her daughter's name, and under interrogation she tried to tell the FBI that her involvement in the underhanded enterprise was all to benefit little Ishtar. While there was no doubt that the child had enjoyed every advantage and had lived in a luxurious, spacious and beautiful home and attended a top private school with fees to match, Sasha Yedid's own lifestyle exposed her self-interest in the profits illegally gained: jewelry, furs and designer clothing were all seized from her million-plus dollar home whose furnishings and appointments had an estimated worth of another million dollars, at least.

And Broadstreet's money was also in an offshore account: what he hadn't spent on squiring Yedid around in the manner to which she'd become accustomed, he'd spent on his own sartorial splendor and accoutrements: Rolex watches, the classic Jaguar, and a regimen of spa services that would make a film star envious.

The five were all locked up in the Berkshire County Jail, partly because the FBI was concerned about possible retaliation at the Hampshire County facility, and partly because Berkshire County was a more up to date, maximum security prison with a Warden who took no bullshit from anyone.

Because the magistrate hearing the initial cases determined that all of those involved were potential flight risks despite their positions within the community, the right to bail was revoked and each would remain in custody until they either struck a plea deal with DA Jenkins on the county charges or had a trial. Then, of course, the state and federal charges brought by the FBI would kick in and they would either plead or go to trial on those.

Either way, Jack told Gracie late on Friday afternoon, all those involved in the JDC scheme would likely not see the outside of a prison wall for a very long time.

"Meanwhile, I have some other interesting news for you," he drawled. He'd given Gracie a call near the end of his day, and was now tidying his desk in preparation for a well-deserved weekend off.

Gracie, who had been varnishing her toenails when Jack had called, waited.

"Monday when the tests came back on your clothes and they were positive for antifreeze, I had Kim Foley brought in," he reminded Gracie.

"When did you have time to question her?" she asked, knowing how busy Jack had been all week.

He chuckled. "I managed. It took a couple days in the Pittsfield PD's holding cell until she finally confessed," he added, noting that he thought several visits from Foley's pastor at the Stockbridge Baptist Church had also persuaded her to 'come clean.'

"What did she say?"

"She's on a mission from God," Jack said evenly.

"I know, she told me," Gracie cut in. "To help people keep their bodies as fit temples for the Lord," she concluded. "Which isn't a bad thing...we all should probably take better care of ourselves."

"Right, but there's more, and it's just what you suspected," Jack replied. And he explained to Gracie how Foley had learned of Sullivan's, and then Ford's and finally Manning's extra-curricular activities, as he phrased it.

"So she killed them?" Gracie queried, surprised in spite of herself that her suspicions had been right: it had seemed a long shot.

Having 'sugar daddies' or working as an escort wasn't a great way to make a living, but it was hard for Gracie to understand that someone would not only condemn a woman for her choice, but take it into her own hands to mete out punishment. Gracie felt that that was between the women in question and their God, as the saying went.

"Yup, she did," Jack answered now. "Said they were a 'scourge on womanhood' and that they deserved to die because they had betrayed the sanctity of their gender." His tone was both disbelieving and sad.

"And so she tried to poison *me*?" Gracie asked.

Jack chuckled again, but wryly this time. "Yes. Apparently you're a better actress than you thought: Kim said you'd hinted that you'd done much the same thing in your, erm, 'younger days' and might possibly still engage in that kind of behavior from time to time. So she thought that you at least deserved to be taught a lesson."

Gracie recalled the conversation between her and Foley at Sure Fit, and her intimation that she had understood, at least, why a young girl just starting out might align herself with a rich, older boyfriend. "Ah, well then, I expect an Oscar, " she joked.

"I'm glad you had explained to me and Carla what you were up to," Jack said, then. "I don't mind telling you I was a little concerned when I thought you'd had a past as an escort or something," he chuckled. He had known what Gracie had planned to tell the suspected murderess to see if she could get her to react, but he couldn't resist pulling Gracie's leg now that it was all over.

"My past isn't that exciting, " Gracie said dismissively. "So what's going to happen to Foley?"

Jack sighed. "Well, Poppinfresh wants to offer her a deal," he answered, sounding resigned.

"Of course he does," Gracie agreed. "But what kind of deal can he make for someone who's confessed to three counts of premeditated and one of attempted murder?" she asked.

Chapter Twenty-nine

Friday Gracie invited Jack as well as his old teacher from Quantico and the FBI training academy, to her house for dinner. "To celebrate the conclusion of two amazing cases," she said.

Jack accepted, and convinced Fitzpatrick, who originally had planned to return home Friday night now that the FBI's work was pretty much done, to come as well, and to delay his flight back to Washington D.C. until Saturday, at least.

"It was nice of her to invite me," Fitzpatrick commented as he and Jack drove to Gracie's that evening. "She's a good reporter, and not a bad investigator, either, Jack." He gave his former student a look. "You train her?"

Jack grinned. "A little. I show her some stuff, from time to time, but a lot of it is Gracie's own brains and intuition, Fitz," he admitted. "Smartest person I've ever known, and although her ideas can be kinda wacky, I will admit they're often right on the nose."

Fitzpatrack nodded. "Good person to have around," he commented laconically, and was silent for the rest of the ride.

Gracie welcomed them in her usual way and soon was involved in a detailed discussion with Fitzpatrick about the parquet floor in her hallway and the finishing work in the Oak Room.

"I've never seen anything like this," Fitzpatrick told Gracie, who handed him the scotch on ice he'd requested. "Where'd you get the idea?"

Gracie explained that she'd seen something similar in an architectural design book and that her contractor Larry had run with the concept and created her beautiful room.

'Fitz' relaxed into Gracie's deep leather sofa and sighed. He looked around. "You've done a beautiful job on the place," he said.

"And you haven't seen the rest of the house," Jack put in, sitting with Gracie on a matching love seat opposite his old teacher.

Fitz smiled and took a sip of his drink. He'd just said, 'scotch' and had figured he'd get something quite drinkable knowing

Gracie's reputation for being a good hostess. He wasn't prepared for the soft, smoky taste he encountered. "Single malt?"

"It's Glenfiddich--40 years old. I hope that's okay?" Gracie asked knowing damn well that it was. She herself didn't like scotch much but she knew Jack occasionally did and kept the limited edition, three-figure bottle mostly for him.

Fitz grinned and took another sip. "I'll say," he commented. If this was Gracie's idea of a 'cocktail' he couldn't wait to see what she'd serve for dinner. Jack had told him his girlfriend was a 'great cook' but depending on who made that comment, it could mean anything from tasty casseroles to a talent for microwaving ready-to-eat dishes from the supermarket.

While they had their scotch--Gracie was sipping a Campari and soda--Jack and Fitz discussed the still unsolved murder of Mike Garnier.

"There has to be a connection," Jack insisted, and Fitz agreed.

"You want to lean on Chacko Salama," he advised his former student. "He's looking at probably forty or more years behind bars for the stuff we already have him on, and I think he's a likely one to have at least arranged the murder," Fitz explained.

Jack nodded. Gracie re-filled Fitz's glass with a smile.

"What do you mean, 'lean on him?' " Gracie asked Fitz.

Fitz shot the cuffs of his blue broadcloth shirt and adjusted one denim clad knee. "Chacko's in construction. And he's from the Middle East. I don't have to tell you to connect those dots, do I Jack?" he asked rhetorically, and Jack shook his head.

"No, I'm aware of the fact that the Middle East, like other ethnicities, has a very efficient Organization here in the states," he replied. "I'm sure Chacko knows a couple of thugs who could have killed Mike."

Fitz shrugged. "So use what we've got against him to get him to name names: Berkshire County's charging him as well as Hampshire County. And we are, too. Even if you offer to mitigate a couple of the charges you've filed against him, he'll still do plenty of time behind bars because of everything else."

Jack made a face and stared at the ice cubes in his glass. "I don't believe in plea bargaining," he said, low. "Maybe because

Poppinfresh does so much of it," he added, and his mouth twisted in a wry half smile.

"Understood," Fitz nodded. "But if you can get the name or names of the guys who killed Garnier in exchange for meaningless leniency, seems like a good exchange to me," he raised an eyebrow and gave Jack a look. Fitz was an ex-Marine, even though he liked to say there was no such thing, and his suggestions still had the tone of command to them.

They were called into the kitchen a short while later by Gracie, who told Fitz she hoped he didn't mind not eating in the dining room.

"I saw it," Fitz commented, since Jack had pointed it out as they'd walked towards the kitchen. "It's a beautiful room, but this is much more my style," he agreed.

They sat at her large barn board table which Fitz exclaimed over. Gracie explained that it had been original, she thought, to one of the outbuildings constructed at the same time as the house, and at least had been a fixture from the earliest records of the house's furnishings she had found, going back to the early 1800s.

"You're really into wood," she commented as she moved expertly around her kitchen, assembling dinner.

Jack chuckled and Fitz made a face.

"He makes furniture," Jack told Gracie. "In his garage."

"It's my wood shop," Fitz protested, but he was smiling.

"Really? What wood do you like to work with the most?" she asked.

"Cherry," Fitz answered promptly.

Gracie nodded, and brought a large platter to the center of the table as well as a bowl of dressed greens.

"Cherry's a beautiful wood," she agreed, preparing to cut into her creation.

"What is it?" Fitz asked, looking at dinner which looked to him like a large, flaky loaf of some type of bread.

"Bison filet mignon in puff pastry," Gracie answered mildly. "And just a plain green salad," she added dismissively.

The bison, which had been marinated before being wrapped in the pastry, was so tender they didn't really need to use knives to cut it, and seasoned perfectly inside the flaky golden crust.

Although Fitz wasn't a big salad man--he wasn't much of a vegetable man altogether--he liked the blend of tangy mizuke and arugula Gracie had spiced up the baby spinach and raddiccio with, and the mustard vinaigrette she'd put on it.

He had seconds, and along with Gracie and Jack finished a wonderfully rich, smooth bottle of Barolo.

"Dessert can be on the porch, " Gracie suggested as she cleared away the dinner dishes. "As I expect you'll want your pipe," she said to Fitz, who said that yes, he'd very much like to have a smoke if that was all right.

Gracie said it was fine out on the porch, especially since it was a pipe, which she liked the smell of. A few minutes later while she was getting coffee and dessert, Jack and Fitz were sitting in the Adirondack chairs on Gracie's screened porch and admiring the summer sunset.

"She's quite the girl," Fitz said quietly, not wanting Gracie to overhear.

Jack smiled. "Yeah, she is," he agreed, his affection for Gracie apparent in his voice.

"I can't believe you let her get away," Fitz went on. Jack had explained that he and Gracie, although they had known each other for a few years and had been dating for much of that time, had also broken up--twice now.

Jack shook his head. "I won't make that mistake again," he assured his mentor, and said no more.

Gracie came onto the porch at this point and presented the coffees and her dessert: strawberry rhubarb upside down cake with custard.

"God, Jack, it's a wonder you're not the size of a house with this woman cooking for you," Fitz said a while later, finishing his dessert and having a second mug of coffee. "And the coffee is excellent, Gracie, thanks."

"I've never heard him compliment anyone on their coffee, Gracie," Jack joked, regarding Gracie fondly. "You must have really made an impression."

Fitz nodded, agreeing. "Like I told you, Jack, Gracie's a pretty good investigator." He turned to her. "You ever think about working for the FBI? I know an instructor down at Quantico could probably get you in," he said temptingly.

Gracie smiled. "Fitz, you don't know how much I appreciate your praise," she said sincerely. "But Jack's the detective on this team. I'm happy helping out and doing the reporting," she replied. But she smiled.

"You sure?" Fitz pressed. "I'd like to have Jack back too, you know. You'd both make good agents."

Jack 'leaned on' Chacko as Fitz had suggested and eventually struck a deal where, in exchange for giving up the two thugs he'd hired to kill Mike Garnier, Chacko's sentences on all the charges he pled to in Berkshire County would be recommended to run concurrent to his state, federal and Hampshire County sentences.

"You understand, that's not a guarantee," Jack warned Chacko. "Judge Norcross makes his own decisions, unlike Judge Elderson," he couldn't resist adding.

Chacko said he understood.

In the course of the questioning about Mike's murder, Jack had discovered what had puzzled him since his friend had been killed: how Mike had found out for sure about what was going on with the JDC scheme.

It turned out that Mike's uncle, who had a home construction business in the central part of the state where he lived, had told Mike about rumors he'd heard that Chacko Salama had standing 'deals' with suppliers for sub standard materials that he in turn billed to his customers at top of the line prices. When Mike had tried to check out his uncle's story, Chacko had caught wind of it and had been afraid that Mike would not only uncover the substandard materials used in many projects in addition to the JDC, but also the embezzlement and money laundering scheme he and Sasha had in place at the Center.

So he'd hired two guys who were subcontracted bricklayers for Salama Construction to kill Mike and make it look like an accident. Chacko normally used the two men, whose names were Zeke Addisio and Nicky Dell'Ossa, for the occasional threat and intimidation intervention, if a worker or contractor ever got out of line.

But a little research on Chacko's part had provided the perfect opportunity for Addiso and Dell'Ossa to accomplish their goal. Chacko had learned of Mike's plans to hike Mount Greylock's north face that spring weekend, and dispatched his thugs to end the state police trooper's life.

Just as Dr. Spears' x-rays had shown, Mike had been strangled: Addisio had distracted Mike when he was atop the north face summit, while Dell'Ossa had come from behind and strangled him. Then they had both pushed Mike over the edge of the lookout point, watching him fall repeatedly on the rocks below until he landed on the outcropping. They had been certain that between the battering his body took and the animal scavenging which was almost guaranteed, the cause of death once Mike was eventually found, would be listed as accidental.

And they'd almost got away with it. Except for Jack's gut instinct when it came to his longtime friend, and the photographs Mike had taken which Gracie had enhanced, that showed two people near the spot where Mike 'fell' to his death just a short while before that had occurred.

Of course, it was Addisio and Dell'Ossa in that photo. They were arrested and charged and when investigation showed they had no credible alibi for the time of Mike's death, and once they were told that Chacko had given them up, Addisio and Dell'Ossa admitted to the murder and were charged accordingly.

While Gracie wrote up the story of Mike's murder being solved, Jack called Sandy, who was back in Maine with her parents, and explained to her everything that had happened. Not only had Mike's murder been solved, but her instincts about what was going on at the JDC had been right.

Sandy had been shocked, saddened and then relieved, but told Jack that she was actually enjoying her return to her hometown and working with her parents in their whitewater rafting and outdoor hiking business, and had no plans to come back to Berkshire County.

"But now, at least, I can come visit if I'm invited without being afraid someone might try to kill me!" she joked, and Jack said he was certain Gracie would invite her to her upcoming 'house party' for Labor Day.

Jack also drove out to Springfield to see Mike's mother, and let her know that they'd solved her son's murder before she read it in that week's newspapers. He knew Mrs. Garnier read the *Intelligencer* and he wouldn't be surprised if the story were picked up by one of the bigger Springfield daily papers as well, since it was so sensational.

Mrs. Garnier was, like Sandy, amazed at the corruption her son had begun to uncover, grief stricken not only by his death but at the senselessness of it, and relieved that it was all over. She was also very grateful to Jack for his tenacity, and for solving the case.

"Mike would be proud," she told Jack, who choked up at her words and gave the older woman a gentle hug.

"Thank you, Mrs. Garnier," he murmured. "That means the world to me."

Chapter Thirty

"Oh, Gracie, I'm so worried," Farida Salama said that Thursday. "I'm afraid no one will come to the Club Cookout!" she exclaimed. She had called Gracie and asked if she could stop over that morning and since Gracie's only commitment was to mow her lawn, she had readily agreed.

Gracie welcomed her friend and had given her a tall glass of mint iced tea and led her out onto the screened porch. Farida had exclaimed over Gracie's house, and she'd sipped at her tea, but the worry was apparent on her pretty face.

"Why, Farida? They've proven that Koshy had nothing to do with what Chacko was up to," Gracie reassured Farida.

That was true. Of course, Chacko's misbehavior had prompted an investigation into Salama Construction as a whole. But it had quickly developed that while Koshy had done the advertising and 'schmoozing' to secure the company construction work, that was where his involvement had ended. And his salary had been paid from the legitimate profits made by the company.

Chacko's money had come from a share of the legitimate profits plus, of course, the excess garnered by the sub standard materials arrangements and from the JDC scheme.

Still, Gracie understood how the name of Salama Construction had been tainted by Chacko's crimes.

"Koshy says he's going to re-incorporate, and re-name the business," Farida told Gracie. "And he's looking for a new partner, someone who can handle the construction side of the business while he continues to do the sales and ad work."

Gracie nodded. "I think that's probably a good idea. And Koshy should be very up front about the whole thing, so people are convinced he's blameless, and continue to trust the company," Gracie advised. "He really never wondered where Chacko got all his money?" she asked her friend.

"No, I mean, Chacko hid a lot of it, so Koshy wouldn't have seen it or known what he had bought with it. And as for the Porsche Cayenne, Chacko told Koshy it was a lease, and a business deduction. Since Chacko handled that side of the company, the money side, Koshy didn't think twice about it," Farida replied.

Gracie nodded.

Then Farida told her that her husband had approached, of all people, Mike Garnier's uncle, Don, and if he agreed to come in as a partner in the new firm, Koshy said it would be called S&G Construction, for Salama and Garnier.

Farida hoped it worked out: the damage done to Koshy's spirit by his brother's--and his second cousin's--crimes had devastated their family, and she had almost decided to cancel the Club barbecue. But when she'd mentioned this to Gracie, her friend had told her that would be like admitting guilt.

"The best way for you and Koshy and everyone else to heal is to go on as much as possible with your normal life, and to surround yourself with good friends," Gracie counseled. She knew: she remembered how she had survived when her parents had died and to this day knew that Susan, Joey and Tyler had been the ones to keep her sane and whole.

"But will people come?" Farida questioned again.

Gracie nodded. "I'm sure they will," she encouraged her friend.

Since the barbecue was the coming Saturday afternoon and evening, Gracie had already thought to canvass most of the Club's members and make sure those who had said they were coming to the barbecue still were. She didn't tell Farida what she'd done, but the responses she'd received had assured her that almost every Club member who had said they were coming was still coming. A couple had legitimate reasons for canceling which weren't related to the criminal charges against Chacko. But to counter that, a few members were now bringing friends they hadn't originally planned to, and a couple more who had at first not been able to attend now were. So she felt certain Farida would have a house full.

"How is Ishtar adjusting?" Gracie asked then, solicitous. Custody of the child, since both her parents were in jail, had been awarded to Koshy and Farida once Koshy had been cleared of criminal involvement; little Ishtar was currently living with them. Yedid's home and other assets, like the assets of all those involved in the scam, would be sold to pay restitution, fines and fees numbering in the hundreds of thousands of dollars.

Farida shrugged. "She's been upset. Of course: the child idolized her mother, thought she was the most wonderful creature on earth. A fairy princess. And now, she's come to live with the poor relatives!" Farida joked.

Gracie's mouth hung open for a split second. "What do you mean, 'poor relatives'?" she asked, askance.

Farida giggled. "Well, to her we seem, if not poor, then definitely a few--how do you say it? A few steps down on the ladder?"

"Rungs," Gracie corrected. "But steps will do. But that's ridiculous!"

Farida sighed. "I know. But I think she'll get used to it," she added more cheerfully.

The barbecue did indeed work out very well, just as Gracie had thought. The day dawned warm and clear and the lovely home Farida and Koshy shared with their children and now with little Ishtar, too, sparkled as it welcomed all of Farida's friends. Koshy, who had been traveling for business so much he hadn't had the time to make a lot of friends, was touched by the support shown to his wife, and was gladdened by the overtures of friendship made to him by some of the Club members' husbands and pals. He vowed to himself to stay home more in the future and nurture those friendships, and be more of a husband to Farida and a father to his children and his new ward, his niece Ishtar.

He was as committed to making S&G Construction a success as he had been committed to the success of Salama Construction.

And that was another bit of good news: Don Garnier had agreed just that morning to join Koshy in a re-born construction company named S&G, as a full partner. They had a lot of work ahead of them, but the challenge energized Koshy. Coupled with the arrival of all his wife's friends, he found himself happier that afternoon than he'd been in a very long time.

Everyone exclaimed over the wonderful food Farida offered for the barbecue. There was the usual chicken and steak, but they'd been marinated in different sorts of spices and had an unusual twist to the flavor. She had made American style potato salad and three bean salad and a green salad, but she'd offered a range of

Syrian appetizers including home made five spice hummus and baba ghanouj and alongside the traditional barbecued meats had made a platter of kibbeh: tender zucchini stuffed with a meat mixture and baked to succulent yumminess in a tomato sauce.

Desserts included several brought by Club members as well as ice cream and home made frozen cardamom spiced yoghurt Farida had made.

Rita came to the barbecue too, and thinking it was best to confront the elephant in the room directly, pulled Farida aside shortly after her arrival.

"I want you to know, Farida, that I don't hold anything Sasha or Chacko did against you and Koshy," Rita explained, adding that she'd been involved with Mark Broadstreet before he'd dumped her for Sasha, but was now only too glad that had happened. "Before all this came out, I might have resented you because you're Sasha's relatives, even though I know you and Koshy weren't close to her," Rita went on. "But now, well, I think we're all on the same side of the fence, if you know what I mean, and I'm glad to be in Club with you and I hope you'll call me 'friend,' " Rita finished.

Farida answered her with a warm, fast hug.

Jack and Gracie had enjoyed themselves, too. As always, they liked being with the group from Club, particularly Jean and Anne. Jean's new beau, Tom, was a wilderness photographer and talked to Jack at length about his work, which Jack found fascinating. He couldn't help thinking of his friend Mike whose photos of the beauty of Mount Greylock had ultimately led to the solving of his murder. And of the photo Gracie had snapped of the golden eagle that day they'd gone up to the cliff where Mike had died, with Sandy.

When the evening wound down, however, Gracie and Jack made their excuses and returned to her house, where Woof and Pumpkin were waiting for them. Jack's parents were coming to Gracie's to join them for Sunday Lunch the following day, and Gracie said she wanted to get a good night's sleep so she'd be bright eyed the following morning to turn out a spectacular meal.

Jack thought she could probably do that pretty much *in* her sleep, but he didn't argue.

As usual, Jack took Woof out when they got back, then brought him inside and gave him a biscuit. He looked around, but didn't see Gracie. It was time to say goodnight.

"Gracie?" Jack called. Where could she have got to?

He mounted the stairs. "Gracie?" He entered her bedroom where a small light shone. The scent of her perfume lingered as though she'd just been there.

Where could she have gone? Surely he would have passed her on the stairs...

"Jack!"

Her call floated up from the ground floor.

Mystified, he followed it, back to the front hall and into the formal living room, where he saw that the doors to the conservatory were ajar.

"There you are!" Gracie smiled from inside the conservatory. She stood next to the hot tub, which was uncovered and bubbling merrily. "I thought it might be a good time to christen the hot tub, if you don't have to leave right away," she suggested, still smiling.

The moon was near new, so the sky shone only with stars. Gracie had turned on a few small flameless votives and placed them around the hot tub's rim and on a couple of the conservatory's shelves where now a few stag-horn and rabbit's foot ferns festooned the area. A couple of spiky cycads and bromeliads provided points of geometrical interest, and several orchids including phalanopsis, Miltonia, catteleyas and more exotic ones Jack couldn't name bloomed in the night, lending color and fragrance to the place.

"Wow, this looks really beautiful, Gracie," Jack said, stepping inside the conservatory. He hadn't seen it since it had been filled with plants, and that was partly the reason Gracie had invited his parents to visit now: she wanted to show Marilyn, who loved orchids, the conservatory in action, as it were.

"Thanks, Jack," Gracie replied with a happy grin. "I hope your parents like it: I'm looking forward to their visit tomorrow," Gracie added.

"I'm glad," Jack said with an answering grin. Then he chuckled: "you know my Mom's going to want a greenhouse after she sees this," he said wryly, with a gesture that encompassed the entire inviting space.

Gracie laughed, "you're probably right, she will!"

FINIS

--33--

www.ingramcontent.com/pod-product-compliance
Lightning Source LLC
Chambersburg PA
CBHW060316260626
47160CB00007B/2634